A CHILD AGAIN

MᶜSWEENEY'S BOOKS
SAN FRANCISCO

For more information about McSweeney's, visit www.mcsweeneys.net.

The stories within originally appeared in *Conjunctions, Daedalus, Epoch, Harper's,
Harvard Review, Iowa Review, Kenyon Review, McSweeney's, n+1, Playboy,
Quarterly Review of Literature, The New York Times,* and *TriQuarterly.*

ISBN: 1-932416-22-6

A CHILD AGAIN

ROBERT COOVER

SIR JOHN PAPER
RETURNS TO HONAH-LEE

PUFF THAT MIGHTY dragon: where is he? He lies, brooding, the
sorry beast, in his wretched cave. Wallowing in his pearls, in his
bits of string and dried-up lumps of sealing wax; in his misery.
Has done, except for occasional forays to wreak dutiful havoc on
the locals, since that gray night when Jackie Paper, old companion, old pride, came no more. Why did he leave? Puff doesn't
know. He was here and then he wasn't here. It's all beyond
Puff's understanding. Yet Puff knows many things, things
Jackie Paper has forgotten. Or never knew. Cannot learn. He
knows this, for example: Jackie will return. To play again perhaps. Or to seek wealth or vengeance, court the impossible—
never mind why. Because he must, that's all. Because magic
dragons live forever. Puff snorts with brute anticipatory joy,
briefly lighting up the dreary cave, and lashes its damp walls
with his excited tail.

* * *

Dragons have no sense of time, nor of the motions of it. All just is. And yet, at times, Puff's green eyes are aglitter with something akin to memory. He is on a boat with billowed sail, Jackie Paper on his tail, and kings and princes grovel, pirates pale. Hah! there they romp! there they frolic! And it's not the honor, the glory, no, shit on all your kings and pirates! It's the blueness, the greenness, the splashiness! All great adventure is ultimately sensual, Jackie would explain were he here. And Puff that mighty dragon would grin back like a happy idiot, rub his belly on the rocks.

Magic dragons may be ageless, but not so little boys. Sir John Paper, distinguished Peer of the Realm, known affectionately to his countrymen as Sir Jack, celebrated orator and devoted equestrian, the one to whose words one turns for solace and inspiration when burdened by life's anxieties or excessive happiness, has reached, as they say, a certain age. Though his style retains the radiant phrasing for which he is so admired, the impassioned romanticism of his youth has given way to a lofty serenity, as befits his later years. But has he, in his august repose, forgotten entirely his old playmate Puff far away in Honah-Lee? No, he has not, and indeed he suffers still, along with occasional back spasms, a residual longing for autumnal seaside mists, a longing that finds its way into his oratory in subtle hidden ways of which even he is not always aware. Something valuable and true, he knows, has been lost, as if a treasure stolen, and he would recover it if he could. His frolicking days, however, are long since over, and a good thing, too.

* * *

HOW JACKIE PAPER SPOILED PUFF. Puff now hates his cave, even though he leaves it but rarely. It is a miserable hole, dank and evil-smelling. It used to be the middle of the world and thus of Honah-Lee, a welcoming place to return to after lapping up virgins or setting the landscape ablaze or bringing the dawn, its sour obscurity like a second skin to him. He played invented games in here back then, lolling about in his treasures, burning whimsical fancies onto the walls with his hot breath, chasing his unpredictable tail. Jackie Paper and his fantastic journeys changed all that. What was a gloomy airless cave after such high adventure? At times in his excitement he actually forgot where it was, or even that it was, though memory was never one of his strong points even in less eventful times. After Jackie left, he journeyed no more, but sank back into his cave, there to brood upon his loss and loneliness, emerging only to unleash an occasional storm of terror on the locals, that he not be forgotten. These outbursts are his more hopeful moments, giving him the momentary illusion of purpose, of something happening, but they do not last long, for melancholy soon overtakes him and he folds his wings and, head bent in sorrow, slips sadly back into his lonely cave once more.

The land called Honah-Lee is a more or less blissful kingdom by the sea, known for its theatrical dreamlike aura and its exemption—or seeming exemption—from diachronic clock time. The kingdom's name is said to mean "the place where the Earth Mother whelped (or whelps) the rainbow," though in fact rainbows have never been seen in Honah-Lee, the weather being unsuitable for them. Perhaps the name somehow alludes to the fabulous treasure said to be hidden here, as if at rainbow's foot, a treasure watched over by a powerful but capricious dragon. Dragons who are guardians of buried treasure are generally thought to be beneficent and worthy of veneration, even to the honoring of them with the occasional virgin princess, but Puff, Honah-Lee's indigenous dragon, while generally viewed more with uneasy tolerance than with awe or respect, is increasingly given to exasperating eruptions of rage, or else of joy, it's always hard to tell, the result in either case being a sudden localized devastation. Of course monsters are monsters and do what they have to do, can't change that, Puff's volcanic convulsions are part of his nature, but it's also the nature of a threatened citizenry to defend itself. One can only take so much. After one outburst too many, Puff's head is finally called for, and his tongue, too, that being the customary procedure in the dismantling of dragons. A task only heroes can undertake. It is time to seek one out.

Puff's poor cave is dark and gloomy, but it is not entirely lightless. Honah-Lee's seaside mist seeps in by day, coiling into penumbral corners, pressing its damp purgatorial murk into the cave's soft walls. Puff vaguely associates this invasion with life. Less reassuring is the terrible nighttime pallor of his treasure store of pearls, those teardrops from the moon as old sailors would have it, thunder-balls, lotus-jewels. Their lurid glow lights up nothing but themselves, causing the barren walls, dimly defined by day, to recede by pearl-light into a vast cosmic night. In all this desolation, Puff sometimes buries himself in his starry pearls like a galactic black hole, haloed by a lightless light, dreaming of the death denied him, and waiting for day to roll mistily in again and snuff out his treasure-store's illusory omens.

ON THE NATURE OF BLACK HOLES. Black holes are the seductive dragons of the universe, outwardly quiescent yet violent at the heart, uncanny, hostile, primeval, emitting a negative radiance that draws all toward them, gobbling up all who come too close. Once having entered the tumultuous orbit of a black hole, nothing can break away from its passionate but fatal embrace. Though eons of teasing play may be granted the doomed, ultimately play turns to prey and all are sucked haplessly—brilliantly aglow, true, but oh so briefly so—into the fire-breathing maw of oblivion. Black holes, which have no memory, are said to contain the earliest memories of the universe, and the most recent, too, while at the same time obliterating all memory by obliterating all its embodiments. Such paradoxes characterize these strange galactic monsters, for whom creation is destruction, death life, chaos order. And darkness illumination: for, as dragons are also called worms, so black holes are known as wormholes, offering a mystical and intimate pathway to the farthest reaches of the cosmos, thus bringing light even as they consume it.

Sir John Paper is delivering an encomium on those splendid particularities of the horse often overlooked or even maligned, such as its tail, its teeth, the golden products of its digestive system, its soft jaws and rising withers, its exuberant sexual behavior, its whinny and its snorts (expression! expression!), when he receives, delivered by hand to the podium, news of the latest depredations by the dragon of Honah-Lee and the open call to all heroes for its severed head, the reward being half the dragon's hidden treasure, said to be worth more than the world is worth. Sir Jack pauses in his oration to contemplate this challenge. Which is not the same for him as it is for others. Other heroes might be willing to risk their lives in an attempt to kill the dragon and win the treasure, but Sir Jack has no use for further wealth and would be loathe to behead his childhood friend and first mount, or even to learn of his beheading. Moreover, it runs counter to his oft-expressed love for wild things, however remote he has become from them. So what is to be done? Puff's appetite for violence must be, being irrepressible (desire is sacred!), somehow transcended. Which is something only he, Sir John Paper, can even hope to accomplish. There is an ancient Chinese saying that "In heaven a horse is made into a dragon, and among men a dragon is made into a horse." That is what he must do. He must make Puff into a horse. Before other heroes get there and make him into a scatter of grisly museum exhibits. He gazes out upon his audience, recalling that green-scaled rascal and the soft pearly light of his cave and wondering where he was in his interrupted oration. Something about beautiful body parts, a favorite theme. Dragons, he says at last, have the outward appearance of giant lizards or crested snakes with the jaws of crocodiles, the head and forelegs of lions, the talons of eagles and hawks, the bellies of clams, soles of tigers, and ears of cows. But they have the heart of a horse.

Puff's pearls lie spilled about, heaped up here and there, some stuffed into fat brown sacks, others imbedded in the cave walls

like drops of some luminous ooze. Beautiful pearls, the wan luster of moons, the nebulous pallor of breath and autumn mist, of
semen, milk, and cowry-shells. Of bones. The white of the eye.
Parchment. COME BACK JACKIE PAPER! the pearls in the
walls would read, if Puff could spell. But he cannot, so they
resemble instead, in their random scatter, the night sky under
which he and Jackie once roamed the high seas. Puff wears a
pearl tucked in his chin, sucks another beneath his tongue. For
pearls are the quintessential "givers of life," more powerful even
than mandrake root or sweet basil or beautiful maidens, though
when he eats them, unlike basil or maidens, they just pass
through, untransfigured. Which might cause others to doubt
their marvelous qualities, but not Puff. Volatile as he is, he is
also a creature of habit and simple beliefs. He has been sucking
pearls for ages and not to do so would cause him to doubt that
he was who he was.

THE PEARL: an emblem of beauty, of fidelity and humility, sign of
self-sacrifice and sorrow, of innocence, integrity, purity, rarity,
tears, and vaginal dew, of virginity and wealth and of wisdom.
Powdered pearl in lemon juice cures lunacy, gut-ache, and
epilepsy. It is an attribute of moon goddesses, Christ, cows,
pudenda, and the Virgin Mary, is used in all Eastern love potions
and protects chastity in the West. Pigafetta, traveling with
Magellan, reported that the King of Borneo dropped his pants
and showed him two as large as goose eggs. The pearl is a
Christian symbol of salvation and a particle of the consecrated
eucharist wafer, the spiritual essence of the universe for the
Chinese and a charm against fire, and a Muslim condition of the

hereafter: the faithful endure forever, encapsulated in pearls, each with his own exquisite virgin, Allah's wages to the orthodox. A pearl, suspended in the belly of the sea monster that swallowed Jonah, provided him light to read by, and among the holy creatures proposed for beatification are the oysters that provided the pearls for the heavenly entranceway, also known as the Pearly Gates. The Chinese in the sixth century believed it rained pearls when dragons fought in the sky, but some beliefs are not true. We now know in fact that such storms are more often triggered by sudden eclipses in the erogenous zones of quasars. Sir Jack has told us so.

When Sir John Paper's departure is announced, his peers caution him against so rash and, well, so unseemly an undertaking. Surely he is past all that, his days of manly glory now well behind him, time to rest on one's laurels, reap one's rewards, etc. The very conventionality of their advice confirms for him the rightness of his decision. He has had to have some of his knightly apparel "let out," as they say, but he feels as fit as ever. Even his chronic aches and pains, his athlete's foot, hemorrhoids, and back spasms, seem to have faded into the background at the prospect of this new quest. But where is this place that he is going, they ask. Is not Honah-Lee much like the mythical islands of Sindbad? And even if it does exist in this world, how will he ever find it? Sir Jack smiles knowingly. One simply, he knows but does not say, follows the east wind. And if he does reach that unlikely place, how does he expect to both save the kingdom and spare the dragon, as he has sworn to do? The creature, by Sir Jack's own report, is into widespread demolition and arson and heavy virgin consumption, a formidable terror. Incomparable equestrian and noble adventurer though dear Sir Jack is, how will he tame such a monster? I do not intend to tame him, Sir Jack replies quite heatedly. "Friendly dragons" are a travesty of nature, mere house pets, zoo animals. I intend to protect his dragonhood at all costs. This is all well and good, they say, relying as ever on the common phrases of the common tongue, but Sir Jack should remember from the ancient wisdom that purity of heart is to will one thing. Instead of risking all in this mad reenactment of his youth, he should continue to focus on his oratory and his horsemanship, of which arts he is an acknowledged genius. Well, that's already two things, replies Sir Jack. Moreover, it is equally true that purity of *will* is to multiply life's creative potential, is it not? And if that will is empowered by revived youthful appetites, then I consider myself fortunate that they have not entirely withered away. He rolls his eyes at the very thought. Now, stand aside, my friends! he cries, licking his finger and raising it to the breeze. I must, in the grand tradition of such adventures, launch forth!

ON THE NATURE OF HEROES. As dragons are to black holes, so might heroes be said to be to comets. Like comets, they project a tragic beauty, a dazzling but ephemeral luster, when they make their rare but significant appearances, hurling themselves out on their brave lonely voyages, cutting their radiant passage, arduous and fraught with peril, across the dark span of human consciousness. There is something forlornly innocent about both comets and heroes as, driven by some mysterious force, not unlike that of desire, they pursue their impossible goals, endure their supreme ordeal. Just as heroes, inspired by misty legend,

heroes as philosophers of invention —

do courageous battle with their fire-breathing adversaries, so do comets, enveloped in their dusty nimbus, defiantly confront the raging solar center, their burning "tails," as they are called, thrust out like a knight's lance into the darkness they seek to illuminate. The meteoric dust trail left by comets as they burn themselves out across the heavens is converted, upon entering the earth's atmosphere, into brief streaking flashes of light known as shooting stars, which capture the attention of mortals in the way that the shining deeds of heroes do, and for about the same length of time. The father of all dragon-slayers is the hero Perseus and, in the heat of a passionate summer, from the so-called Perseid radiant near the fork of his constellation, shooting stars seem to emanate like sparks struck from clashing steel, little bits of hot light flung at the universal darkness. Nearby, Draco glimmers approvingly. Unlike ordinary earthbound mortals, who are reluctant even to look up at the celestial abyss for fear of losing their balance and falling over, heroes are able, like comets, to live serenely with the icy incomprehensibility of the universe. This is their unique gift, though the earthbound grudgingly call it stupidity, noting that, on average, they themselves last longer.

When Sir Jack's peers admonished him for the inappropriateness, at his age, of such a quest, they had in mind, in part, the very nature of that land called Honah-Lee, a land, as they understand it, of almost miraculous gratification of the ego (there was no doubt a touch of envy commingled with their honest fear for him), where dreams of honor and glory are said to be realized as soon as dreamt—or seem to be, for in the foggy

timelessness of Honah-Lee, no thing endures, it only is or else
is not. Giddy Sir Jack, his sober peers believed, was not embracing reality, as he has always vowed to do, but was fleeing from
it, probably on the wings of some dubious aesthetic principle or
other. Little is known of Honah-Lee's landscape, described usually in terms of what is not seen due to the pervading mist, but
it is generally held to be shapely and green, rich in flowery effu-
sions and secret places, Puff's cave being but one of many. It is
an island whose contours shift with the tides and whose limits
therefore remain unmapped, giving rise—on the grounds that
what cannot be measured cannot exist—to those rumors,
expressed by the peers, of its imaginary character, rumors bol-
stered by the land's most characteristic feature, its legendary
mistiness. The mists of Honah-Lee conceal what is and evoke
visions of what is not or is doubtfully so, and as things appear
and disappear, it is said that one can call up whatever appari-
tions one desires— or, rather, that one's desires are made spec-
trally manifest as though the mists were reading the heart of the
intruder. Thus, there is reason to fear for visitors to that strange
inconstant realm, for it is one thing to enter it and another to
find one's way out again. For fearless Sir John Paper, however,
the mists of Honah-Lee are not so much a threat to his well-
being as access to it. To enter into them, he explains to himself
even as he does so, with his customary search for the pungent
phrase to define his passage, is to enter the meaningful and
numinous void of the mystics, the essential condition for the
rediscovery and emergence of the fully conscious self, somewhat
submerged in the company of his peers. Better: To be lost in
nothingness is to be found again. He smiles contentedly and
blinks his eyes: already he seems to see, coiling up out of the

gray mist, towering castle turrets and pirate ships with billowing sail, smells sulfur in the air.

Dragging his tail home through Honah-Lee's mist after another
listless assault on the natives, that old rascal Puff, still petulantly
spitting pale tongues of bluish fire, waddles past the seashore to
catch a glimpse of sky. He should perhaps go for a little paddle,
get out past the haze, sun his weathered hide, air out the pipes.
His scales are growing moss, his roar is thick with phlegm. But,
in his morose disquiet, the gray murk better suits him, his miserable old hole does. Creature of routine, this is what he does:
wreak havoc, wait for Jackie. Suck a pearl. He discovers on arriv-
ing they have left another virgin at the mouth of his cave,
together with an array of condiments and spices. She is chained,
he can see by her arched back, to a rock, but he cannot see the
rock, cannot see any rock, any more than men can see the wind,
visible to him in all its feathery hues. Jackie and he used to
describe these impossible things to each other. The maiden is
glitteringly moist from the mist, or from terror, a little thing, no
more than a bite. But he has no appetite. He leaves her there.

ON VIRGIN PRINCESSES. Just why dragons are to be appeased by virgin princesses may be clear to men, who themselves find them a
consoling delicacy and a cure for melancholy, but it is not clear to
dragons. It is just something that is, along with everything else
that is. If given a choice (never asked), they might prefer wild asses,
say, or errant doves, griffins, pelicans, or roasted swallows, the
latter known to be a particular draconic favorite, and all certainly

less pestilential than royal maidens—these squealing things attract heroes the way honey attracts flies. Which are much less of a nuisance. The wide-mouthed Phrygian and Libyan dragons were sensibly more partial to herdsmen and their herds, the Drakon of Ethiopia to whole elephants, not to everyone's taste or capacity, while the Laidley Worm of Lambton was quite content with a daily ration of cow's milk; some were known to eat their own tails, others light or oceans, and sweet-toothed Greek dragons accepted offerings of marzipan from virgin damsels, turning vicious only if they sniffed out deflowered impostors. No one knows how they did this, but nothing, other than tiger bones in their drinking water, seemed to anger them more. Or so goes the legend, composed by men, dragons lacking the literate knack and, so, probably blame-less. There are many such morality tales, meant to terrify the young, about the mortal dangers of approaching a dragon without one's innocence intact. Perhaps these legends grew up around the suggestive eroticism of dragons themselves, generally held to be symbolic of the wilder human passions, at least those of men, who often have a way, when they are feeling bigger than they really are, of identifying with these sinuous insatiable monsters. The Chinese associate dragons with the essence of yang, the male element, and have strange tales of palacefuls of crossbred pregnancies, while in the West congealed dragon seed is identified with quicksilver and the philosopher's stone and is said to bring about the renewal of youthful potency. The peers did not speak directly about all this with Sir John Paper, but they were thinking it.

Sir Jack, following his nose, has come a long deep way and he is exhausted, more so than he'd anticipated. He had felt so vigorous and able-bodied—puissant!—upon setting out. Now he wonders if he might have, at his advanced age, undertaken one adventure too many. Enveloped in a dim gray mist without that echoes his fading vitality within (no more coiling images of castle turrets and billowing sails, what he envisions now are the civilized comforts of his study, a warm bath, his well-stocked cellar, his eiderdowns), he slumps against a tree to rest his aching limbs, too weak even to groan, musing, as he often does, on his mortality. He seems to have arrived here at dawn. Or else dusk. Doesn't matter which. This is a place where time is more like space, something to be explored, not something that races past. Of course, it probably races past all the same. And not much left of it for him, he knows. He is exploring this tree, the few feet of ground that he can see without his glasses, maybe that's it, finis. Everything hurts, all the way down to his insteps. His sinuses are clogging up, his throat is sore, he may be getting a fever blister, his toes are itching again, other things as well, it's exasperating. Why has he come here? Well, he feared for his old friend, against whom a death warrant had been issued. Was that it? Or had he, far removed from his heroic past and close to the end of things, ostensibly fearing for Puff, really been grieving for himself? Was he, as the sneering remarks of his peers implied, merely a foolish old man trying romantically, hysterically, to recapture his lost boyhood, to be a child again, to relive once more some of that timeless excitement, that untrammeled joy? No. Please. His project, as always, has been to break through the half-truths of conscious thought to reconnect with the submerged truths hidden below in the noble striving for full consciousness: this is what it means to seek out, once again, Puff's cave. Even these meditations on time and death are part of it. Are they not. With such heady rationalizations is Sir John reassuring himself (but he *is* a foolish old man, he knows this!) when the tree suddenly twitches and sends him flying. When he picks himself up from the damp earth and goes looking for it, the tree is gone. He finds instead a dewy young maiden chained to a rock outside the mouth of a malodorous cave. He unbinds the terrified creature, nymphet-like in her tender proportions, and tells her to scamper on home. No need to thank me, I'm merely doing my duty, he is about to say with a kindly nod of his head, but she has already, after staring up at him in horror, vanished without a word.

Desire is held by some of Sir Jack's peers to be an affliction, a per-version, a refractory but inescapable medium into which humankind is born, and by which it is helplessly victimized, and Sir Jack is not averse to this opinion, though he holds others as well, nor does he for that reason, as some do, seek to repress it. On the contrary. Desire is the soul, the soul desire, he has often said, it being his only known use of the word "soul," except to add on occasion, in fond remembrance of his childhood: My soul is the dragon in me. Sometimes he says: My soul is the horse in me, by which he means, but does not add, the free unbroken horse. This remark usually evokes approving laughter. Growing up and joining one's peers, then, is, comically, to stifle the soul, break the horse, behead the dragon. Or at least forsake it. "Transcendence" is the word he likes to use when guilty of it, thereby easing the pain, though what he means by it he's not exactly sure, nor has he ever, so far as he knows, achieved it. It's just an idea that keeps him going on, noble hero that he is, an idea strangely more attached to memory than to quest, though quest has also often kept him going. As what has not? When as a boy at sea he kept a lookout, perched on Puff's gigantic tail, what was he looking for then? For his own future perhaps, unable, as Puff was able, to enjoy wholly the immediate present. He was always going somewhere, desiring to, and, though Puff gave him momentary power and meaning with his mere name and presence, he knew, even in the delirium of play, that, sooner or later, he would leave him, for this would be the heroic thing to do. For Puff, too, his desirous soul is the dragon in him, which is to say, it is what he is, and, unlike conflicted Sir Jack, purely so, a purity Sir Jack has always envied. Puff's desires are often thwarted, but, when so, simply replaced with other desires, no troubling residue remains. Except for the lingering image of little Jackie Paper. He who has no unrealized desires, knows no tense beyond the simple present, dreams no dreams, is, in this one regard, possessed by longing and by sorrow. Little Jackie is like a canker in the purity of his dragonhood. A bone between the teeth, an unscratchable itch at the far end of his tail.

When engaging with dragons, the official wisdom is that it is wisest to approach them head on. Terrible as are their reptilian jaws and searing breath, breath so foul it poisons oceans and sends birds flopping down out of the sky, much more lethal are their enormous coils of tail. Pliny tells us that their tails can kill elephants, being "of such greatness that they can easily clasp and wind them around the elephants, and withal tie them fast with a knot," and if that doesn't do it, there's a fatal sting at the tip to finish the job. A mere whip of their tails can mow a town down and belt its populace into the farthest reaches of the cosmos. Even the general region of that great appendage is hazardous, for dragons have been known to void the fiery contents of their bowels upon those to the rear, their excrement fouling as much as three acres and so potent it can set off forest fires and cause the seas to boil and cough up its fishes, poached to a fragrant turn. Nor is cutting off the dragon's tail a useful ploy, it simply grows another more lethal than the one it has lost, although the flesh of the severed tail, if found by survivors, is a well-known remedy for dysentery, arthritis, gallstones, impotence, nosebleed, boils in the bowels, squinty eyes, weak hearts, and bad complexions, and can teach those who eat it the language of the birds and how to change the weather. A dragon's tail is a thick muscular scaly thing and so more or less insensible, although, as Puff raised his and entered his cave, he did receive the vague sensation of something pressing against it. He shrugged and shook it off, too weary to think more about it. Now, however, he hears a shout from out there. Just another damnable hero no doubt. Foo. He's exhausted from his depredations and only wishes to sleep for a century or two, let him be. But the shout comes again. Irritably, he pokes his flaming eyes out the cave's entrance. There's an ugly old man standing there. Wobbling a bit on his thin pins, his belly hanging low. A wizard maybe. He opens his jaws to toast him with his breath, but the old man raises his hands and calls out: *Puff—?*

Sir Jack has stood some time in doubt before the mouth of the cave, feeling ancient and feeble and somewhat ill (he has just been swatted by a dragon's tail!), the admonitions of his peers resounding in his ears. Yet again his passions have overruled his wisdom, such as it is (he has no illusions), although, to be fair, it was his reasoning mind that said: Let the passions rule! If one can be separated from the other. In Sir Jack, avowing life and all that's in it (herein lies his nobility, he knows, fool though he is), they cannot. Thus, his mind (he feels overtaken by galloping senility!) drifts in and out of parenthetical musings, seeking justifications for the madness that has brought him here and courage to face his immediate future. Or flee from it. Will Puff remember him? Will he even recognize him? Though he still feels like little Jackie Paper, ever more so since entering the mists of Honah-Lee—indeed, in spite of all his knightly accoutrements acquired over the years of his maturity, he has never *stopped* being little Jackie Paper—he is well aware this would not be obvious at first glance. Which may be all the time he will have. Gazing into the black hole, wreathed by gnarly bushes ominously charred, he is no longer certain about his oft-declared love of wild things. His knees feel watery, he is finding it difficult to breathe (though he has grown accustomed to the dense odor—in fact, more than anything else, it is this that has brought him home again), his back spasms have returned, his stomach is acting up. He is not up for this. He pities himself and decides that he has adventured all that he can adventure. Just by revisiting Honah-Lee, he reasons, he has more or less accomplished his mission, he will just slip quietly away before he is noticed. And it is precisely while making this decision and backing away that he shouts out Puff's name.

 WHEN OLD FRIENDS MEET. Changes will have inevitably taken place. Few for the better. Age, disease, folly will have added their dread cosmetic. Eccentricities will have hardened, hopes vanished. One will find, in short, that the bloom is off the rose. It is not easy at first encounter, behind the prophylactic scrim of nostalgia's storehoused imagery, even to see, much less to recognize, the friend one once knew. Puff stares at this apparition before him in utter disbelief. There was nothing familiar about this stranger's gravelly wail, yet only one creature could have cried out, as this old man has cried out, the name that Jackie Paper called him. But this sour decrepit old thing cannot be little Jackie Paper. And even if it is, it cannot be! Puff snorts and smoke curls masklike round his eyes and ears. Sir Jack sees Puff's bewilderment and knows that it is a dangerous moment, for bewilderment can turn to anger in a tick. He should do something. But he, too, is in a state of shock. Things that seemed large to a child often appear shrunken and ordinary when revisited years later as an adult, he knows that, and so has prepared himself for a less grand and glorious creature than the one he holds in memory. But his dragon friend—if it is really he—is more monstrous than ever. Sir Jack could walk into his jaws and down his gullet standing up. He recalls sitting on bright shiny scales the color of emeralds, but these scales are like dark pitted plates of iron, more brown or black than green, the greenest thing about them being the moss growing between them. Puff has reared up into the heraldic rampant position as though about to pounce, his shaggy wings aflutter, claws flexed, smoke curling out of his cavernous nostrils. His eyes are aglow in the old way, yes, even more so, but Sir Jack perceives a strange unbeastlike melancholy behind them. Gazing into them is like gazing into the abyss. Old Puff is, truly, more than he'd ever realized, a monster from the deeps. Each stares, frozen, at the other. It is another timeless Honah-Lee moment.

* * *

Monsters from the deeps: often have they risen from the terrible abyss to serve as disquieting subjects of Sir John Paper's oratory. Sometimes they represent the destructive forces of nature, sometimes the dark forces in ourselves, sometimes both as a within/ without continuum, our hearts unwitting cradles of the cosmic horror, a horror that is both appalling and erotically compelling. Why do these monsters even arise? It is our terrified fascination that draws them forth. A fearful obsession with the Possible. This, Sir Jack likes to say, is the very nature of eros and that which distinguishes it from love or compassion. All of which (this is usually when he introduces the theme of transcendence) makes an appealing sort of sense, until one is actually face to face with such a nightmare and quaking in one's boots. In his orations, Sir Jack often likes to propose the gift of beauty—especially, he is wont to insist, the beauty of language—as a kind of palliative against the disturbing truths from the abyss, but now, voiceless, breathless, even that gift escapes him. Which, however, does remind him. Cautiously, hoping not to trigger a catastrophic gesture from the wheezing rampant Puff, he reaches into his pockets.

Sir Jack's gifts to Puff are simple: a ball of string, a stick of sealing wax, his gifts to Puff of old. Puff raises his horny head and lets loose a fiery roar as if enraged, lashing the mouth of his cave with his gigantic tail, and for a moment all goes dark and thunder cracks and the earth wobbles, and Sir Jack, alarmed, staggers back, feeling his teeth loosening and rattling in his mouth. But

Puff is only expressing his happiness, having recognized by the gifts his old playmate at last. Already he has replaced that old dim image of little Jackie Paper with this new wrinkly one. Little Jackie Paper wasn't here and now he is here, that's all that matters. It's time to make the fishes dance! Bring on your princes and pirates! Puff wants to play!

ON MOUNTING. To mount one's steed, the noble Xenophon has said, as Sir John now dutifully (and desperately) recalls, the rider "must hold the leading-rein fastened to the chin-strap or the nose-band ready in the left hand, and so loose as not to jerk the horse whether he means to mount by holding on to the mane near the ears or to spring up with the help of the spear. Then, when he has made his spring in order to mount, he should raise his body with his left hand, while at the same time he helps himself up by stretching out his right; for by mounting in this way he will not present an awkward appearance even from behind by bending his leg as he throws it over. Having brought the foot over, he must then tenderly ease his buttocks down on the horse's back..." Of course, Puff does not have a leading-rein fastened to a chin-strap, nor even a mane to grab, clearly a different kind of horsemanship is required. How was it they used to do this? Puff comes to the rescue, uncoiling his tail and offering it to him by spreading it on the ground. Whereupon Sir Jack recalls the old drill. All he has to do is secure his seat atop this coil, and Puff will do the rest, curling his tail into an S and lifting him on high. But whereas he used to scramble up the side of the scaly tail with boyish ease, now it's a laborious slippery hand-over-hand crawl over heavy shifting plates, clasping his mount like Xenophon's disdained barbarian with all the arms and legs he has. Presenting an awkward appearance from behind is the least of his worries.

Puff is ecstatic. His unhappiness has been forgotten, gone as though it never was. Little Jackie Paper is perched once more on his tail as, it seems (such is his beastly memory), he has always been, and all's right with the world. He is galumphing joyously through the mist down Cherry Lane toward the sea and the prospect of glorious adventures, trumpeting his pleasure as he goes, when he chances to glance back to feast his eyes again on his playmate and rider and discovers Jackie is no longer there. Puff staggers to a stop. Oh no. He was there and now he is not. Is it happening all over again? With a heavy heart (a sensation once strange to him, no longer so), Puff lumberingly retraces his steps. He finds Jackie sitting in an awkward, limbs-akimbo position, probably propped against something, must be a big rock. Jackie emits a sound that might be a groan, or might be a greeting or a curse, or a disquisition on life's little agonies, wordless Puff has no idea, it's all the same to him. He's happy just to see Jackie again and know he hasn't gone away.

Great men have lost their seat in the past, this is no disgrace. There was Bellerophon attempting to ride the winged Pegasus into Olympian glory, for example, on which occasion Jove sent a gadfly to sting Pegasus in his lively wide-hammed arse, causing him to buck his impertinent rider all the way back to earth again. It was a rather serious fall, though at the moment Sir Jack's feels no less so (fatal, that is to say), his impertinence no less punishable.

He came here to save his old friend from his sentence of death by helping him to transcend his own nature. He wanted in effect to bring out the horse in Puff. What unbridled arrogance. He could not even hold his seat atop that majestic old rascal's tail. A good seat teaches the intimate relationship between hips and hands, he knows, but in his case these parts did not seem to know each other. A good seat further depends on balance and sympathy and should be natural, comfortable, supple, and strong, without being stiff or cramped, but he had no sooner got his bent stick of a leg over than he began suffering the most awesome back spasms and he soon found himself slumping back into the notorious "old gentleman's seat," a knees-high, feet-up travesty of riding, and hanging on desperately by the "crash and bang" style, well-named for what happened next. He remembers now that he had many falls when riding Puff's tail, but somehow they didn't hurt then. He could very much use a calmative, a strong painkiller, and something to restore his meditative powers, but, alas, he seems not to have packed his medications, a further sign of his onrushing mental infirmity. *Tant pis.* Everything is dangerous, he would like to tell Puff, hovering above him like a worried mother, everything is tentative, nothing is certain. Except perhaps uncertainty itself. And that great absence men call the abyss into which fall certainty and uncertainty alike.

Puff the magic dragon, gazing gratefully, mournfully down upon little Jackie Paper, sprawled below him in his bruises and forlorn innocence, is feeling something of that anticipation of loss that accompanies the realization of all desire, and so is getting another fleeting glimpse of the tragic and awesome beauty that is the human condition. It is a feeling not unlike gas on the stomach. He shakes it off with a whip of his tail and a mighty roar, searing the tops of the trees lining Cherry Lane, then spreads his reptilian jaws to grin down at crumpled Jackie. Come on! Get up! Let's go! The pirates and princes are waiting!

Sir John Paper's dark voyage of fantasy, wonder, trial, and tempest, as they say (Puff, if he could speak, would call it a frolic), is nearly over, its end perhaps hastened by his impetuous revisit to the misty haunts of younger days. If so or not, he has no regrets, suffering only the familiar pangs of passionate longing that there might be more of it. There was a moment, so fleeting that perhaps "moment" is an exaggeration, when he felt, just as he was lifting his leg over while rising high on the elevator of Puff's curling tail, a rush of joyful exhilaration: that he was here! that Puff was here! that such a moment in such a cosmos could transpire! Although the mists of Honah-Lee now present him with no images other than that of the portentous and inscrutable void, in that brief rapturous moment aloft they were coiling into the glorious shapes of life itself in all its exuberant and voluptuous manifestations. From up on high, amid such phantasmal delights, he seemed to catch a tantalizing glimpse of the trembling sea in dawn light with its promise of noble adventure and, though surely it was an illusion (*life* is an illusion, as he has often declared), he embraced this promise (it was about then that the back spasms began) with open arms. He gazes up now at the toothy old rascal grinning down at him and perceives something of the scaly wide-bellied grandeur of his own inner being, the wild, winged strangeness of it, the unspeakable enigma at the core. Which core is not his, he is only of it. As though in response, Puff, once more presenting his tail, snorts an impatient, or perhaps celebratory, plume of fire, and roasted birds fall like rain. Well, he has been flattering himself. Though expression is his métier, he can't do that. Puff is Puff and he is only fancy-ridden Sir John Paper. Yes, Puff, he says, we shall go. All too soon. Sir Jack can hear the thundering hordes of heroes out on the periphery coming after his dragon friend, unless that is the pounding of his own heart in his ears. He struggles, groaning, to his feet and recommences the hand-over-hand climb. If he joined the heroes he would probably be spared to live another day. But of what use would that be if the dragon in him were no more?

original song
lords of childhood

- Just about all
words of song
weaved into story —

unintrusive —
yet commentary
narrator —

31

PUNCH

HERE COMES JUDY. Popping up. Mad about the baby. If you'd been walking by, I say, you could've caught him. My bitter half carries on in the grand style. Oh my poor child, my poor child, and so on. What a peach! I kill her with my stick. It's what I do best. I'm laughing. Roo-tee-too-ee-too-it. That's the rusty sound I make. They say it's not natural. They're right. It's not natural. Now here comes the law. I don't get a minute's rest. No respect for a poor widower. Doesn't take long. Bop. He's gone, too. More to follow. I can't help it. It's this big finger in my head. It points and says: Kill. I don't hesitate. If I did, they'd knock my hooter off and use me for the hangman. Anyway, it's fun. Something like fun. Biff, boff, another corpse. Roo-tee-to-to-toot. The baker: Roo-tee-toot. A lawyer. That's the way to do it. A yapping dog: shut him up. Root-to-too-it. He's now the dog that everyone's as dead as. Joey comes to help me count the bodies. Too many. We lose track. Who cares. Stack 'em up. Joey's my pal. He's a brain-less wall-eyed knockabout but a pal. Not big on the ladies, but it takes all kinds. My werry merry companion, as they say in the trade. I don't kill him. Probably couldn't if I tried. In fact, I have tried, but he's too quick. Straight out of the circus, that pecker-less greaseball, and no hump or belly to slow him down. Let's for-give and forget, Joey, I say, and aim a blow at him, but he's behind me suddenly with a stick of his own. Ow, Joey, ow! I give up! Come on, let's go drown our sorrows. Is that like drowning cats, Mister Punch? Like enough, Joey. Well, here, put 'em in this bag, then. All right, Joey, here they are. Very good, Mister Punch. Now give 'em a widdle and they're gone to glory. The fin-ger's out of my head and sticking out below and, after I wag it around a bit just to give it an airing, it's in the bag. Pssshh! is the sound it makes. That did it, Mister Punch, says Joey, your sor-rows have gone out with the tide, they've crossed over the waters, they're on the other side, and he snaps the bag shut around my psshher. Help, Joey, I'm caught! We have to get rid of those dead sorrows, Mister Punch, says Joey, and throws the bag out the window. I nearly follow it out but I don't. My arse is well-anchored. The bag dangles out there on my psshher, swinging back and forth like a pendulum, making a watery tick-tock sound. You shouldn't have done that, Joey. Why not, Mister Punch? I'll be arrested for deceitful exposure. They'll say I was inflaming the masses. Inflaming them whats? Come here, Joey, you scoundrel. Just look at that mob out there! Shaking their bel-lies and gapping their jaws! You think they want to eat my sor-rows? Joey comes over to the window. I stiffen up and hit him with the bag, send him flying. Got him at last. Or maybe not. He bobs up again with another stick. Maybe it's mine. We fence in the heroic style, Joey with his stick, me with my stiffened psshher and bag of sorrows. The bag flies off and Joey's gone. I'm a happy man again. Free and frolicsome. Sorrows gone and psshher tucked safely away between my ears. But I miss Joey. Killing's no fun without a pal, and before I know it my head's getting diddled and I'm at it again. Roo-tee-toot, and so on, what I do best, down they go. Corpses everywhere. And now it's the hangman. You've broken the laws of the country, he says. I never touched them, says I. Just the same, your time is up, he says. Up whose? I ask. Ask the devil, he says. I just did. Enough of this impertinence! It's back to the woodpile for you, blockhead. Sawdust thou art and unto sawdust shalt thou return. And he sets up the gallows, the sanctimonious blowhard. Looks very like a puppet booth, I remark. That's right, Mister Punch, and you're going to dance in it, says he. Do you have any last words? Yes. I'm off. Good-bye. But police have popped up and are holding me. It's not that easy, you villain, says the hangman with a cruel laugh. Prepare to meet your Maker. I already know him, says I. He's a drunken wanker. That's enough now, Mister Punch, just put your head in here. I've never done this before, I say, I don't know how. Show me. He does and I jerk the rope and hang him. There's nothing to it. He's dancing on air. I whistle a little tune. The mob loves me for it. I'm a fucking hero.

Oh oh. It's Judy again. Thought I did her already. Must be her ghost. Probably. I killed her too soon, she wasn't done with her nagging, she has to come back and finish it. Can't be sure, though. She's as hard as ever. Take that, she says. And that. It's a real thumping I'm getting. Can you hit a ghost? Where's my stick? Somebody took my stick! She's got the baby. Or the ghost of the baby. The one I threw out the window. She hits me with

it. Blow after blow. It's yowling fit to be tied. I'm yowling, too.
Like a stuck pig. You can hear me for miles around. I'm a real
crybaby when it comes to it. The dead brat and I're into a bawling duet that is sort of like roo-tee-too-it and sort of like boo-
hoo and tee-hee. No, the tee-hees are Judy's. She's having a party.
Her beak is lit up like a lantern, she's grinning ear to ear, her
skirts are flying. Always one to give the mob a glim at her
underparts, such as they are. But finally she poops herself out
with so much strenuous haunting and, with a final whack that
knocks me right off my pegs, she flits off with her squalling
cudgel. It's all right. My hump's sorely blistered and I'm not
likely to rise soon, but I'm not dead yet. Not quite. I've apparently got more killing to do. More fun. It's not over. I've got my
stick back. I'm lying on it. Who's next? It's the doctor. We know
how this is going to turn out. Well, well, it's my old friend
Punch, he says. Looks to have paid the debt to nature at last, and
high time, too, he owed it a potful. Are you dead, Punch? Dead
as a stone, I say. Well, that's good news, but you're a terrible liar,
why should I believe you? Feel my pulse, I say. He gropes about
and my knuckled gap-stopper pops out. Zounds! What's that?
cries the doctor with some consternation. It's my brains oozing
out, I say. I always supposed yours were down there in the dreck,
Punch. It stiffens up. Great snakes! Now what's happening?
exclaims the learned man, aghast at the dreadful sight. Rigor
mortis, says I, and I bat his spectacles off with it. I think all you
need, Punch old boy, is a sturdy dose of medicine. I prescribe a
rum punch with extract of shillalagh, he declares, and he takes a
swing at the offending digit with his cane. But it's already
buried away again, so in remedy he cracks my nose instead. It
honks like a goosed gander. I give him a taste of his own medicine

with my stick, but it's evidently not a strong enough dose, for his condition worsens, I must improve on it. He tries to run away but I catch him with that clever thing between my legs and, holding him with it, chin in my chest, apply my therapeutics until he's physicked to a lifeless pulp. Roo-tee-too-it. Way to do it. The police are back. There's a law against killing doctors in broad daylight, they tell me. My watch must have stopped, I say. They take me to the judge. You're incorrigible, Punch, he says. A vile pestiferous reprobate, a murderer, a heartless foulmouthed bully, a coarse loathsome unrepentant knave without a single redeeming feature. The mob is eating this up. How do you plead? Innocent, Your Honor! The mob boos and laughs. Innocent? Of all what you say, Your Honor, and lots more besides! The mob's cheering, he's banging his gavel. I'm feeling eloquent. I'm going to kill him, it's all I can do in this world except fall down, but I feel a spell of rhetoric coming on, so I rear back and let fly. By my oath, Your Worship, I am but as my Maker made me. His hand is in my head. By the smell, I think it's the same hand the sodden letch wipes his ass with. So what can I do? Whomsoever he hates, I hate, and he hates everybody. Even me, I think, that's why he takes it out on me from time to time. And whomsoever he hates, we dispatch. It's as much a law of nature, Your Honor, as that for which we need boghouses. The judge is immovable. Is that your final plea? Not quite, I say. Here it is. And I let a loud blattering fart that causes my shirttails to ripple out behind. The guards fall back, fanning their faces. The mob howls and I peer out at them and grin my rigid grin. Then I take the judge's gavel away from him and club him with it until he's a bag of mushy robes. That might have been Joey wearing a wig, but if so, too bad. I kill the guards before they can recover their senses and all the jury and it's time for a rest. Maybe I can find Polly.

And here comes Polly, popping up. No sooner maybe'd than here she is in all her silks and satins. Life's like that. A miraculous sequence of joys and sorrows. Punch, says the beautiful pink-cheeked strumpet, you're looking a touch woebegone. What's the trouble, my darling? Hemorrhoids again? No, Polly, love of my life, the pain's not in my arse but in my heart. Didn't know you had one, Punch, my precious knob, I'm gratified to hear of it. Maybe we can boil it up and have it for supper. Do not make light, Polly, of my little inquietudes. Oh dear, are they swoll up again? No, Polly dear, I speak of my mortified soul. My vexation of spirit. On the subject of spirits, she says, and she reaches into her skirts and pulls out a bottle. This should make you feel better, she says, or if not better, less, and in her loving way she drinks most of it off and hands the dregs to me. Now lie back and pull out that fidgety widget of yours, my dearest darling, she says with a tender burp, and let us dance our dance before your Judy comes round with her vengeful stick again. A sweet innocent child, Polly, still given to euphemisms. It's out and she's on it, doing her little gavotte, as one might call it. Perhaps there is music playing. A panpipe. Lovely. But I feel emptied out in heart and head. It's sad. You know me, Polly, as a happy bawdy fellow without a care in the world. I get to do a lot of killing, it's great fun, and the mob loves me for it, especially the ladies, whom as you know I never disappoint. I'm immortal and handsome and find the wherewithal for all my daily needs in the pockets of the recently deceased. I should be a most satisfied gent. But something's missing, I add with a tremulous sigh, my hands clapped to her bouncing bum, and I don't know what it is. Polly has got carried away with her dance and has nothing to say except: Oh! Oh! Oh! Some pleasure I'm missing out on? If I don't know what it is, I reply, conversing with myself, I'm not missing it. A reason for being? A tautology, dear heart, if you'll pardon the French. Meaning, am I missing? Pah! I don't even know what meaning means. Love? I'm drowning in it. Polly lets out a wild shriek, quivers all over as if caught by a sudden fever, then collapses over the mound of my belly, conking her head on my nose but seeming not to notice. Her little bum continues to rise and fall gently as if trying to remember something. Maybe, I say as her dance dies away, it's just that everything seems to happen as it must. Even what I'm saying now. Polly grunts in sympathetic understanding and tweedles a pretty fart out between my fingers, perhaps an answer of sorts. Yes, I can always count on wise Polly.

But no time to contemplate it. Her flatus raises the dead. Here comes Judy's ghost again, mad as ever, swinging the howling baby. The kid's had a tough life. Or death. I maybe should have been a better father. Judy, bellowing in her termagant fashion, rains blows on the both of us with the poor brat, intent, it would seem, on belting us both into her own domain of the dead. What rage! She's a real beauty! My sweet duck! For a moment I love her all over again and am sorry I killed her. Maybe I can take it back. Pretty Polly, though, just a wisp of a thing and drained by her dance, unable even to get disconnected from my digit, squeezed up tight in terror as she is, is no match for my Judy, and I worry for her health. She is not part of our little circle and does not understand why she is being walloped by a dead baby. Some things are best kept inside the family. Grateful still for her fragrant little whiffle of wisdom, I ease her off me, and cover her with my hump until she can drop out of sight, being myself somewhat inured to the baby's blows. More than to its cries. It's a maddening din. If I could, I'd throw it out the window again and the yowping mother with it. But they're ghosts. They'd just fly back in again. In the pandemonium, I have forgotten to put Polly's dancing partner back where it belongs and now dead Judy clamps her jaws on it, trying to bite it off. It's my tenderest part. It hurts so much I can't think. Even though she's got no teeth. All I can do is try to pull her off. She bites down the harder, her nose and chin joining like the pincers of a crab. Having her head there, for all the excruciating pain of it (if I could cry, there'd be tears in my eyes, maybe there are tears in my eyes), reminds me of happier times, though I can recall none specifically. All the melting moments. There must have been some. Where did we go wrong? Better not to ask. Finally, in desperation, I yank so hard, I rip her body away from her head. The body, silent at last, flies away with the baby, but her head, still wearing the Georgian mobcap, remains clamped on my suffering instrument of mercy and thanksgiving, my great animator. Without it in prime and proud condition, I'd be disgraced, unable to hold my head up in public. I'll have to call for a doctor, if there are any left, or else a carpenter, and have her sawn off. Then I'll have to kill the doctor or carpenter, roo-tee-too-it, how you do it, et cetera. Because I must. And then I'll do it all again. As maybe I've done it all before. So much happens in this world. I can hardly keep up with it from minute to minute. But then it's gone. There's no residue. Ah. Well. Maybe, dear Polly, that's what's missing. The price of immortality. When nothing ends, nothing remains.

THE INVISIBLE MAN

THE INVISIBLE MAN GAVE up his life as a crime fighter, it was too hard and no one cared enough, and became a voyeur, a thief, a bugaboo, a prowler and pickpocket, a manipulator of events. It was more fun and people paid more attention to him. He began inhabiting horse tracks, women's locker rooms, extravagant festivities, bank vaults, public parks, schoolyards, and centers of power. He emptied tills, altered votes, made off with purses and address books, leaked secrets, started up fights in subway cars and boardrooms, took any empty seat he wanted on planes and trains, blew on the necks of naked women, moved pieces on gameboards and gambling tables, made strange noises in dark bedrooms, tripped up politicians and pop stars on stage, and whispered perverse temptations in the ears of the pious.

Theft was particularly easy except for the problem of what to do with what he took. To be invisible he had to be naked, and there were not too many places on or in his body where he could hide things which themselves were not invisible. And these places (notably, his mouth and his rectum, which served as his overnight bag, so to speak) were often filled with other necessities. So, except for small jewelry store heists which could be slipped in, he was generally limited to what he could hold in his closed fists or squeeze under his armpits or between his buttocks, his daily spoils comparable then to those of a common panhandler, from whom on bad days he also sometimes stole. Still, there was not much on which to spend his wealth, whatever he wanted he could simply take and he could travel and live as and where he pleased, so he soon amassed a small fortune and, privy to all the inside information he needed, became a successful day trader on the side.

Though drawn into a life of crime without remorse, and tempted like anyone else to kill a few people while he was at it, he had no place to conceal a suitable weapon, indeed it would be dangerous if he tried, so his new career was necessarily limited to lesser felonies. Of course, he could discreetly misdirect the aim of others, but in fact he steered clear of armed persons, as well as reckless drivers, busy kitchens, operating rooms. He could still be hurt. Stray bullets could wound him, knives could prick. He was only invisible, not immortal. And his insides were not invisible, his excretions weren't, his blood. What a sight, a wound in view and no wounded! Moreover, if wounded, who would heal him? Perhaps he could find a blind doctor, though probably there weren't many. And if he died, who would mourn him? Who would even see him there to bury him? He'd become a kind of odd speed bump in the road for a month or two. Such were the handicaps of an invisible person, no matter how rich they were or how much secret mischief they enjoyed.

He was also obliged to stay away from cold places. Though his nakedness was apparent to no one and he himself was accustomed to it, it was a reality he could not ignore. Cold winds drove him inside, air conditioning out. Sometimes, to warm himself or to conduct some business or other such as fencing his stolen goods, or perhaps simply in response to a deep longing, he made himself visible with masks, wigs, and costumes. So as not to have to steal these things over and over, he bought a house to store them in, and took up stamp and coin collecting and growing orchids on the side. There were many choices amongst his costumes, many characters he could be, and this added to his existential angst: who was he really? Without a costume, he was invisible even to himself. In the mirror he could see no more than anyone else could see: a blurry nothingness where something should be. "You are a beautiful person," he would say to it, more as an instruction than a comment.

When costuming himself, he had to dress carefully from head to toe. One day he forgot his socks and caused something of a sensation when taking his seat on the subway. "Sorry, a... a kind of cancer," he explained to the people staring aghast at his missing ankles, fully aware (he exited hastily at the next stop) that the mouth on the mask was not moving. On another day in a crowded elevator (when visible, he loved to mingle with the human masses, feel the body contact, something that usually had to be avoided when invisible), his scarf fell off, which was even worse. A woman fainted and the other passengers all shrank back. "It's just a trick," he chuckled behind the deadpan mask, which no doubt appeared to them to be floating in midair. He riffled a deck of cards enigmatically in his gloved hands, and when the door opened, he turned his empty eyes upon them to mesmerize them long enough to make his escape. After that, he took to wearing body suits as the first layer, a kind of undercoat, much as he hated getting in and out of them.

Mostly, though, he went naked and unseen, committing his crimes, indulging himself in his manipulative and voyeuristic pleasures. Women fascinated him, and he loved watching them do their private things, frustrating as it was at times not to participate. Even when they were most exposed, they remained unfathomably mysterious to him, and an unending delight. And it was one day while hanging out in the ladies' room of a grand hotel during a hairdressers' convention that, when things were slow, he stepped into a stall and raised the seat to relieve himself, only to have the door open behind him and the seat lower itself again, and he knew then that he was not alone in his invisibility. Was she (he assumed "she") sitting on the seat or was this merely a gender signal and a warning? Taking no chances, he backed out silently, hoping he wasn't dripping, the opening and closing of the stall door no doubt telling her all she needed to know.

After that, he began to feel pursued. Perhaps she had been following him for some time and he hadn't noticed. Now he seemed to sense her there whether she was or not, and whether or not, he had to consider his every move as if she were. She might still be an active crime fighter, just waiting to apprehend him or to avenge some crime that he'd committed in the past. He retreated from more than one burglary, sensing her presence in the room, and sometimes it seemed there was another hand in the pocket he was trying to pick. He watched the women on the street carefully in case she, like he, occasionally made herself visible, and they all appeared to him to be wearing masks. He was jostled by absences, felt a hot breath often on his neck. His income dropped off sharply and he was even inhibited from acquiring his daily necessities. Her possible proximity made him self-conscious about his personal hygiene and interfered with his voyeuristic routines. He felt especially vulnerable inside his own house and went there less often, with the consequence that the food in his refrigerator spoiled and his orchids died.

How did she know where he was if she couldn't see him? By following the clues the invisible always leave behind: footprints in the mud, snow (of course he never walked in snow), and sand, bodily excretions, fingerprints (he couldn't wear gloves, nor carry them without getting them messy), discarded costumes and toothbrushes, mattress indentations, floating objects, swirling dust, fogged windows. She could watch for places where the rain did not fall and listen for the noises his body made. He had always stumbled over things; now he could not be sure she was not placing those things in his path to expose him, so just moving about was like negotiating a mine field. He had to eat more surreptitiously, not to exhibit the food flying about before vanishing, and so ate too fast, giving himself heartburn. But when he started to steal a packet of antacids, he thought he saw it move as he reached for it.

Then it occurred to him one day that she might not be a crime fighter after all, merely another lonely invisible person seeking company, and as soon as he had that thought, she disappeared, or seemed to. He should have felt relieved, but he did not. He found that he missed her. Though she had not been exactly friendly, she was the nearest thing to a friend he'd ever had. He went back to where they'd first met and raised and lowered the toilet seat, but there was no response. He should have spoken up that day. He did now: "Are you there?" he whispered. No reply, though the lady in the next stall asked: "Did you say something?" "No, dear, just a frog in the throat," he wheezed in a cracking falsetto, then flushed quickly and swung the door open and closed before the woman could get up from where she was sitting and peek in. But he remained in the stall for a time, reflecting on how something so ordinary as a toilet seat can be transformed suddenly into something extraordinary and, well, beautiful...

Now he left clues everywhere and committed crimes more daring than before. If she was a crime fighter he wanted to be arrested by her. If she was not, well, they could be partners. She even had more room to hide things, they could tackle bigger jobs. As he moved about, he swung his arms freely, hoping to knock into something that did not seem to be there, but caused only unfortunate accidents and misdirected anger. Twice he got shot at in the dark. He figured it was a small price to pay. Perhaps if he were hurt she'd feel pity for him and make herself known. He began to see her, even in her invisibility, as unutterably beautiful, and he realized that he was hopelessly in love. He thought of his adoration of her as pure and noble, utterly unlike his life in crime, but he also imagined making mad impetuous love to her. Rolling about ecstatically in their indentations. Nothing he'd seen in his invisible powder-room prowls excited him more than these imaginings.

Still, for all his hopes, she gave no further evidence of her existence. In his house, he left messages on the mirrors: "Take me, I'm yours!" But the messages sat there, unanswered, unaltered. When he looked in the mirrors, past the lettering, he could not see his cheeks but he could see the tears sliding down them. His love life, once frivolous, had turned tragic, and it was all his fault. Why had he never *touched* her? A fool, a fool! He was in despair. He hung out in bars more often, drinking other peoples' drinks. He got sick once and threw up beside a singing drunk peeing against a wall, sobering the poor man up instantly. He knew that rumors about him were beginning to spread, but what did it matter? Without her, his life was meaningless. It had not been very meaningful before she came into it, but now it was completely empty. Even crime bored him. Voyeurism did: what did he care about visible bodies when he was obsessed by an invisible one?

He tried to find some reason for going on. Over the years, he'd been collecting a set of antique silverware from one family, a piece at a time. He decided to finish the set. He didn't really want the silverware, but it gave him something to do. He successfully picked up another couple of pieces, operating recklessly in broad daylight, but then went back one time too many and, with a soup spoon up his ass, got bit on the shins by a watchdog the family had bought to try to catch the silverware thief. He got away, doing rather serious damage to the dog (in effect, it ate the soup spoon), but he bled all the way home. He supposed they'd follow the trail, didn't care if they did, but they didn't. Maybe they were satisfied not to lose the spoon.

But the wound was slow to heal and he couldn't go about with it or the bandage on it exposed, so he donned the costume of an old man (he was an old man!) and spent his days in cheap coffee shops feeling sorry for himself and mooning over his lost love. He went on doing this even after the dog bite had healed, drawn to coffee shops with sad songs on their sound systems. He no longer stole but bought most of what he needed, which was little, but now included reading materials for his coffee shop life. He avoided newspapers and magazines, preferring old novels from vanished times, mostly those written by women, all of whom he tended to think of as beautiful and invisible. He would sometimes sit all day over a single page, letting his mind drift, muttering softly to himself, or more or less to himself, all the things he should have said when she was still in his life.

Then one day he saw, sitting at another table, also greatly aged, an old police captain he used to work with back in his crime-fighting days. He made himself known to him (the captain did not look surprised; perhaps he'd been tailing him) and asked him how things were going down at the station. "Since you left, Invisible Man," said the officer, "things have gone from bad to worse. You became something of a nuisance to us when you took up your new career, but it was a decision we could understand and make allowances for. Now there are gangs of invisible people out there committing heinous crimes that threaten to destroy the very fabric of our civilization." The Invisible Man stroked his false beard thoughtfully. "And since I stopped being a crime fighter, have you had help from any other... person like myself?" "No. Until these new gangs came along, you were unique in my experience, Invisible Man." So, he thought, she might be among them. "It's why we're turning to you now. We're asking you to come back to the force, Invisible Man. We need you to infiltrate these gangs and help us stop them before it's too late." "You're asking me to turn against my own people," he said, somewhat pretentiously, for in truth he never thought of himself as having people. "These aren't your people, Invisible Man, it's a whole new breed. They create fields of invisibility so even their clothing and weapons and everything they steal is made invisible when it enters it. And now they're into bomb-making." This was serious, all right; but he was thinking about his beloved. His former beloved. He understood now that she might have been trying to recruit him for her gang, but had found him unworthy, and he felt hurt by that. "They think of you as old-fashioned, Invisible Man, and have said some very unflattering things about you. In particular, about your personal habits, of which of course I know nothing. But they also look up to you as a kind of pioneer. And though their power is greater than yours, their technology is less reliable. They've suffered catastrophic system crashes, and we want them to suffer a few more. It's a dangerous job, Invisible Man, but you're the only one we know who can handle it."

So once again he took up his old life as a crime fighter, but under cover of renewed criminality, drifting somewhat cynically through the city in his old invisible skin, targeting the city fathers for his burglaries and vandalisms, dropping inflammatory notes to draw attention to himself, and even, with help from the captain, blowing up the captain's own car, which he said was anyway in need of extensive clutch and transmission repairs, so he was glad to get rid of it—in short, making himself available, waiting to be contacted. Would she be among them? He felt misunderstood by her, undervalued, and in some odd way misused. A victim of love. Which he no longer believed in, even while still in the grip of its unseen power. And if he found her again, would he crash her system? Or would she succeed in seducing him into the gangs' nefarious activities? Who knows? He decided to keep an open mind about it. The future was no easier to see than he was.

THE DEAD QUEEN

THE OLD QUEEN HAD a grin on her face when we buried her in the mountain, and I knew then that it was she who had composed this scene, as all before, she who had led us, revelers and initiates, to this cold and windy grave site, hers the design, ours the enactment, and I felt like the first man, destined to rise and fall, rise and fall, to the end of time. My father saw this, perhaps I was trembling, and as though to comfort me, said: No, it was a mere grimace, the contortions of pain, she had suffered greatly after all, torture often exposes the diabolic in the face of man, she was an ordinary woman, beautiful it is true, and shrewd, but she had risen above her merits, and falling, had lost her reason to rancor. We can learn even from the wretched, my son; her poor death and poorer life teach us to temper ambition with humility, and to ignore reflections as one ignores mortality. But I did not believe him, I could see for myself, did not even entirely trust him, this

51

man who thought power a localized convention, magic a popular word for concealment, for though it made him a successful King, decisive and respected, the old Queen's grin mocked such simple faith and I was not consoled.

My young bride, her cheeks made rosy by the mountain air, smiled benignly through the last rites, just as she had laughed with open glee at her stepmother's terrible entertainment at our wedding feast the night before, her cheeks flushed then with wine. I tried to read her outrageous cheerfulness, tried to understand the merriment that such an awesome execution had provoked. At times, she seemed utterly heartless, this child, become the very evil she'd been saved from. Had all our watchfulness been in vain, had that good and simple soul been envenomed after all, was it she who'd invited her old tormentor to the ball, commissioned the iron slippers, drawn her vindictively into that ghastly dance? Or did she simply laugh as the righteous must to see the wicked fall? Perhaps her own release from death had quickened her heart, such that mere continuance now made her a little giddy. Or had she, absent, learned something of hell? How could I know? I could vouch for her hymen from this side, but worried that it had been probed from within. How she'd squealed to see the old Queen's flailing limbs, how she'd applauded the ringing of those flaming iron clogs against the marble floors! Yet, it was almost as though she were ignorant of the pain, of any cause or malice, ignorant of consequences—like a happy child at the circus, unaware of any skills or risks. Once, the poor woman had stumbled and sprawled, her skirts heaped up around her ears, and this had sprung a jubilant roar of laughter from the banqueters, but Snow White had only smiled expectantly, then clapped gaily as the guards set the dying

Queen on her burning feet again. Now, as I stood there on the mountainside, watching my bride's black locks flow in the wintry wind and her young breasts fill with the rare air, she suddenly turned toward me, and seeing me stare so intensely, smiled happily and squeezed my hand. No, I thought, she's suffered no losses, in fact that's just the trouble, that hymen can never be broken, not even by me, not in a thousand nights, this is her gift and essence, and because of it, she can see neither fore nor aft, doesn't know there is a mirror on the wall. Perhaps it was this that had made the old Queen hate her so.

If hate was the word. Perhaps she'd loved her. Or more likely, she'd had no feelings toward her at all. She'd found her unconscious and so useful. Did Snow White really believe she was the fairest in the land? Perhaps she did, she had a gift for the absurd. And thereby her stepmother had hatched a plot, and the rest, as my father would say, is history. What a cruel irony, those redhot shoes! For it wasn't that sort of an itch that had driven the old Queen—what she had lusted for was a part in the story, immortality, her place in guarded time. To be the forgotten stepmother of a forgotten Princess was not enough. It was the mirror that had fucked her, fucked us all. And did she foresee those very boots, the dance, that last obscenity? No doubt. Or something much like them. Just as she foresaw the Hunter's duplicity, the Dwarfs' ancient hunger, my own weakness for romance. Even our names were lost, she'd transformed us into colors, simple proclivities, our faces were forever fixed and they weren't even our own!

I was made dizzy by these speculations. I felt the mountain would tip and spill us all to hell or worse. I clutched for my bride's hand, grabbed the nose of a Dwarf instead. He sneezed loudly. The mourners ducked their heads and tittered. Snow White withdrew a lace kerchief from her sleeve and helped the Dwarf to blow his nose. My father frowned. I held my breath and stared at the dead Queen, masked to hide her eyes, which to what my father called a morbid imagination might seem to be winking, one open, the other squeezed shut. I thought: We've all been reduced to jesters, fools; tragedy she reserved for herself alone. This seemed true, but so profoundly true, it seemed false. I kept my feet apart and tried to think about the Queen's crimes. She had commissioned a child's death and eaten what she'd hoped was its heart. She'd reduced a Princess to a menial of menials, then sought to destroy her, body, mind, and soul. And, I thought, poisoned us all with pattern. Surely, she deserved to die.

In the end, in spite of everything, she'd been accepted as part of the family, spared the outcast's shame, shrouded simply in black and granted her rings and diadems. Only her feet had been left naked, terribly naked: stripped even of their nails and skin. They were raw and blistery, shriveling now and seeming to ooze. Her feet had become one with the glowing iron shoes, of course, the moment we'd forced them on her—what was her wild dance, after all, but a desperate effort to jump out of her own skin? She had not succeeded, but ultimately, once she had died and the shoes had cooled, this final freedom had been more or less granted her, there being no other way to get her feet out of the shoes except to peel them out. I had suggested—naively, it seemed—that the shoes be left on her, buried with her, and had been told that the feet of the wicked were past number, but the Blacksmith's art was rare and sacred. As my Princess and I groped about in our bridal chamber, fumbling darkly toward some new disclosure, I had wondered: Do such things happen at all weddings? We could hear them in the scullery, scraping the shoes out with picks and knives and rinsing them in acid.

What a night, our wedding night! A pity the old Queen had arrived so late, died so soon, missed our dedicated fulfillment of her comic design—or perhaps this, too, was part of her tragedy, the final touch to a life shaped by denial. Of course, it could be argued that she had courted reversals, much as a hero makes his own wars, that she had invented, then pursued the impossible, in order to push the possible beyond her reach, and thus had died, as so many have believed, of vanity, but never mind, the fact is, she was her own consummation, and we, in effect, had carried out—were still carrying out—our own ludicrous performances without an audience. Who could not laugh at us?

My sweetheart and I had sealed our commitment at high noon. My father had raised a cup to our good fortune, issued a stern proclamation against peddlers, bestowed happiness and property upon us and all our progeny, and the party had begun. Whole herds had been slaughtered for our tables. The vineyards of seven principalities had filled our casks. We had danced, sung, clung to one another, drunk, laughed, cheered, chanted the sun down. Bards had pilgrimaged from far and wide, come with their alien tongues to celebrate our union with pageants, prayers, and sacrifices. Not soon, they'd said, would this feast be forgotten. We'd exchanged epigrams and gallantries, whooped the old Queen through her death dance, toasted the fairies and offered them our firstborn. The Dwarfs had recited an ode in praise of clumsiness, though they'd forgotten some of the words and had got into a fight over which of them had dislodged the apple from Snow White's throat, and how, pushing each other into soup bowls and out of windows. They'd thrown cakes and pies at each other for awhile, then had spilled wine on everybody, played tug-of-war with the Queen's carcass, regaled us with ribald mimes of regicide and witch-baiting, and finally had climaxed it all by buggering each other in a circle around Snow White, while singing their gold-digging song. Snow White had kissed them all fondly afterward, helped them up with their breeches, brushed the crumbs from their beards, and I'd wondered then about my own mother, who was she?—and where was Snow White's father? Whose party was this? Why was I so sober? Suddenly I'd found myself, minutes before midnight, troubled by many things: the true meaning of my bride's name, her taste for luxury and collapse, the compulsions that had led me to the mountain, the birdshit on the glass coffin when I'd found her. Who *were* all these people, and why did things happen as though they were necessary? Oh, I'd reveled and worshipped with the rest of the party right to the twelfth stroke, but I couldn't help thinking: We've been too rash, we're being overtaken by some-thing terrible, and who's to help us now the old Queen's dead?

The hole in the mountain was dug. The Dwarfs stepped back to admire their handiwork, tripped over their own beards, and fell in a big heap. They scrambled clumsily to their feet, clout-ing each other with their picks and shovels, wound up bowling one another over like duckpins and went tumbling in a roly-poly landslide down the mountain, grunting and whistling all the way. While we waited for them to return, I wondered: Why are we burying her in the mountain? We no longer believe in under-worlds nor place hope in moldering kings, still we stuff them back into the earth's navel, as though anticipating some future interest, much as we stuff our treasures in crypts, our fiats in

archives. Well, perhaps it had been her dying wish, I'm not told
everything, her final vanity. Perhaps she had wanted to bring us
back to this mountain, where her creation by my chance passage
had been accomplished, to confront us with our own insignifi-
cance, our complaisant transience, the knowledge that it was
ended, the rest would be forgotten, our fates were not sealed,
merely eclipsed. She had eaten Snow White's heart in order to
randomize her attentions, deprive her of her center, and now, like
her victim and the bite of poison apple, she had vomited the
heart up whole and undigested—but like the piece of apple, it
could never be restored to its old function, it had its own life
now, it would create its own circumambience, and we would be
as remote from this magic as those of a hundred generations
hence. Of course... it wasn't Snow White's heart she ate, no, it
was the heart of a boar, I was getting carried away, I was forgetting things. She'd sent that child of seven into the woods with a
restless lech, and he'd brought her back a boar's heart, as though
to say he repented of his irrational life and wished to die. But
then, perhaps that had been what she'd wanted, perhaps she had
ordered the boar's heart, or known anyway that would be the
Hunter's instinct, or perhaps there had been no Hunter at all,
perhaps it had been that master of disguises, the old Queen her
self, it was possible, it was all possible. I was overswept by confusion and apprehension. I felt like I'd felt that morning, when
I'd awakened, spent, to find no blood on the nuptial linens.

The wedding party had ended at midnight. A glass slipper
had been ceremoniously smashed on the last stroke of the hour,
and the nine of us—Snow White and I and, at her insistence, my
new brethren the seven Dwarfs—had paraded to the bridal chamber. I had been too unsettled to argue, had walked down the

torchlit corridors through the music and applause as though in a trance, for I had fallen, moments before, into an untimely sobriety, had suddenly, as it were, become myself for the first time all day, indeed for the first time in my life, and at the expense of all I'd held real, my Princeship, my famous disenchantments, my bride, my songs, my family, had felt for a few frantic moments like a sun inside myself, about to be exposed and extinguished in a frozen void named Snow White. This man I'd called my father, I'd realized, was a perfect stranger, this palace a playhouse, these revelers the mocking eyes of a dying demiurge! Perhaps all bridegrooms suffer this. Though I'd carried my cock out proudly, as all Princes must, I'd not recognized it as my own when the citizenry in the corridors had knelt to honor it—not a mere ornament of office, I'd told myself, but the officer itself, I its loyal and dispensable retinue. Someone, as I'd passed, had bit it as though to test its readiness, and the pain had reached me like a garbled dispatch from the front line of battle: Victory is ours, alas, all is lost...

But once inside the nuptial chamber, the door clicking shut behind me, Snow White cuddling sleepily on my shoulder, the Dwarfs flinging off their clothes and fighting over the chamber pot, I'd returned from my extravagant vagrancy, cock and ceremony had become all mine again, and for some reason I hadn't felt all that grateful. Maybe, I'd thought, maybe I'm a little drunker than I think. I could not have hoped for a more opulent setting: the bed a deep heap of silken eiderdowns, the floors covered with the luxuriant skins of mountain goats, mirrors on all the walls, perfume burning in golden censers, flasks of wine and bowls of fruit on the marble tables, lutes and pipes scattered decorously about. In the morning, I'd vowed, I shall arise before daybreak and compose a new song for my bride to remember this night by. Gently then, sequentially, as though being watched and judged, as though preparing the verses for my song, I'd embraced and commenced to disrobe her. I'd thought: I should be more excited than this. The Dwarfs had seemed to pay us no attention, but I'd begun to resent them: if I failed, they'd pay! One of them had got his foot stuck in the chamber pot and was clumping about in a rage. Another had seemed to be humping a goatskin. I'd nuzzled in Snow White's black tresses, kissed her white throat, whence she'd vomited the fateful apple, and wondered: Why hadn't I been allowed to disenchant her with a kiss like everybody else? Of course, with the apple there, it might not have been all that pleasant...

Her nimble hands had unfastened my sashes and buckles with ease, stroked my back, teased my buttocks and balls, but my own fingers had got tangled in her laces. The Dwarfs had come to the rescue, and so had made me feel a fool again. Leave me alone! I'd cried. I can do it by myself! I'd realized then that Snow White had both her arms around my neck and the finger up my ass certainly wasn't my own. I'd gazed into the mirrors to see, for the first time, Snow White's paradigmatic beauty, but instead it had been the old Queen I'd seen there, flailing about madly in her redhot shoes. Maybe it had been the drinking, all the shocks, or some new trick of my brethren, or else the scraping of the shoes in the scullery that had made me imagine it, but whatever, I had panicked, had gone lurching about drunkenly, shaking off Dwarfs, shrouding all the mirrors with whatever had come to hand, smashing not a few of them, feeling the eyes close, the grimaces fade, the room darken: This night is *mine*! I'd cried, and covered the last of them.

We'd been plunged into night—I'd never known a dark so

deep, nor felt so much alone. Snow White? Snow White! I'd
heard her answer, thought I'd heard her, it was as though she'd
called my name—I'd lunged forward, banged my knee on a marble table, cut my foot on broken glass. Snow White! I'd heard
whispering, giggling, soft sighs. Come on, what're you doing?
I've cut myself! Light a candle! I'd stumbled over someone's foot,
run my elbow through a lute. I'd lain there thinking: Forget it,
the state I'm in, I might as well wait until morning, why has my
father let me suffer such debasement, it must be yet another of
his moral lessons on the sources of a King's majesty. The strange
sensation had come to me suddenly that this bride I now pursued
did not even exist, was just something in *me*, something locked
and frozen, waiting to be released, something lying dormant, like
an accumulation of ancestral visions and vagaries seeking corpor-
eity—but then I'd heard her struggling, gasping, whimpering.
Help me! Please—! Those Dwarfs! I'd leaped up and charged into
a bedpost. *I'm coming!* Those goddamn dirty Dwarfs! Ever since
the day of Snow White's disenchantment, when I'd embraced
them as brothers, I'd had uneasy suspicions about them I couldn't
quite allow myself to admit, but now they'd burst explosively to
the surface, in the dark I'd been able to see what I couldn't see in
full daylight, from the first night she'd shared their seven beds,
just a child, to the unspeakable things they were doing with her
now beneath the eiderdowns, even their famous rescues had been
nothing more than excuses to strip her, play with her, how many
years had the old witch let them keep her? *Leave her alone! You
hear?* I'd chased her voice, but the Dwarfs had kept shifting her
about. They worked underground, it was easy for them, they
were used to the dark. I'd kept pushing toward her muted voice,
scrambling over goatskins and featherbedding, under bed and

tables, through broken glass and squashed fruit, into closets, cracking my head on pillars and doorjambs, backing my bare nates into a hot oil lamp, recently extinguished. I'd tried to light it, but all the oil had been spilled. In fact, I was sitting in it.

But never mind, I'd begun to enjoy this, I was glad to have it out in the open, I could beat those Dwarfs at their own game, yes, I'd got a real sweat up, and an appetite, too: Whatever those freaks could do, I could do better! I'd brushed up against a couple of beards, grabbed them and knocked the heads together: *Hah!* There'd been the popping sound of something breaking, like a fruit bowl. I'd laughed aloud, crawled toward Snow White's soft cries over their bodies: they'd felt like goatskins. The spirit had begun to wax powerful within me, my foaming steed, as they say in the fairytales, was rampant, my noble lance was at the ready. Hardly before I'd realized I'd begun, I'd found myself plunging away in her wet and eager body, the piercing of her formidable hymen already just a memory, her sweet cry of pain mere history, as now she, panting, breathed my name: Charming! *Oh dear dear Charming!* She'd seemed to have a thousand hands, a mouth everywhere at once, a glowing furnace between her thrashing thighs, I'd sucked at her heaving breasts, groped in her leaping buttocks, we'd slithered and slid over and under one another, rolling about in the eiderdowns, thrice around the world we'd gone in a bucking frenzy of love and lubricity, seven times we'd died in each other, and as at last, in a state of delicious annihilation, I'd lost consciousness, my fading thoughts had been: Those damned Dwarfs are all right after all, they're all right...

And we'd awakened at dawn, alone, clasped in each other's arms, the bed unmussed and unbloodied, her hymen intact.

The Dwarfs had returned from their roll down the mountain, patched and bandaged and singing a lament for the death of the unconscious, and we prepared to enter the old Queen in her tomb. I gazed at her in the glass coffin, the coffin that had once contained my wife, and thought: If she wakes, she will stare at the glass and discover there her own absence. I was beginning to appreciate her subtlety, and so assumed that this, too, had been part of her artifice, a lingering hope for her own liberation, she'd used the mirror as a door, tried to. This was her Great Work, this her use of a Princess with hair as black as ebony, a skin as white as snow, lips as red as blood, this her use of miners of gold! Of course there were difficulties in such a perfect view of things, she was dead, for example, but one revelation was leading to another, and it came to me suddenly that maybe the old Queen had loved me, had died for me! I, too, was too prone to linger at still pools, to listen to the flattery of soothsayers, to organize my life and others' by threes and sevens—it was as if she'd lived this exemplary life, died this tragic death, to lead me away from the merely visible to vision, from the image to the imaged, from reflections to the projecting miracle itself, the heart, the pure snow white...!

One of the Dwarfs had been hopping about frantically, and now Snow White took him over behind a bush, but if this was meant to distract me, it did not succeed. The old Queen had me now, everything had fallen into place, I knew now the force that had driven her, that had freed me, freed us all, that we might live happily ever after, though we didn't deserve it, weren't even aware of how it had happened, yes, I knew her cause, knew her name—I wrenched open the coffin, threw myself upon her, and kissed her lips.

If I'd expected something, it did not occur. She did not return my kiss, did not even cease grinning. She stank and her blue mouth was cold and rubbery as a dead squid. I'd been wrong about her, wrong about everything...

The others had fallen back in horror and dismay. Snow White had fainted. Someone was vomiting. My father's eyes were full of tears and anger.

Though nauseated, I pitched forward and kissed her again, this time more out of pride and affection, than hope. I thought: It would've helped if the old clown had died with her mouth shut.

They tore me away from her body. It tumbled out of the coffin and, limbs awry, obstinately grinning, skidded a few feet down the mountainside. The flesh tore, but did not bleed. The mask fell away from her open eye, now milky white.

Please! I pleaded, though I no longer even hoped I was right. Let me try once more! Maybe a third time!

Guards restrained me. My father turned his back. The Dwarfs were reviving Snow White by fanning her skirts. The Queen's corpse was dumped hastily back into the coffin and quickly interred, everyone holding his nose. The last thing I saw were her skinned feet. I turned and walked down the mountain.

Thinking. If this is the price of beauty, it's too high. I was glad she was dead.

PLAYING HOUSE

ONCE THERE WAS a house, whispers someone in the dark (we are learning about another house, our own house, the one in which we live), and it had windows everywhere and walls as thin as skin and it was full of light.

Even at night?

There were no nights.

Our walls are thick and windowless, but alterations can be made. Even now someone can be heard chipping away with a hammer and a chisel.

Inside that house, the outside came and went by whim or will, not as a guest, but as though it too resided there, continues the whispering storyteller, until the inside felt more like a visitor inside the house that was itself.

Inside our house, the outside remains no more than an architectural project, in the planning stages still. We imagine it in terms of the unseen walls and floor and ceiling. The absence of.

To possess the light is to be possessed, the storyteller whispers, and in the dark we can see that this is so, and a great longing overtakes us. To be possessed!

Unseen, the structures of our house—the rooms and so on—but known to us; we get about by touch, our toys our tools, and dream, a game we play, of building light. Though out of what, we're not yet sure. The materials used so far—steel, stones, bones, water—have yielded only obstacles to light, suggesting that, as that fable we've all been told would have it, light cannot be built or even found, but someone must bring it in.

Another game we play is naming things. We call the hammer hammer, chisel chisel. Claw hammer, we say. Cold chisel. Some say that naming things creates them, but we've named the light and no light comes. We call the new hole under construction a window, though as we understand windows (not well), it is really more a window-yet-to-be. Or more likely only another door. We take turns peering into it and describing what we see there, or rather, what we wish to see. I see a tree! The moon! A lake, a bay! Another house! Perhaps this wishing *is* the light and all there is of it.

With the outside in, whispers the storyteller, the inside withdrew further in, and that is how the dark began. Oh well. Another happy ending. Presumably. We've heard this nursery tale before. We leave it and its teller and squeeze through one of the old holes we've made that we call doors.

These doors, most of which began as windows, lead to other rooms, the rooms we play in, or else to a corridor. We think there may be fifteen or twenty of these rooms and corridors, but now and then a new one's found, brought about perhaps by the making of our doors, or else an old one, subtly altered, feels like new, our imagined floor plans thus less like storied gameboards than the pieces moved about on them. So, several, maybe, better said. Several in a cluster (new doors sometimes find old rooms thought several rooms away: if these rooms are like beads on a string, as some believe, then that string is knotted).

These several rooms in which we play all have walls (from one to many, curved or straight), floors (just one each, though sometimes stepped), and ceilings (entire or not) some ways above us, known to us only by the knocks we hear when we throw things up at them, the corridors these elements as well, though sometimes in the corridors the ceilings can be touched. Tunnels might be another word.

Once there was a house, goes another story we have heard, called the House of Anxiety, in which the corridors all led onto other corridors, provoking ceaseless motion without respite, the rooms all trapped somehow between, if in fact there were any. The story says there were, but how can a story know? We suppose these rooms exist in a story where they do not exist simply because a house *qua* house is unimaginable without them. We call it the Fallacy of the A Priori Judgment. Still naming things.

In our story, as we might call our lives, rooms do exist, even if as yet unseen; we play in them. We make things in them with our tools, more doors, for example, and play, among others, what-am-I-holding and where-are-we-now games. We tell stories, kiss, stack stones, and read the walls with our fingertips. In the legendary House of Anxiety, there was nothing to read; the corridors, though well-lit, were all smooth-walled and empty and identical to one another, their precise dimensions chilling to the touch and to the naked but illumined eye, the dubious moral of the story being: Light is not what's missing.

In our lightless rooms and corridors, some walls and floors are smooth, but most are rough, uneven, woolly even; we like the rough ones best of course. They're more our own somehow, and we know them when we've returned to them; the smooth ones could be anywhere and sometimes we get lost in them. Here's one! someone in such a room will shout, meaning a door, and everyone will then scramble toward the voice and out through the opening there, afraid to be left behind in a space where nothing can be known.

The objects in these rooms are few and mostly things we've left behind ourselves when playing here before, some made by us, some found: an awl, a teaspoon, a cuplike thing, a piece of pipe, small heaps of stony rubble from the doors we've built or come upon, but in one such room, newly discovered, a large one-walled one (it is circular, or nearly so), we find a cupboard standing in the middle, one unattached to any wall. Have we made this? No, someone must have come, we think. And if, as fabled, they've brought the light, then the light they've brought may be inside!

The prospect of light in a house so long unlit fills some of us with exhilaration—at last!—but others with deep disquiet, a fear of pain and disenchantment: Leave it alone! Don't touch! Here's one! (A door, they mean.) Come on, let's go! But few follow. There are always those who plead for caution and those who blindly rush ahead; we rush ahead, blindly by necessity.

The tall boxlike cupboard, standing free, has four sides at least—a fifth and sixth if roofed and floored—and one of them, we all suppose, must have or be a door, though none have handles; barrel hinges felt down one side's edge soon give the game away, and tools are sought to pry it open. A slender tack lifter's tried so as to limit damage to the frame and door, and then a putty knife, but both are quickly bent and, our patience soon evaporating, a wrecking bar is used.

No light flows out when the door at last pops open with a splintering crack and we all fall back. We're left still in the dark. Sighs of relief are heard, but also of exasperation. But if not light, enlightenment (we know now what next to do), for what's found inside's a ladder, aluminum by weight and feel, extendable, with rope and pulley to make it easier to raise and lower, far better than the toy ones we have made.

The holes we've constructed as windows-yet-to-be as yet lack sashes or casements and panes of glass before they can be proper windows. Such finished windows come in many shapes and sizes, imbedded flat within the walls or bowed or set on piers or bressumers as bays and oriels, some louvered or fitted with mechanisms to pivot, tilt, and turn; we have imagined all their kind, and have fashioned prototypes for most. But, as someone cries out now (the ladder did it): Of course! There are sky lights too!

As architectural elegance is frequently the consequence of conceptual economy, so wisdom springs most often from the simplest thought. We have supposed light to be something that exists independently of us and have sought it laterally, but where light might be found in such a maze no one can say; that it's overhead somewhere, if the universe is not without it, seems beyond all doubt.

And so we set about with fresh enthusiasm to build a sky light, astonished only that we never thought of this before. The room we're in is cavernous, but the ceiling's within easy reach of the ladder when extended, so we decide to start in here, remembering to sandbag the ladder's foot for safety's sake and to use wall hooks and ring bolts at the top. Even so, tampering with a stony ceiling, especially in the dark, is dangerous, soon bits and pieces are raining down, there are casualties, but they're removed and eagerly we press on, break through at last.

What we discover, however, is not light, but yet another room, a kind of loft, we think, perhaps too hopefully, for we might as easily be deeply cellared beneath a structure of countless subterranean levels. One by one, we crawl up into it to see what it contains, and what by touch we find is a large stack of lumber in different shapes, wood for making things, hammers, nails, sheets of glass.

We are at first somewhat bemused, but then someone whispers: I remember now. Once there was a house... We gather round to listen. These family stories have eased us past perplexities in the past. Once there was a house, the storyteller continues, which was struck by a hurricane and turned inside out, the outside enclosed within it, its own dimensions infinite and unknowable at what was once the core, now more like edge. Those within moved out, which of course was further in, and there they built a new house looking out in all directions upon the inverted old. Over time, they enlarged the house and as they added rooms, the old house gradually backed away and faded out of sight. Of course it was not forgotten and there were those who left the new house and set off in quest of the old, but they were never seen again, so the continuing existence of the old house was never proven and ceased in time to be an article of faith, and became instead a story, one idling in the depths of memory, unneeded until now.

Inspired by this legend of the house turned inside out, we

lower a portion of the wood supplies to the room below—that is to say, we drop them: it's a hardhat area now—and commence to construct a new house, a kind of playhouse, as it were (we call it that as what at least we'll have if all else fails), within the house in which we live, but a proper house with, above all, proper windows, through which the light we seek might find us.

To take advantage of work completed, as good builders do, we decide to start with the cupboard and build the new house around it. But what kind of house? someone asks, thereby unleashing the chaos of architecture, said by some to be the cause of the invention of madness. Disputes arise, some quite violent (stones are thrown in the dark, tools are used improperly, the chamber echoes with angry black shouts), as to the intended house's size and shape, disputes of a nature at once functional— the treatment of space, scale, scope, surface and depth, elasticity, connection and obstacles to connection—and ontological: to wit, what is a "house," or what might, here within this other house, if it is a house, yet be one? In short: the mind-body problem as expressed in a war of invisible floor plans.

Insofar as the ontological questions are largely, because of the darkness, epistemic in nature, and in any event understood by almost no one outside of architecture's more esoteric cults (goddamn them all), it is finally resolved that they are, at least until there is light, irresolvable, a resolution that does nothing, however, to temper the enflamed passions of the disputants, who have momentarily forgotten, alas, that the goal is not the house but a window. Such is the maddening power of schism. There is the clash of timber swung blindly, a *whutter-whutter* through the black air of T-squares flung like boomerangs, the bellowing of ancient dogma.

In such a melee, the search for common ground is doomed. Though we all acknowledge that a house is largely made of air, for example, we can none agree on how much air is to be used and in what proportion it is to be boxed and parceled, the more impatient among us wanting, quickly, one simple room alone (let's get the walls up and those windows in and see what happens!), the more ambitious wishing to construct a proper multileveled house with play den, bathroom, domes and bartizans, solarium, nursery, and perhaps a central well as a neutral linking space through which to get from room to room, arguing that the structure must be of sufficient quality and intricacy to attract the light to it, else all our efforts will be in vain. Even the question of ornament is no small matter, they cry out (the din is terrible), for if there is light we will see and be seen and we must want what is seen to be seemly!

A cessation of hostilities is suddenly achieved when it is recognized that all the competing designs include what might be called a hallway or vestibule and, though those demanding a single room are loathe to call it that instead of a house, we all agree to start there, and let all thereafter each go our own way.

But the peace is short-lived, for calling it a room instead of a house does not free us from sectarian conflict, and soon there is the danger that what we make, if we ever do, will become more martyrium than vestibule. There are those, for example, who insist on a simple cube, crisp and clean and precisely figured according to the sophisticated laws of harmonic proportions, while others, referring bitterly to these "suffocating laws of barbaric contortions," cry out for more exuberant and curvaceous forms akin to rumors about nature: a flower, a cocoon, a termite hill, a womb, a bird in flight, a peapod. As no one has actually seen these things and despite threats of sabotage from the self-styled naturizers, a simpler boxlike or diamond shape with the ladder cupboard in one corner is finally decided upon and work begins.

The decision to corner the cupboard, though controversial (*corners* are controversial!), is a practical one, making maximum use of the structure already in place, for simply by extending the two incorporated walls (the advocates of a design based on a bird in flight are momentarily pleased), nearly half the new construction will already be completed, lacking only two walls and a ceiling—or a roof as some, still screaming, prefer to call it.

First, however, trenches must be dug for the foundations, so work details are sent out to round up picks and shovels, quarry stones, make mud, while the rest of us gather up the scattered missiles and weapons, now known once more as tools and building materials, restack the timber, count and measure it (in the dark the shouted estimates vary wildly), and seek to pacify the last of the belligerents with singing, kissing, and guess-what games, the telling of old family stories.

Once there was a house—! someone cries out; then, still breathing heavily, that person firmly exclaims· Once there was a house..., and finally manages to whisper (and can be heard, as the clamorous dissent dies away at last as though drifting off into other rooms): ...Once there was a house... built of water...

Have we heard this story before? If so, we have forgotten it. But the very thought of water has a soothing effect on us all. Tell us, someone says, and the room is awash in a ripple of concurring murmurs. Tell us about the house made of water!

Its pure clean form, the storyteller continues, was deemed the most beautiful in the world, praised for its elegance, clarity, and cool restraint, yet at the same time—and this was part of its universal appeal—it was utterly amorphous and so infinitely mutable, its shape changing from hour to hour as the mood or climate changed, or for no reason at all other than to exhibit its own inimitable and multiform beauty. Nearly perfect though it was, however, embracing all other forms as it did, it could not be lived in, for it lacked one utterly necessary element, which, if incorporated into it, would have caused it to cease to exist.

The storyteller pauses, leaving the riddle of the house made of water floating heavily in the hushed air like a balloon filled with the very material with which it had been built.

Ah! someone gasps. A door! It could not have a door!

And we all take it up: A door! Yes, a door!

And so (our family stories never fail to instruct) a door is imagined for our new house within a house, and not merely a disappointed window like those before, but, hung on powerful hinges, a proper door, framed by an architrave and broken up into rails, stiles, and panels, with a brass knob and lock on the shutting stile and a knocker on the muntin. A door, in short, that stands as hinged postulate of an inside and an outside, opposing states than can abut but never intersect or partake of one another, a thought that excites us and spurs us on.

The trenches are forsaken, the walls, foundations, floor plans, house, our fevered imaginations focused entirely now upon the making of the door. The work crews return to lend a hand, skilled craftsmen among them, caught up in the infectious enthusiasm—it all makes sense! It's as if a mathematical problem has been resolved by factoring it to its irreducible components: door ➤ light.

A six-panel rail-and-stile door with mortise-and-tenon joints is the carpenters' choice. With the hint of arches in the upper rail, softly sanded to feel like the inside of a knee, they add, carpenters being of an infamously sensuous nature. That's so old-fashioned, proponents of the new school of architecture object, eager to press on without delay. This is a matter of function, not beauty! A simple batten door will do! Slap it together, let's get on with it! Light, respond the carpenters, is also old-fashioned. Also beautiful. And what, if our stories be true, could be more sensuous? We must do it honor, draw like to like. Bah! Elitism! scream their adversaries, suffering from a hallucination of efficiency and functionality, and again there is the clatter of thrown tools. Schools of architects can be compared to schools of fish only if the fish are species that eat each other.

We need carpentry more than doctrine so the carpenters win the day. The new-schoolers are relegated to tool-gathering tasks (they may be right but they cannot be tolerated) and the percussive melodies of carpentry soon fill the air, soothing all spirits, the darkness suffused with the invigorating fragrance of fresh-cut wood. Aromatic hours pass, perhaps days (days! will we soon experience what till now have been but the stuff of legend? or will light just come and stay like the darkness has?), filled with heady imaginings. And with trepidation: the fear of failure; the fear of success (what is light? does it hurt? will our kissing in it be the same?). We stand, as the door comes together, on the edge of the unknown. Perhaps the unknowable.

Once there was a house, someone says, and even the carpenters pause in their labors. A house whose doors and windows moved about as if in search of a perfect arrangement, forever denied them. This restlessness disturbed those living in the house, dizzying them with endlessly shifting outlooks, and they sought some way to fix the doors and windows in their places. But nothing worked, not even steel restraining bars. They moved a few of the walls, hoping to confuse the doors and windows, only to augment their anxiety and accelerate the shuffle. To spare themselves the giddy flutter of changing views, they blackened all the windows, whereupon, in their blindness, the windows collided with one another and with the slower-moving doors, sending explosive shatterings of black glass flying and knocking doors off their hinges. Finally, those living in the house decided simply to let what must happen happen in the hope that one day the doors and windows would discover their longed-for arrangement and settle down. So far as we know (we have murmured our understanding), this never happened, but in time the occupants grew accustomed to the ceaseless shuffle and came to believe that their everchanging perspectives defined them, and indeed they did.

We return to the building of the door, prepared for come what may. Our anxieties are not lessened, but they are contained, in the way that a verb is contained in a sentence. The door itself is nearly finished, the carpenters applying their final rubdown. We all take turns stroking the door for luck and courage, and it's true, the subtle arches in the upper rail are soft as the softest parts of us. A door, however, cannot stand alone. Lacking a wall's rough opening in which to install it, a frame of header, trimmers, and threshold is built and a platform is constructed to set it on, the raw planks of the mock rough framing hidden behind a finished casing, complete with jambs and architrave. This solves another problem: by building the frame around the door, any geometric irregularities (our levels are made of strings and weights) are conveniently echoed in the frame. When it is finished, the door is hinged and hung and the latch installed.

So the moment has arrived. We line up behind the door. We don't know if the light will come blindingly, all at once, or only individually to each of us as we step through. The carpenters are given pride of place, though cowardice by others may have pushed them there. Our breaths are held. The latch is turned.

The well-oiled hinges are soundless but the carpenter's steps can be heard on the wooden platform as he steps through. Nothing happens, at least nothing the rest of us can see. But no one's breathing yet. The door clicks closed. The carpenter is silent, perhaps struck dumb with awe, more likely stilled by disappointment. The rest of us take turns, opening the door, stepping through, closing the door. There's a certain thrill in doing this, but there is no light. We take a count, making certain all step through at least once. Even the skeptics take their turn, obliged but also, however faintly, hopeful. But: no. A failure. One elaborate and abject. We have suffered others but none so painful as this.

It is a moment ripe for another family story. Perhaps about illusions puffed up into belief, or about shortcuts taken and rued—the story of the hasty house doctor and the pantry by-pass, for example. We wait in a silence heavy with despond. And wait in vain. Well, no need, the story awaited is the one we've just constructed, building a door to welcome light without a house to hold it. Those to come will be regaled by our brainless folly.

Back to the original floor plans, the site preparations, the trenches and foundations. We are determined now to press on with the task in all its detail, though our appetite for nuance has withered. We are one with the functionalists: get it up, get on with it. No further self-deceptions, frivolous aesthetics. Angled by the cupboard, the four walls are paced off, marked with pegs

and cord, and we commence to dig the trenches for the foundations with the shovels, picks, and spades collected by our crews.
If one pauses to remark on the noble beauty of the shovel, say, or
the erotic symbolism of cubes, the warp and weft of wall and
floor, no audience is found, and those who trip over the staked
cords in the dark get only barked scoldings for their clattering
pratfalls, our sense of humor gone with our appetite for frill. And
perhaps, somewhat gone as well, our hopes: we are preparing,
even as we strive, to accept the unending dark. How long has the
cupboard been there? Perhaps it has always been there, our dis-
covery of it far too late. Perhaps we put it there ourselves in
another time and forgot about it.

The trenches, excavated, are filled with stones quarried from
the walls, framing posts are sunk at the three new corners, and
those who have to go, go now, sealing the stone-filled trenches
with the mud they make. The corner posts are long enough to
reach the stony ceiling overhead, so we decide to build the walls
that high, avoiding rafters, beams, a wooden ceiling (with only
one ladder, scaffolding would have been necessary), and incorpo-
rating the new-found loft into our house, as most of us still
choose to call it, and the carpenters, humbled now into a gloomy
silence, dutifully take over the construction of the frame. Mud
sills are set in place, floor joists, subfloor and sole plate, top plate
more like a capping frame, a plank floor's laid.

Decisions must be made about doors and windows before the
studs are set in place, and once again disputes break out, more
surly now than exhortative. Doors will be needed for internal
walls, windows for external walls only, and the issue is, as before,
one room or many? If one, no internal walls exist. Our impatience with décor is matched by our impatience with sectarian

discord. The disputants are drowned out by a loud voice vote, electing a wall opposite the cupboard for the front door, already built, the two side walls for door frames, either internal or external, the narrow back wall for a patio door (a passing whim), with a fanlight overhead. Large windows are chosen to flank the front door, the twinned hopes we skeptically cling to, but simple frames are put in place where once were imagined bays, a decision distressing to some, uninspiring to all. The game that we began with has decayed to labor, obligatory and dull.

Once there was a house, someone says suddenly, startling us. Sighs of relief are heard. Tools are downed. A communal smile can be imagined. Once, the storyteller continues, voice ringing in the fallen hush, there was a house with copulating parts, a design feature installed by the architects seeking a more fluid, evolutionary architecture and organic paths to innovation. The imagined smile widens. Out of it almost immediately came the inverted dormer window, the floating family-room module, undulating rooflines, and the lickable split-level candy-coated X-frame. New economies were realized with the intimate commingling of the plumbing and electrical systems, flowing ecstatically into one another, though a premature attempt at a ménage-à-trois with the gas boiler temporarily melted the circuit breakers. These bursts of passion were difficult to restrain. New designs were born, but to increasingly short lives, and others rushed hotly past utility into self-demolishing excess, bringing down bearing walls and chimney stacks and pulverizing the masonry. And though a limited feature originally intended for the basic structures only, the erotic fever soon spread to peripherals, décor, and outbuildings, where copulations were less conventional and also, or consequently, less generative, lascivious delight displacing the productive function. The raucous interplay of the cornices, drain tiles, hipped gables, finials, festoons, flashing, and ginger-bread vergeboards was far short of exemplary, architecturally speaking, though it did introduce baroque elements into the waste pipes and boot room and turned stairwells into exotic dancers. In spite of the restrictive building codes, watching the copulations soon became a popular entertainment, audiences drawn more to the perversities of the superficie, needless to say, than to the stodgier reproductive behavior of the structural elements. All this passionate agitation could be hazardous: there was a ceaseless seminal spray of shingles, tiles, and shattered glass, and fatalities occurred the night the ceilings tragically embraced the floors. Prophylactic I-beam kingposts—now known as nay-beams—were inserted, though that only seemed to provoke splintering back porch and crawl space eruptions and lethal high-speed appliance riots. But in spite of the dangers, the crowds kept coming. The house was no longer even minimally habitable—it was as though what was erotic was also, at the root, deeply dysfunctional—yet everyone wished to inhabit it, making of this architectural experiment both a radical failure and a crashing success.

The story is applauded. It was meaningless, teaching us nothing. Except to laugh at ourselves. Which is to say, it has taught us everything. We all kiss and mate happily with one another and go back to our house-building with lighter hearts.

Which now proceeds speedily, the rough framing quickly completed and the sheathing no sooner begun than done: simple wallboards with board-and-batten siding, the historic dialogue between the frame and its infilling reduced to plain declarative sentences, stripped of superfluous modifiers. The side doors, too, are kept simple: hollow-core and flush, the veneer to follow when the light comes, if. The patio door and fanlight are postponed, their framing boarded up, all attention now upon the paired windows at the front. The carpenters suggest shuttering the windows on the inside so that, if there is light (there is no longer a real belief in light, nor even much desire for it, its mythic existence merely a tenet to be acted upon for lack of any other), we have a shield against it if it tries to hurt us. Moreover, shutters would give us something to open as a welcoming gesture, like a friendly handshake or a kiss. The suggestion of the carpenters is accepted without dissent, but not solely for the reasons they advance. Our headlong rush to complete our house, or at least this room of it, has aroused old fears of light's possible malevolence and, with the erecting of the walls, apprehensions about what might be outside now that an outside exists. (There *is* an outside. We are all now inside.) Building shutters takes time, time we can use to consider what we are doing and brace ourselves. None of us, however, wish all our labor to have been in vain, merely for lack of courage, so, doing what we call singing, we lend the carpenters a hand when we can and our encouragement when we cannot, reassuring one another with our hopeful odes to light.

But when, with appropriate ceremony, the completed shutters are hung and, with caution, opened, the result is as it has always been. The dark remains. Defeat feels final. We have worked so hard. Despair sets in. Where did it come from, we ask, this mad dream of light? We feel betrayed by our own restless natures which want but cannot have. There is no consolation. The game of building light, which has filled and defined our lives, is over. We cannot step into light, but we cannot step back into our old games in the dark either. When, in desperation, old family stories are launched—Once there was a house...!—their tellers are cursed and rudely shushed. Fuck it, someone says. Who wants a game of mating tag? There are no takers. Another proposes opening the door we've made and taking turns running at it full tilt in the dark: those who miss the door and hit the wall lose. Why not? says someone and opens the door.

And light floods in, swirling about our ankles, splashing against the walls, swooping upward to crash against the ceiling, falling upon us with such force we are thrown to the floor, then exploding silently outward to the remotest corners and beyond, its punishing brilliance ever more searing. We could not see in the dark. We can see even less in this fierce thing called light. One can hear cries but of a strangled whimpering sort as if the light had invaded throats and stifled the chords' vibrations there. All of our orifices feel penetrated by the light, our brains, too, the light without indistinguishable from the light within. We carried the dark within us, too, for that is what the light's displacing, but this is not the same. We were together in the dark as though the dark were a sea we swam in hand in hand. Now we are alone, disconnected from everyone and everything except our own shocked perceptions. In the dark we could see with our imaginations and our other senses and did not think we did not see, but now all imagination has been stunned by light, all thought and sensation has. Light is everywhere. We cannot shut our eyes against it. Even the insides of our lids are lit. We have a fleeting remembrance of that storied house in which all wishes, catastrophically, came true, and then that too is blotted out.

Then, slowly, the walls emerge, the ones we've made, luminous shapes within the general luminosity, and we begin to see other radiant forms, lumpy and quivering: each other, cringing in terror on the floor. Windows come into view, the open door, the impenetrable sea of light beyond. It is not as if the light is retreating, but as if it is relaxing, trying to, making itself at home, adjusting its density just to be more at ease, while folding us into itself the way that lovers do. Do we feel loved? No, more like netted by a hunter, overpowered, possessed. But we are adjusting, too, shock and fright gradually giving way to awed curiosity, the thrill of seeing. Everything, still soaked in light, is strange, yet oddly familiar. With our first glimpse of forms, it is as though we have always seen them: our house with its shoddy workmanship, our scattered tools, and our bodies, which are both more beautiful and less beautiful than we'd imagined, yet in form no different than we'd supposed.

Gathering courage, we creep toward the open door, peer out into the candescent glow beyond the threshold. Some say that they can see the encircling wall of the room in which we built our house. It is like a far horizon, they say (we already know about horizons), but others say: No, no, that *is* the horizon! If so, there is nothing on it. The space beyond the door is as barren as our room once was. We step cautiously out into it, out onto the vast white plain, and as we do, things seem to grow from it, bushy things and piles of rocks and what must be trees and even hills, if those are hills, a landscape shaping itself before our eyes—or perhaps our eyes, adjusting, are seeing now what has been there all along, light slowly releasing its humbling grip on us, and as these things appear, it is as if we are not discovering them so much as remembering them, returning to some place we've been before. Another cautionary house tale comes to mind but immediately vanishes just as the dark has vanished, a shadowy whisper from the dead past. No more of that. Already, it is the dark that is becoming unimaginable. We are enraptured by the present moment and where our feet are now (we can see our feet! they are dancing!) and—no more whispers!—we are shouting, calling out in our exhilaration to the more timid, still hiding in the house, to come out and play.

Our old games, played in the dark, the where-are-we-now, guess-what, and find-the-door games, no longer amuse us. We invent new ones, using the things we find, sticks, stones, holes full of water or else of air, old tools we'd lost, and other things as yet unknown to us by touch alone. The game of naming things becomes the game of filling old names with all the things we see. We fill "sky" with sky and "grass" with grass, if that is what it is, and not moss or weeds or hair. Everything is beautiful. We can't stop looking. Details excite us, colors do, the motions of things, being looked *at* does: we perform for one another's looking, amazing ourselves with ourselves. Distance fascinates us, now that we can see it, and we play running, throwing, measuring, and find-the-horizon games in it. We leave our house far behind, and caution, too, and spread out on the flowering plain, reveling in boundlessness and all its wondrous stuff, and when at last, to catch our breath, we return, the house has grown new wings and towers and more levels, with accoutrements like loggia, balconies and terraces, parapets and onion domes. The carpenters, it seems, have been busy. A new construction is sprouting like a mushroom (we have already considered the word "mushroom" and filled it up) on the side of a rising cube, even as we watch.

Inside, too, there have been changes. Gone is the rough-hewn vestibule with the cupboard in the corner, the little anteroom some grandly called a house, and in its place a glittering rotunda with spiraling staircases and ornate balustrades, tiled walls, high arched doorways, filigreed columns, fountains and statuary (we are immortalizing ourselves!), colored glass pictures in the windows and a painted cupola high above. The carpenters, now the chief among us, reply to our expressions of amazement: It's simple. We are merely the servants of light. That is the secret of construction. There is a chaotic profusion of corridors and rooms leading off the rotunda and its staircases, all kinds of rooms—kitchens and pantries, dining halls, exercise rooms, ballrooms, toilets with white ceramic walls for drawing messages on (drawing!), theaters and art galleries, carpenters' workshops, pools, patios, and amusement parlors—indeed the house seems bigger on the inside than out. No bedrooms unless in some distant unseen corner, but who can sleep with so much to see and do. We run through the rooms, playing our games, and sometimes the rooms play games with us, walling us in and hiding the doors, opening their floors to drop us into other rooms, rotating suddenly to tumble us out of our mating games. Sometimes they divide up into a cluster of tiny rooms, isolating us from one another, then expand outward as if stretching (a new wing is forming!); sometimes they merge with other rooms, a ballroom invading a laundry room, shower stalls appearing in the dining hall. There's no pattern in this; it's just mischief, a kind of playful restlessness in a house still trying to understand itself. As we it, in our eager explorations.

And so a certain time passes, one cannot say how much, the light is constant as the dark was, unmarked by phases or transitions, as we search out the marvels of house and landscape, of sight itself, filling up the names we know with things we see and making new names when the old run out. The question arises: But what of the old house, the one we used to play in in the dark, where is it now? And that room we built, the cupboard and the storehouse loft? The ladder: is it still propped against a wall somewhere? These are names that are empty still of the proper things to fill them. We ask the carpenters, they can't remember. Probably behind some door, they say. And so a new game of find-the-cupboard is launched, just for fun for most, though some want to honor it somehow, create a kind of shrine. We spread out through the house, opening door after door, in search of the place where light found us, or we it, feeling as if caught up in one of our old family stories, which have also got lost somewhere. Our task is complicated by the house's ceaseless multiplication of doors and rearrangements of the old, the house our playful, if playful, adversary in this new game.

Rumors arise as rumors do: that the cupboard is constantly receding ever more deeply into an inaccessible black core into which the entire house will eventually implode; that some have actually stumbled upon the original cupboard and have vanished, sucked back into the dark; that darkness leaks from there as from an unclosed wound, a darkness destined to overtake the house entirely, flooding in as light once did; that our search for the cupboard is inspired by the spirit of the dark and puts at risk the entire community. There are many now who have forgotten dark-ness or who never knew it, nor believe it ever was, and simply think us mad. There is a movement to outlaw our cupboard-hunting games as a dangerous breach of the building code. Corridors are walled off and some doors grow locks.

Such rumors, threats, and obstacles only provoke a greater longing to know again the dark, remembered more for its peaceful depth than for its agitated length, and when now it's walled away from us, it returns as an illegal substance, purchased in soft little bags the size of scrota. Is it the real thing? Who can say? It's said to be gathered from the cupboard's leakage, and real or not, when squeezed against the eyes or tongue or down the throat, it seems to obliterate for a moment or at least to dim the omnipresent dazzle of the light and isolate us from the loud voracious frenzy of the busy house, wherein maddening regulations have broken out like a malignant rash and the architecture wars have returned and even the carpenters are squabbling among themselves. Once there was a house, someone whispers as a signal, and we slip away into locked bathrooms to share our bags of dark and listen to old family stories thought forgotten.

Once there was a house, the storyteller continues (we quietly applaud the existence of the storyteller as a gentle dimming settles in and furtive shadows are glimpsed), whose inhabitants lived in total darkness. They got about by touch, their toys their tools, and dreamt, a game they played, of building light...

RIDDLE

IT IS THE LIEUTENANT'S first execution. Five men are to die by firing squad, and his company has drawn the assignment. He does not look forward to it, but he will not falter in his duty. He is a hunter and has killed often, creatures large and small. Nor will these five be the first men he has killed, though they will be the first he has put away in this manner, tied helplessly to a post and shot on command. At least, he believes, they should be allowed to run free and be chased down as fair game. He is a sportsman and a soldier, not a butcher. Still, what's to be done will be done. The five—a priest, a truck driver, a labor organizer, a student, and a farm worker—will not see the morrow. Their fate is a harsh one, but it is not an undeserved one. Directly or indirectly, with arms or with words, they have brought about the deaths and injuries of many, have sown the seeds of lawlessness, and have even threatened the downfall of the state. They have their reasons, their causes, but they do not justify the havoc they have unleashed on orderly society. Which is, at best and by necessity, as all know well, an unsatisfactory compromise. Not all rules are good rules, but they must be obeyed until better ones are found, else all collapses into anarchy and humankind returns to that condition from which it has so laboriously emerged, one ruled by blood, not by mind.

That is anyway what the lieutenant, dedicated keeper of law and order, believes: that civilization such as that he serves is hard-won over many centuries and all too easily lost in a day, man being the capricious undisciplined animal that he is. He understands, as the student Lázaro Luján would say, his own weaknesses and urges, and fears them in others, the law their safe container. Lázaro Luján, known to his comrades as the Reader, also believes in civilized society but does not believe that he lives in one. Moreover, civilization is not a condition or an achievement or even an ideal, but a process, demanding constant renewal, its good health dependent upon periodic upheavals, such as this one he is presently guilty of fostering. He does agree with the lieutenant that civilization does not come without hard work and sacrifice. There is always a price to be paid, and in his case that price is high. He has suffered expulsion from the university, rejection by his family, the deaths of friends and loss of lovers, injustice, incarceration, and torture, and now must pay with his life. His remote austere father, a judge with high connections, might have saved him but did not. As Lázaro Luján himself fiercely demanded: Hands off, this choice is mine! Thus, he feels at once respected and abandoned. When the lieutenant asked him if he had any final request, he asked that he be allowed to say in what order they will stand for their executions, placing himself at one end.

Which is why Carlos Timoteo faces the firing squad with the labor organizer on his right. The lieutenant understands the student's choice. He knows that Carlos Timoteo has no ideology at all unless it be that of a primitive and superstitious religion which even the priest would scorn. He seems confused by life, speaks only in incoherent mutters. The labor organizer beside him is a brave man, brazen even, devoted to his dangerous politics, ambitious, well spoken, proud. He has lived a life of confrontation, this thus its natural conclusion, whereas Carlos Timoteo is a man who finds himself on history's stage without quite knowing, though his crimes were many, how he got there. The lieutenant therefore supposes that the student wanted the least committed of the condemned to stand alongside someone who might give him courage and a sense at the end, however illusory, of purpose. Actually, however, Carlos Timoteo's purpose is clear and free of illusions. His has been a long life of humiliation and abuse. He has been beaten, chained, mocked, knifed, used as a human mule, kicked, branded, tied to a tree and whipped. Even now, his gnarled calloused hands are suppurating at the fingertips where, until yesterday, his nails were. They laughed, who tore them out, as many have laughed before. Carlos Timoteo was not born to wealth or power, nor has he even dreamed of it; all he has sought his whole life through is dignity. Which at last today he has found. For once, he signifies. He will face his executioners with his head held high.

It's true, the populist creed of Carlos Timoteo is not that of the priest, but he would not scorn it. In fact, simple as it is, it is more reliable and steadfastly held than his own. All the poverty, injustice, corruption, cruelty that he has witnessed have taken their toll. Suffering humankind has won his love at the expense of his lost love of God. Which is an idea he no longer trusts, any more than he trusts the church which propagates it, handmaiden to the venal state. The priest's logic is simple: If God is good, He cannot exist. If He is not, He should not. All but the student have asked him for spiritual guidance at this moment of extremity, even the anarchist. He has told all of them that in the eyes of the church they are saints and will be blessed by the best the afterlife has to offer. Which, he knows but does not say, is nothing; he could provide the lieutenant and his soldiers the same consolation, or even the corrupt and ruthless leaders they have struggled against, the lascivious bishop who denounced him. The soldiers will raise their rifles, silhouetted against the blank whiteness of the overcast sky, and the door will close. The priest, unlike Carlos Timoteo, has no one on his right to give him company and strength. I am merely one of the thieves, he thinks bitterly, and what's more, I will it so.

The anarchist, Umberto Iglesias, sees no conflict between anarchism and religion. Indeed, he thinks of God, in His absolute freedom and cosmic violence, as the ultimate anarchist. Order stifles and is the devil's realm. Look only at the devils who maintain it. He's not as smart maybe as the Reader beside him, but he's not stupid. He knows that violence is the natural state of things, the universe a boiling pot of ceaseless eruption, destruction, and renewal, life itself a mere fleeting aberration, the nation-state life's mad invention. Destroy it, Umberto Iglesias figures, you're doing the universe a favor. The labor leader cries out now for justice, and the others mutter their assent, poor fools. They just don't get the joke. They're like a comedian's nightmare audience, probably they deserve to die for that reason alone. But, then, who doesn't, and for whatever reason? Umberto Iglesias has never actually blown anything up, but he's trucked the explosives around for those who have. He's dreamed of hitting the floorboard one day and driving his loaded truck at top speed into the capitol or the stock exchange or even the casino where over the years he has been robbed of all he's ever earned, but much as he disdains life, he's been reluctant to give it up, having too much fun in it. Especially with the women, fucking being the best thing about being alive, maybe the only good thing, and at the same time the weirdest thing of all. Now, it's too late for revolutionary glory (fuck glory of any kind, history is a farcical delusion), too late for anything short of shitting himself. Already, he is shackled to the post, the firing squad is standing at attention, the lieutenant is giving the soldiers their final instructions. Umberto Iglesias has had his eye on the lieutenant, that jaunty bastard, recognizing in him a kindred spirit, but one warped by fear and ambition into its contrary, that sickness men, suckered by reason, call sanity. The lieutenant is calling out their names. So how is Umberto Iglesias going to meet the end of things? By thinking about the open road and about all the women he's had. See if he can remember them all in order and how they smelled and what they did.

The lieutenant has also been aware of Umberto Iglesias— while being bound to the post, the condemned man winked at him and grinned—and he too recognizes that there is something that they have in common, though the lieutenant supposes this simply to be the love of women. Umberto Iglesias is a handsome man with dark eyes and sensuous lips and a dissolute air, no doubt a favorite with the ladies. Perhaps he should have had the insolent wretch emasculated before executing him, but, though this has on occasion happened under the lieutenant's command, he has never himself ordered it, being respectful of the authority of love as of all authority. He has never even neutered animals, his own possible neutering in warfare his worst and most persistent nightmare. The lieutenant is not a superstitious man—even his gambling is grounded in a mathematical logic—yet he fears (irrationally, he knows, and reconsiders the truck driver's wink) love's reprisal should he in any way interfere with its sweet mechanics. He could at least have blindfolded Umberto Iglesias, but he, like the other prisoners, chose as his final request to face his executioners with open eyes, and this, because it suited him, he granted them. He too, as with the animals that he hunted, wished to gaze into their eyes before killing them, watching them as they watched death's advent. Noting Hugo Urbano standing to the right of Amadeo Fernández while calling out the names of the condemned, the lieutenant realizes that there was a purpose after all to the student's lineup, an unexpectedly ironic one, and that consequently he will have a riddle tonight for his riddle-loving lover. He raises his hand as a signal.

As the members of the firing squad raise and cock their rifles, the lieutenant having turned toward him with a bemused gaze, his hand in the air, Lázaro Luján suddenly, with deep chagrin, realizes his mistake. His last chance to raise a word against the gun, and he has, yet again, written, not for his audience, but for himself. Trapped as always in his own ego, just as his mentors and peers have so often said. What a pity at such a moment as this to feel their scorn. His comrades have fallen silent. In the distance, he sees a lone black bird, scribbling its riddles on the white sky. Its message is obscure but, Lázaro Luján realizes with a sudden flash of insight, it is not completely illegible. If only…

Later that night, the lieutenant describes the day's events to his lover while she works aromatic oils into his chest and abdomen. He does not tell her about his personally giving each of the condemned the coup de grâce with his pistol while they were still hanging from their posts, nor about the stripping of the bodies of their possessions by his soldiers, but he has left in the truck driver's knowing wink. I think my men found too much pleasure in the killing, he says. Pleasure? Well, excitement. Thrills. One is never so aware of consciousness as at the moment of annihilating it in another. They are probably all with their lovers tonight, as am I, and no less rampant and awake. I'm afraid I don't understand such excitement, she says. Is that the riddle you spoke of? No. From what I have told you, can you tell me who were each of the condemned and in what order they were standing? And what was the message the student wished to leave behind? I had supposed he might have been given to some jejeune romantic gesture, and so I was surprised by its bitter irony. I have already solved it, his lover said with a smile, and told him the names and occupations of each and where in the line they stood. And as for the message, she added, spreading the oils between his thighs, perhaps you yourself have not entirely puzzled out the riddle left you.

THE FISHERMAN AND
THE JINN

THE OLD FISHERMAN HAS had another shitty day, hauling up the dead detritus of the sea. He's already cast his net three times, four's his limit. Why? He doesn't remember but that's it, one to go. He tucks up his shirt tails, wades in waist-deep, casts again for the thousand-thousandth time, give or take a throw or two. He waits for the net to sink. He can feel fish swimming between his legs, tickling his cods. Praise God, the bountiful sea. But this time his net snags on the bottom. It's not fair. He works his scrawny old ass to the bone, and what does he have to show for it? Wet rags and an empty belly. Even if he caught a fish, what would he do with it? He'd sell it to a rich man, go hungry, and cast his net again. His existence is a ceaseless punishment. He throws off his clothes and dives under. The net's about all he's got in the world, he has to rescue it.

This time it has caught a brass jar with a lead stopper. Looks old, maybe he can sell it in the copper market. It's heavy, not easy to drag it out of there, he nearly drowns trying, and the net gets shredded. Maybe there's a jinn inside, he thinks. If he doesn't kill me, maybe I can wish for enough money to be free from these stupid labors, eat other people's fish. Or get my youth back, the old dangler functioning again. New teeth. The apple of Samarcand to cure my crotch itch. A young beautiful wife who talks less. A rich princess maybe. Rule a kingdom. Ride horses. Kill a few people. Sure enough, the lead seal has been stamped with an ancient seal ring. For once in his life he's in luck. He gets out his knife, but then has second thoughts. If there's a jinn bottled up inside, squashed in there for centuries, he could be in a pretty explosive mood. Life's shit, sure, but does he really want to end it, and no doubt in some horrible way only jinns can imagine? But what other way does it ever end? Even now he can feel things in his bones that suggest bad times coming. Best to take a chance. He scrapes away at the lead stopper until he pries it loose.

What comes out might be smoke, it might be dust, smells like death. Maybe just somebody's ashes. But the muck continues to curl out of the neck of the jar, slowly rising into the sky over him and spreading out over the sea, more and more of it, until that's all he can see. The sun's blotted out, the sea's brighter than the sky, it's as if the world is turning upside down. Then the dark mist gathers and takes shape and suddenly, with a great clap of thunder that sets his knees knocking, there's a monstrous jinn standing there, feet planted in the shallow waters at the shore, head in the clouds, eyes blazing like there's a fire in its head, its teeth, big as gravestones, gnashing. Sparks fly. If the old fisherman had any boots, he'd be quaking in them. As it is, naked still from his dive, he's trembling all over like a thin pale jellyfish. The jinn, in a pent-up rage, kicks the brass jar far out to sea. There goes his ticket to the copper market. The jinn might be talking to him, but he can't hear a thing. He's pissing himself with terror, his ears are popping, his tongue is dry, his jaws are locked as if hammered together. "What? What?" he croaks at last. "I said," says the jinn, his voice like the wind on a violent day, "make a wish, Master! Choose carefully, for I've only time for one!"

Master? Ah, it's true then, the old stories, it's really happening. He's just been making a list, he can't remember it. Wealth, yes, heaps of it. But of what use is wealth if he dies before he can spend it? Likewise, bedding down with princesses. Marrying a princess without youth would be like fishing with a torn net. But wishing for youth without a princess would be like casting his net on the desert. Can he wish for more wishes?

"You cannot, Master, as I will not be here to fulfill them! Make haste, while there's time!"

"Oh, I don't know! I can't think! I wasn't ready for this!"

The jinn is bigger and scarier than ever. He has long snaky hair and claws where his fingernails should be. But he's harder to see. It's as if his edges are dissolving. There's less of him even as there's more of him. Come on, think, think! The end of all disease? World peace? No, fuck the world! It's his turn! How about healthy and alert and virile for at least two hundred years: is that one wish or several? And what would happen when the two hundred years were up, how could he face that? What about simply a long life, get it going, what the hell, see what happens? He knows what happens. Just prolonging the misery. Some sort of toy? A flying carpet? An invisible cloak? A bottomless beer jug?

"Hurry, Master! Before it's too late!"

"I'm too old to hurry, damn it!"

The jinn is huge now. Almost as big as the cloud from which he was formed. But you can see the sun shining through him and the fire in his eyes has dimmed to a flicker. His voice has become thin and echoey, his face is losing its features, his extensions are growing vague, bits and pieces blowing away when the wind blows. Which may only be his own heavy breathing.

"I know! Power! I want power! No! I want endless joy!"

"What...?"

"Endless joy! I want—!"

"I can't he-ea-ar you-u-u-u...!"

"Wait! Stay where you are! Joy! Just make me happy!"

Nothing left of the jinn now but a few beardy wisps floating on the breeze, and then they too fade away.

"Please! Come back, damn it!" he cries. "At least mend my net!"

But the jinn is gone. Not a trace. It's too late. Praise God, fucked again. The old fisherman hauls on his shirt with its wet tails, rolls up the rotten shreds of his net. On the sand, he spies part of the stamped lead seal. Ah. So, he got something out of the encounter after all. A story. You see this lead seal? Let me tell you what happened. Trouble is, he's told too many stories like it before, none of them true, so no one will believe him now. Why would they? He wouldn't believe himself. They might even put him away. Lock him up as an old loony. He *is* an old loony, he wouldn't have an argument. And even if they did believe him, they'd want to know what he did with the jar. They'd think he stole it and cut off his hands for thieving. Fuck that. He pitches the lead seal into the sea. He'll repair his net and have another go tomorrow. Maybe he'll catch a mermaid.

ALICE IN THE TIME OF THE JABBERWOCK

WHEN THE RED KING awoke, Alice found herself back in Wonderland, still at timeless tea with her demented companions the Hatter and the Hare and being used as a cushion by both of them, her armchair occupied by the snoring Dormouse, his little two toothed rodent mouth slackly agape, and she knew then that her whole life aboveground had been only a dream, the King's dream, just as that ill-tempered little fat boy Tweedledee had foreseen, his puzzle about who was in whose dream bitterly resolved, and she was back where she had always been.

"What's that Dormouse doing in my chair?" she complained with a yawn squeezed to half a yawn, feeling dreadfully suppressed. The Hatter's ten-bob-six hat was pushed under her chin, holding it up, and her upper lip was mustached by the March Hare's unwashed ear. "Off with its head," she added despondently and closed her eyes, hoping to fall asleep again and dream the

Red King back to sleep so that she might, at least in his dreams, return aboveground once more to play with her cats and her games and take those lovely rowing expeditions on the magic river with her dream-sisters and the older gentlemen, so like wizards and magicians. Ah, those golden afternoons! Vanished like summer midges, and the rest of the century (that's what they called it up there) with them.

"The rule is," muttered the Hatter, shifting about to make himself more comfortable and Alice even less so (the Hare's ear twitched and she sneezed), "to get ahead, you must start behind."

"All right then," grunted Alice, elbowing free of her tea-sodden companions and rising heavily, "off with its behind." And she rolled the slumbering Dormouse out of her chair and collapsed into it, curling not into one corner as she used to do, but into both at the same time. Indeed, she did feel a great temptation to sink back into Dreamland, envying the oblivious Dormouse at her feet, who once told her (it was in the dead of night after one of those frumious battles, she couldn't sleep, she felt like she was going crazy, or if everyone here in Wonderland is already crazy, then like she was going sane, which was even more terrifying) that he sometimes went to bed so soon after getting up that he found himself back in bed *before* he got up. She was so tired now all the time that just *being* awake was an insufferable labor, but whenever she tried to sleep she found herself back in the Jabberwock's blistering grip, her body cramping and itching and her head pounding, a fearsome experience whose mere anticipation made her irritable and nervous whenever she was awake, which was, however dimly, most of the time.

"What, pray, is the reason," she asked, noticing them now,

tied to the chairs and to the teapot handle, "for are all those black balloons?"

"Inasmuch as a reason is a premise to an argument," replied the Mad Hatter in his haughtiest manner, perhaps somewhat put out at losing his cushion, "I suppose what you really wish to know is what is the argument? And the argument is a party."

"A party can't be an argument!"

"It is seldom anything else!" declared the March Hare, dropping his paw in his teacup, then gazing at it with a puzzled expression. "Oh! My paw's wet!" he exclaimed in a soft whining voice that reminded Alice of one of her dream-sisters from long ago.

"Of course it's wet, you poor crazed creature," said the Hatter. "Take it out of your teacup!"

The Hare raised his paw to his face and stared at it quizzically, his ears adroop. "It's *still* wet!"

"You might try sitting on it," suggested Alice, trying to be helpful.

The Hare peered up hopefully at Alice and tucked his paw beneath him. "Oh dear! Now my *tail's* wet!"

"Of course it is," said the Hatter. "That's called effect and cause."

"No," said Alice. "Cause and effect. The cause comes first."

"Nonsense," said the Hatter with a deprecatory snort that caused the tea to overflow his cup beneath his nose. "What came first was that his tail is wet. You heard him. *Now* comes the cause!"

"The cause..." insisted Alice, desperately weary of such madness, but unable to stop herself.

"There!" exclaimed the Hatter triumphantly. "You see?"

"...Is his wet paw. His paw was wet before his tail."

"Exactly!" said the Hatter, feeling quite proud of himself.

"Just as I said! It's like the balloons. First come the balloons, then comes the birthday party!"

"Birthday? Whose birthday?"

"Why, yours, dear child," said the March Hare, now sitting on both front paws, the second presumably there to dry the first and the tail as well. "The rest of us don't even *have* birthdays!"

"Mine? Again? But which—?"

"Your seventh, of course," said the Hatter with a patronizing grimace, as though speaking to an idiot or a small child.

"But it's *always* my seventh birthday! It was my seventh birthday when I *came* here!"

"I don't know about that," replied the Mad Hatter, "but last time, or some other time or times before or after that, it was, if I am not mistaken, your tenth birthday. And all the other numbers have had their party, too, it's only fair. I don't even mention your crowning party, which was your four thousandth *un*birthday—at *least!* Have you forgotten?"

"No, I remember. How could I not? It was the first time I stained my pinafore."

"An historic occasion!" pronounced the Dormouse, still fast asleep under the table.

"It was the Queen of Hearts' fault, she made me do it. It was just spite."

"It?" asked the Hatter. "You mean the stain?"

"No, the Queen. It—"

"Then you mean 'she.' *She* was spite."

"No, she was not," said Alice with an impatient sigh, feeling another headache coming on, the heartless red-eyed Jabberwock looming not far behind. "Spite was the *reason.* I was young and she was old." She'd thought about that tyrant often of late: all her dreadful moods, her furious passion, how she could become like a wild beast, screaming, shouting, crimson with fury, and what the poor old thing must have been going through.

"And the Queen was the argument?"

She sighed again, this time more in exasperated resignation. She'd promised herself never to come here again, but the truth was, she'd never been anywhere else. "You could say so."

"Thank you! I *will!*" exclaimed the Hatter, and he rose from his chair and put down his teacup and removed his hat, cradling it in his elbow, and solemnly declared in a manner he might have thought was singing:

"Alice had a little stain,
Which brought on royal laughter,
For everywhere Queen Alice went,
The stain would follow after.

It followed her to tea one day,
'Twas quite a sight to see;
It made us all faint dead away
To see a stain at tea!

The Red Queen screamed and pointed to
The cause of our confusion.
If the argument was she, we knew,
That stain was her conclusion!

And though Queen Alice washed it out,
The stain came back again,
And went on following her about
As a banner of her reign!

> But all of this was long ago,
> It happened yesterday!
> Where now's the stain? I do not know!
> Nor should I, could I, say!"

From underneath the table, as the Hatter took his bows, came the little click of the Dormouse's clapping paws, and the sleepy remark, punctuated by low rumbling snores, "My point exactly!" The March Hare tried to clap while sitting on his paws, which made him bob up and down in his chair and caused his ears to waggle stupidly, but Alice only slumped into her armchair and said: "It wasn't like that at all." But maybe, she thought, because "confusion" and "conclusion" had wormed their way into her mind somehow like little tunneling centipedes, it *was* a bit like that *now*, now when it *had* stopped following her about, another cruel joke and she again the butt, so to speak. And, oh dear, *did* she have centipedes in her head? Was *that* her problem? She clutched her furrowed brow with both hands. It seemed best to change the subject. "When *did* I come here?" she asked, probably not for the first time.

The Mad Hatter removed his large round watch from his checkered waistcoat pocket and put it to his ear, which was half-hidden by his high stiff collar. "At least two hours ago," he said matter-of-factly, then put the watch in his mouth and sucked on it like rock candy. "Give or take a yard or two," he added, mumbling around the watch.

Alice scowled. "Do you even know *how* to tell time?" she demanded.

"Of *course*, I do!" he shouted with such vehemence that the watch flew out and landed with a plunk in his teacup. His notorious quarrel with Time had never ceased, and it showed now in his pallid tea-stained face, which wanted to grow old but couldn't. "What do you wish me to tell him? And make it short! He's very busy, you know!"

"Tell him," Alice said, more to herself than to the Hatter, with whom one did not really converse, but only reparteed, "to get lost!"

"Ah, no need to tell him *that!*" exclaimed the March Hare, squirming on his forepaws. "Time is easily lost without needing reminders!"

"Even if you can keep Time, beat Time, or take him by the forelock," declared the Mad Hatter portentously, ticking these items off with his fingers as though enumerating a bill of particulars, "Time gets lost just the same."

"I know," said Alice wearily. Reparteed, she thought; that's rather good, I can use it later at the re-party. If I don't forget it as I forget everything else these days. Probably I should make a memorandum. "Time flies and all that "

"Time flies?" cried the Hatter, falling back in alarm.

"She must mean horse flies," whispered the Hare.

"Butterflies," suggested the sleeping Dormouse from under the table.

"Bread-and-butterflies, *he* means," whispered the Hare.

"Speaking of that," said Alice, "are there any sandwiches for my party? I'm desperately hungry!"

"There *were* sandwiches," the Mad Hatter said, stirring his tea with his pocket watch. "But someone stole them."

"Maybe it was the Knave of Hearts," said Alice gloomily. "That's in his line."

"In one of them anyway," agreed the Hatter somewhat patronizingly.

"No," squealed the March Hare, and he removed one paw from beneath him and pointed it at Alice. "*She* ate them all!"

"Did I?" They were all staring accusingly at her, all those with their heads above the table, that is. Well, it was possible. These days, she consumed all things edible, and some things not, as soon as her gaze fell upon them—EAT ME! DRINK ME! the whole world urged, and she did—but she was always as hungry afterward as before, everything eaten reduced instantly to ash in her inner oven. Even her droppings, as they called them here in Wonderland where animals, after all, were animals, were hard as agates and scorched-looking, dark little pellets of the sort left by the dear old White Rabbit in his dithery ramblings. It was all so sad. So woefully mome and mimsy, as they were wont to say. She looked down at the spots on the backs of her hands and began, as she had so often done of late, quite without reason as if reason had any business here, to cry.

"Now, now!" exclaimed the Mad Hatter, putting down his cup with a clatter as though rapping a gavel. "No tears, please! Definitely out of order at birthday parties!"

But still the tears kept flooding out of her as though having been bottled up in there for years, maybe that accounted for the terrible dryness she'd been feeling recently, inside and out, and now she was just wasting what precious little moisture she had left, it was pouring out of her from everywhere, tears or whatever, she couldn't hold any of it back. "Oh boo hoo!" she was wailing. Her face was wet, her pinafore, she was wet all over, there were puddles collecting at her feet.

"Now stop that, stop that!" cried the Hatter, scrambling up into his chair for higher ground. "A great girl like you, you ought to be ashamed of yourself! Stop this moment, I tell you!"

Oh, she *was* ashamed! And not just of the crying, but of everything that was happening to her! A great girl indeed! What was she doing here in this crazy nightmare, looking like this, leaking like this, her whole body like a huge squeezed sponge? It was hideous! *She* was hideous! She wanted to wake up! She wanted to go home and be a little girl again! She nearly did once, nearly did escape this terrible place—she could still remember this, though she'd forgotten almost everything else—for it happened one day that she found, in a corner of the White Queen's Castle, a looking-glass through which she might have passed, just as she had passed this direction long before, it might even have been the same one. But she had been so alarmed by the huge baggy thing she'd seen in it coming straight at her (the creature's upper arms were flapping like wings! and all those *chins!*), she'd screamed and fled, and she'd never found her way back again. "Oh boo hoo hoo!" she sobbed. "I'm so miserable!"

"There, there," said the March Hare, who had got up off his front paws and splashed around the table to comfort her. The entire back garden was under water. The Hare cradled her head in his starched shirtfront and patted it tenderly. "Perhaps it was the Knave of Hearts who stole the sandwiches! Yes, yes, I'm sure it was!"

"But what's *happening* to me?" she bawled. "I can't stop *changing!* Who *am* I? *What* am I?"

"Why, you're a little girl, of course," snapped the Mad Hatter in something of a peevish temper, still squatting in his chair above the flood like an angry toad. "Just like you've always been! As large as life and—!"

"No, no! *Much* larger! *Look* at me!"

"Now, now," said the March Hare, still patting her head.

"We love you just as you are, dear child!" He gave her a rather smelly hug, then reached under the table to pick up the snoring Dormouse by his long tail and save him from drowning. "And not to worry about the sandwiches," he added, tying the Dormouse's tail around a tree limb overhead. "The Duchess is bringing one of her turnip and trotters birthday cakes with her famous black pepper frosting!"

"Oh no!" gasped Alice damply, but somehow the thought of the peppery birthday cake and the ugly mustachioed Duchess, who was *altogether* uglier than Alice, even as she was now (hairs had appeared on Alice's lip, too, but she'd pulled them all out), finally did bring the tears to an end, though her snuffles continued and her breast heaved in wobbly little spasms. Above her, the upside-down Dormouse, looking wet and bedraggled, but still sound asleep, swung idly back and forth like the pendulum of a clock, an image all too prevalent of late. If only she could get rid of all clocks. Clocks and looking-glasses. And birthday parties.

"Are you all right now?" asked the Mad Hatter, offering her, with some reluctance, the small square of linen he kept tucked in his cuff. Alice nodded and blew her nose in it. Her fat nose. With the creases above it that looked like the March Hare's ears. "Very well and good!" he said as though he were concluding a difficult argument. "Have some more tea then!" And he handed her a cup from an empty place across the table.

"I shouldn't," Alice said with a snuffle, taking up the cup. It was the worst thing for her really. "It just makes my hot flushes hotter." Not to mention worse things. She felt moist and faint and limp in all her joints as if she'd just been wrestling again with the whiffling Jabberwock, and there was a wet stinging tingle in that tender unseen place, a sensation she had come to associate now with moments when she was overswept with feelings of regret. Maybe all that talk of the Knave of Hearts had set it off. That shameless roué. She remembered how she first saw him (he seemed so old then and so much younger now), proudly bearing the King's crown on a crimson velvet cushion as though carrying a great piece of fragile pastry. He was quite royally enrobed, though an accidental glimpse when he slipped sideways suggested to Alice that he was more decorously attired on the near side than the back, which was quite bare. And then later she saw him for the second time at his trial, cruelly clapped in chains and threatened with execution and looking very pleased with himself in a tragic sort of way. When she rose to give evidence and knocked over the jury box, he winked at her with the one eye she could see as though to say he understood what she was doing, even though she did not. It caused a brief little flutter in her chest, rather like indigestion, a flutter that returned whenever he was near. Over the years, if they were years and not, as the Mad Hatter would have it, yards, he had attempted countless advances, using all his deceptive finesse, and she had always cut him cruelly, dealing him insult after insult, telling him he didn't suit her at all, then bidding him a frozen farewell, that flutter fluttering all the while. Perhaps she had not played fairly. With him. With herself. This was what the tingle said, had been saying ever since the flushes began. "Are other people really coming to my party?" she asked with a rueful sigh.

"They can't *come*," said the Mad Hatter, settling back into his chair as the waters receded. "Not the way Time's behaving! But they will be here all the same."

Alice understood this. It was the way things happened here. Not at all or all of a sudden. "I rather wish they wouldn't," she said, feeling damp all over. "I don't think I want to see anyone."

"Then close your eyes," said the March Hare.

"That's not what I meant."

"Then you must say what you mean," admonished the Hatter.

"And mean what you say, I know, I know," said Alice snappishly.

"No, no, that's not the same thing, not the same thing a bit!" exclaimed the Mad Hatter vehemently, his polka-dotted bow tie bobbing.

"You might just as well say," said the March Hare, "that 'I like what I get' is the same thing as 'I get what I like!'"

"Yes, yes," sighed Alice, having heard all this before, "or that 'I see what I eat' is the same thing as 'I eat what I see.'"

"I'm afraid it *is* the same thing with you, dear child," sniffed the Hatter.

"Oh," cried Alice, "why did I come here? How did this happen to me?"

"The question," said the Hatter, raising a pedagogical finger into the air, "is not how but whether!"

"*Stop it!*" screamed Alice, so loudly that her empty teacup cracked and two of the black balloons popped. "I can't *bear* this any longer! Think of something *else* to do!"

The Dormouse, swinging idly overhead, opened his eyes when she screamed, but now closed them again. "We might play games," he murmured sleepily.

"You mean, like Chest or Chuckers?" asked the March Hare. "Or Dafts or Chin Rubby?"

"Double Chin Rubby, more like," said the Mad Hatter, catty as ever.

"Or Hide and Shriek!" shrieked the March Hare, clapping all four paws. "Or Rings Around the Nosy, Alice Fall Down!"

"Or Drop the Rag," continued the Mad Hatter with a superior smirk. "Or Lacie Loosic!"

"That's much too clever," remarked Alice, repressing her urge to scream again. "And not very nice."

"Quoit," agreed the sleeping Dormouse, speaking up quite clearly, whereupon the March Hare, as if it were his turn to do so, said, "I vote the young lady tells us a story."

"All right," said Alice, mopping her brow with the Hatter's soggy bit of linen, for though she did not know what story she might have to tell, she certainly did not want to hear again about the three little sisters in the nauseous treacle well, or any other nonsense her mad companions might dream up. She felt headachy and grievously weary and bloated and as parched within in as she was wet without. "Once upon a time—"

"I beg your pardon!" interrupted the Hatter.

"I'm not offended," said the March Hare.

"I was speaking to the little girl, you mindless beast!" exclaimed the Hatter. "Did you say 'once *upon* a time?'" he asked, turning to Alice accusingly.

"It's how a story begins," replied Alice, though she knew her explanation was far too sensible to suffice.

"I'm afraid then it begins quite wrongly," sniffed the Mad Hatter. "One cannot be upon Time. Ahead of Time perhaps. Behind the Times when they are out walking together. But never upon Time! He would not allow it!"

"Very well," sighed Alice, a bit desperately. "Once within time, then?"

"Scandalous!"

"Beyond?" The Hatter plucked his watch from his teacup and consulted it, but said nothing, so she hurried on. "There was once beyond time a little girl, an eager curious child who thought the world a wondrous place, and she was very pretty and loved by everyone, especially older gentlemen, and so small she could curl up in the very corner of an armchair. She lived aboveground with her cat named Dinah and two darling little kittens—"

"Was one of them white, the other black?" asked the Hatter.

"Yes. Have you heard this story before?"

"Before what?"

"Before now of course."

"I'm afraid that's impossible," said the Hatter with just a trace of melancholy, wiping his watch on his long coat tails. "It's always now. It can't be anything else. Before and after are just make-believe."

"Well, so is my story, then," said Alice, "for all this happened long ago and in another place. I don't remember what it was called, but there was an 'X' in it and a great river ran through it."

"How curious!" exclaimed the Hatter. "I never saw a river run!"

"I saw a river fall once," said the March Hare.

"I saw a river wave," muttered the Dormouse in his upended sleep.

"Above*ground*," Alice said with determination, for she could be stubborn, too, "rivers run."

"It must be a strange place indeed!" observed the Hatter, pocketing his watch after staring into its face as though to see the strange place there. "I suppose next you'll say that cause comes before effect up there!"

"Yes, and punishment always follows the crime, and two and

two always make four, and time is not a person and never goes backward, and when you say 'once upon a time,' that is exactly what you mean!" Alice was not certain about any of these declarations, shouted out so fiercely, for she had not been aboveground, except in her dreams (or the Red King's), for a very long time, and at least two of them seemed quite likely false, but she felt she had the upper hand at last in this conversation, and she did not intend to lose it by displaying any doubt.

"Two and two make *whom?*" the March Hare squealed with some amazement, counting his paws in a circular way such that he never came out with an even number. "I can't believe it! They must be out of their minds up there!"

"And animals don't speak aboveground! They are only spoken *to*, and often quite severely!" cried Alice, feeling another of her tearful rages coming on. The Jabberwock wouldn't come here, would he? Not to her birthday party! "And the only hares they have up there are jugged hares!"

"My ears! What a nightmare!" yelped the March Hare, and he knocked over the milk jug in his alarm and fell off his chair.

"Now look what you've done with your cruel aboveground talk, you silly goose!" shouted the Mad Hatter, skimming some of the spilled milk into his teacup. "You've frightened the dear fellow half into his wits!"

"I'm sorry. I take it back," said Alice, regretting her outburst, for she was at heart a considerate person even in her present bitter and sometimes uncontrollable condition.

"You *can't* take it back! Not if it's been said! You couldn't take it back even if you tried with both hands!"

"I wouldn't *try* to take it back with my *hands*," sighed Alice, pushing herself with effort out of her armchair, which was in any

ROBERT COOVER

case still soaked through from her flood of tears and gave one the disagreeable sensation of snuggling amongst wet sheep, and she plodded around the table to give the March Hare a helping hand. Before she could reach him, however, they were suddenly surrounded by the party guests, all her Wonderland friends, everyone from the stammering Dodo to the pedantic Red Queen, all laughing and screaming and sneezing (the black pepper cake had arrived and had been consumed almost before it had been cut) and hopping about in the traditional birthday party fashion—aboveground, they had a phrase for this mad hopping, but she'd forgotten it—and the poor Hare found himself being quite soundly trampled until finally a kindly gentleman dressed in white paper, or else made of it, discovered him there and, with a thin folded bow, helped him to his feet again.

"You can't think how glad I am to see you again, you dear old thing!" said someone with a deep muscular voice, tucking a fat arm into Alice's and digging a sharp chin into her shoulder. It was the ugly pocket-mouthed Duchess, she who'd brought the cake, making her usual clumsy and annoying show of affection, if it was affection and not something more sinister. "Isn't it a lovely day!" she added, her hoarse voice squawking a few notes higher, for she had to stretch up on her tiptoes now to lodge her chin on Alice's shoulder as was always her custom during their conversations. "It's simply perfect for your crowning party!"

"You're too late for that, I'm afraid. This is more like a croning party," said Alice miserably.

"Too late? Well, the moral of *that*," said the Duchess, "is that it is never too late to say you're sorry."

"It's always too late," said Alice, for she had just spied the

116

Knave of Hearts shuffling in with the rest of the pack, "or too early."

"You are quite right, my dear, time and tide run with the Hare and hunt with the hounds, making haste slowly, waiting for no one, who is always late anyway, the moral being, it is better to be safe than be sorry."

"Oh dear," exclaimed Alice, wondering if in fact it might not have been better to be sorry, "are there hounds here, too? It's getting very crowded!" Indeed, they were pressed in on all sides now by royalty and commoners alike, two-legged and otherwise, some in party hats and blowing little paper horns, others singing birthday songs of the rather unflattering "saggy/baggy, frumpy/dumpy" sort ("Happy birthday to Alice!" they were singing. "And to her spreading hips! To her varicose veins! And her tender nips!") or telling impenetrable riddles, like why is a bearded lady like hot mustard or a candle flame like a fat bum? Just so much stuff and nonsense, which, together with the heavy presence of the overbearing Duchess with her squeezes and pinches, left Alice feeling quite put out.

"I know one," wheezed the Duchess in her ear, her sharp chin drumming on her shoulder as she spoke. "A riddle, I mean. Two make it, two bake it, two break it. What is it?"

"That's easy," said Alice. "Bread."

"No, it's a baby," corrected the Duchess, "the moral being, you know, as you brew so shall you bake!" And she gave Alice a thick suffocating hug as though clapping her in an oven.

"Don't do that, please! I hurt there!" she complained, and pushed the Duchess's hands away. All around her now, they were popping the black balloons, or else she was developing another savage headache.

"Oh, dear child! Are you not feeling well?"

"No, it's, well... the time..." Alice hesitated, for she did not like to admit even to herself what the trouble was (she glanced at the Knave of Hearts who was flirting quite openly with Lily, the White Queen's daughter, proposing to her a game of vingt-et-un in the March Hare's private chambers), but she was near to tears again and in need of a friend who might understand. "It's, you know... the Jabberwock," she allowed at last.

"Ah! The Time of the Jabberwock! I remember it well!" announced the Duchess to all present, and released a windy sigh, though whether from nostalgia or anguish, it was hard to tell. "It was in those mimsical and frabjous days, as they are called, that I acquired my passion for black pepper. And for other things, not all as savory. Baby soup, for example. The moral being, of course, that one's passions are irresistible but too often indigestible."

"I'm afraid I don't know much about passions, or babies either," said Alice mournfully.

"Well, they're a little bit like fashions and rabies," said the Duchess, stroking the hair on her lip, "though somewhat less civilized."

Around her, her party guests were behaving in *very* uncivil fashion, carrying on like the indiscreet animals that many of them were, and showing manners little better, those that weren't. Some like the Lion and Pat the Guinea Pig had taken off all their clothes, if they'd had any on to begin with, and the Unicorn was doing very improper things with his horn, eliciting violent squeals of alarm and laughter wherever he went. "Sure, I don't like it, yer honor, at all at all!" cried Bill the Lizard, flying through the air, and the Queen of Hearts kept fluttering her skirts and shrieking for the Unicorn's head. Even the old White

Rabbit seemed quite undignified in his stiff exaggerated bouncing, his eyes glazed over and staring blindly as though he might have been back at his snuff pot again.

"I was just dreaming about you, my dear," said the Red King, passing by, looking utterly exhausted, his eyes the color of his regalia.

"A nightmare!" added the Red Queen with an accusing scowl. "He's been suffering from insomnia ever since!"

"Perhaps you should have a little lie-down for a few days," Alice suggested hopefully, but the Red King only looked horrified and fled, he and the Queen speeding backward in the direction from which they'd come.

Led by the Mad Hatter, many of the partygoers were still singing her birthday songs, or one of them anyway, Tweedledum and Tweedledee now taking turns reciting in their twittery little schoolboy voices alternating lines of another unpleasant verse:

"She's losing her hair,
There are pleats in her seat!
Her tummy's so big,
She can't see her feet!"

And here they wobbled their own round bellies in mockery, while all her friends howled out the Happy Birthday chorus.

"There's a moral about that," said the Duchess in her ear, "but I can't think what it is. It might be 'Honesty is the best policy,' or else 'Experience is the best teacher.' Or maybe 'All's for the best in the best of all possible worlds?'"

"I think I'm going to be ill again," said Alice dizzily, for she was feeling a sudden rush of the most intense heat to her chest, spreading quickly like a hot burrowing animal to her neck and face and arms, and she could feel the sweat breaking out all over and the wild palpitations of her heart—it's the Jabberwock!— and there was a terrible burning itch below that part of her they'd just been singing about as though their singing might have enkindled it. "Oh!" she gasped. "It's like being set upon by some dreadful storm!"

She turned to face the monster head-on then, quite willing just to die and have it over with, *no* one should have to suffer this, but it was only the ugly Duchess there behind her, smiling faintly, if that twitching of her massive jowls could be called smiling. "Just remember, dear," she growled gently, her dark scowl softening, "no matter the weather, old trots stick together!"

"I'm *not* an old trot!" she screamed.

"No, of course not, my love, who said you were?"

"I-I'm a little girl!"

"Yes, dear, aren't we all? The moral being—Ah! But take care of yourself! Something's going to happen!"

Something did. Someone sneezed behind her shoulder, and the heat immediately drained away, sinking into her tummy like heavy fog, and, more noisily that she might have hoped, left her by the ordinary passage.

"Ho! List! Who is it speaks so eloquently?" asked the Knave of Hearts with a sideways smirk at the vast landscape of her hinderparts, touching a kerchief plucked from his sleeve to his nose.

"I-I beg your pardon," whispered Alice, knowing that she was both pale and blushing at the same time, which probably gave her a very peculiar mottled look. The Knave was carrying a slice of the black birthday cake with a candle burning on it which he offered to her with a little bow and another sneeze into his kerchief, and because she was too embarrassed not to, she accepted it, though she hated black pepper and feared it would bring on another devastating flush.

"It makes you hot, you know," he said with a wink, pointing at the pepper.

"I certainly need no help for *that!*" replied Alice glumly.

"Do tell!" grinned the Knave with a suggestive roll of his eye, and he reached out to give her hip a thin papery pat. "I'll call that!"

"No, I mean *hot*, hot," she snapped, slapping his hand away with her free one. "Blistering hot. Sweaty sticky sickening hot. Not your kind of hot."

"Well, we won't know about that until we crack the deck, will we?" he murmured seductively, and stroked his waxed mustache, bobbed his eyebrow. "How about it, oh my queen? Just a round or two? Face up and jokers wild?"

All this was a mere routine, she knew, one he practiced like the rules of a game, for he was a Knave by design and could do no other, but should she ever play along and call his bluff, his hearts would blanch and he'd fold and flee in an instant. And why *had* she never played along? He was a notorious deceiver, of course, a thief and a seducer who casually discarded all the hearts he won or stole, and he could be insufferable with his knavish winks and nudges and his naughty innuendoes, which he probably thought were flattering but which were really quite insulting. She knew how to deal with him when he got out of hand, of course, and did—but what *was* out of hand on such occasions, and why was she so unbending? When asked at his trial, so very long ago (if it was not yesterday), what she knew about this business, she had to answer, "Nothing whatever," and she knew very little more now, and that learned more from watching her animal friends than from personal experience. She looked the Knave over. She could have done worse. He was handsome enough in a flat-headed sort of way (he was rather overly fond of his profile, she'd often told him so), and his attentions always gave her own heart a little flutter as it was fluttering now. Wasn't that supposed to mean something? Perhaps it was not too late; perhaps, if she gave him just the least bit of encouragement (if only she knew how to *do* that!), he might still have a go. Well, the next time he suggested that she try playing stud poker or hearts or gobang instead of old maid or solitaire, she should just follow his lead and say yes, thank you, do his bidding for once, why not? What did she have to lose but the infinite tedium of her Wonderland life? All these years of senseless tea parties! Whatever happened to her spirit of adventure?

Now, inspired perhaps by the loud singing going on around them and her own flushed hesitation, he bent toward her and asked: "Do you know the song, 'Tinkle, tinkle, little twot?'"

"I've heard something like it," she said politely, uncertain what a "twot" was, but supposing it prudent not to ask. She smiled hopefully.

"It goes," said the Knave, "this way—

> Tinkle, tinkle, little twot,
> How I wonder what you've got,
> High above your dimpled thighs,
> Like a clam up in the skies!"

"That's really very rude, you know!" gasped Alice, somewhat aghast.

"There's more."

"I think that's quite enough!"

But the Knave only pursed his lips as if to blow a kiss, and she knew this was why she'd never said yes: he was so pompous and ill-mannered and utterly inconsiderate! Just like royalty. You played the game his way or you didn't play at all.

"Tinkle, tinkle, little twot," he sang now, "High above the chamber pot "

"*Stop it!*" cried Alice, and all her guests turned around to watch. "That's completely *stupid!*"

But he only grinned out of the side of his mouth and went right on:—

"How I wish I were a flower,
Underneath your golden—!"

"*NO!*" stormed Alice, her fury rising, hating herself for this shrill hysteria ("Off with his head!" is what she *felt* like screaming, and nearly did, unsure who she even *was* any more), but unable to stop herself "You think you're a real *card*, don't you!" she cried out, and she took the lighted birthday candle from the cake and stabbed him with it in the middle of his royal pantaloons, burning a big brown hole there. "Now, dummy, you're a *marked* card!"

"You can't *do* that!" he shrieked. "*It's not allowed!*"

"Hmm. If that's your argument, yer honor," observed the mournful Carpenter, hovering nearby with a bitter tear in his eye and a toothpick in his blackened teeth, "there seems to be a hole in it," and the Walrus, stroking his long mustaches while gazing at Alice as though into a looking-glass, nodded solemnly. "Ah yes. Callooh, if I am not mistaken," he said, quite nonsensically. "And so, Callay."

The Knave shrieked again and flapped off in a rage, his hearts as black as spades, all the party guests now idiotically calloohing and callaying in his wake. Alice flung the slice of cake at his retreating backside, its plainness marred now by an ugly little brown hole, but hit the poor old Dodo on his beak instead.

"S-s-sorry!" exclaimed the Dodo, never at a loss for words or for a few extra syllables as well, and he looked up apprehensively at the sky as if it might be falling on him. "Always in the w-w-w-way! I sh-sh-shouldn't even *be* here! Just a dod-dod-doddering old r-relic! I do-do-do-do apologize!"

"Poor old thing," growled the Duchess at Alice's shoulder. "Always lingering about as though afraid of being forgotten. He's become quite dot-dot-dotty in his old age."

"He was born in old age," said the Mad Hatter with a disparaging sniff. Well, thought Alice, still aflame, that's true, what with the way time works here. She must be quite a novelty for them. "Which reminds me, my dear, would you like to hear 'You Are Old, Father William'? It's one of your favorites."

"No, I wouldn't," sighed Alice, the rush of blood to her head and elsewhere slowly subsiding, aware now that she had just made her relations with the Knave very difficult, very difficult indeed. Why was she so out of control all the time? But the Hatter, one hand tucked inside his waistcoat and hat in hand, began to recite anyway, as she knew he would:

"You are old, Mother Alice, and big as a door—"

"That's not 'You Are Old, Father William.'"

"Well, almost," said the Hatter. "Only a few of the words have got altered."

"It is wrong," she snapped, depression and perspiration flooding her, respectively, inside and out, "from beginning to—!"

"Don't interrupt, my child! Have you forgotten where you

are?" he cried, then resumed his oratorical stance:

> "You are old, Mother Alice, and big as a door,
> And all covered with wrinkles and fat...!"

Forgotten where she is? Oh no, more the pity!

> "...And yet you still wear your old pinafore,
> Pray, what is the reason for that?"

> "I'll tell you, good sir," Mother Alice replied,
> "And I hope you'll not think that I'm bitter;
> Since I've grown I could not get it off if I tried
> For it won't lift off over my sitter!"

"Oh, stop, please!" She felt a pressure something like that of a closing nut cracker just behind her eyes, and her legs seemed suddenly as thick and ponderous as those of an elephant. "You're giving me a dreadful headache!" But there would be no stopping him, she knew, for the Hatter's madness was of the theatrical sort, and now all her guests had gathered around and were clapping rhythmically, spurring him on. In the end she'd have no choice but to run away.

> "You are old, Mother Alice, your hair has turned white,
> And your skin is as rough as sandstone!
> And yet you go chasing after each knave and knight,
> Why don't you leave them alone?"

> "I'll tell you, good sir," said Mother Alice in haste,
> "If you'll spare me a thought for my lot;
> All my life I've not been the chaser, but chased,
> It's high time that I ought to be caught!"

"You are old, Mother Alice, and to be quite blunt,
You seem to have run out of luck;
It's clear that you've got a cork in your"—

But she never heard the rest. She had already fled, holding her head, the heat back, pounding at her temples, a kind of blindness overtaking her, and when she stopped running, if running could be said to be what she'd been doing (whatever, it exhausted her), she found herself standing, weak-kneed and fat legs aspraddle, wheezing heavily, in an old weedy garden, gone, as she, to seed. She wiped her dribbly nose on the apron front of her faded pinafore, sensing that the end of her story might not be very far away, whether or not she got past these duellos with the manxome Jabberwock, and she was frightened by that, and terribly depressed.

She knew well of course this sad garden which so reflected her own sad spirit. Alas. Her fault it looked like this. The flowers here, once quite lovely, used to talk. But then one day, enraged at her old tormentor the Rose, who liked to remind her that she was dropping her petals and fading fast, and who on that particular day had taken to reciting in her shrill little voice, "Alice, Alice, full of malice, why is your garden so dry," she'd simply plucked the wicked thing. "That will be enough of *that!*" she'd cried and snapped her fat little red head off. All the flowers had lost their color and withered away with a gasp of horror and had been utterly silent ever after, though sometimes, passing through, Alice thought she heard dry bitter whispers trailing in her wake.

Well, death, death and madness—the madness, as it were, of soldiering on for all the pointlessness of it, all the cruelty—these seemed to be the very essence of Wonderland, it was a wonder one should wonder. And—living garden, dead garden—did that mean that time really did pass in Wonderland? she asked herself, pressing her throbbing head between both sweaty palms. No, she replied, talking to herself as had ever been her wont. It only passed for her, fabulous otherworldly monster that she was. This garden appeared to her perhaps as sere and devastated, but to others it was no doubt as bright as ever and full of chatter; it had to do with something happening within one more than without, there was probably a word for it, at least aboveground, where things always got named no matter how crazy or useless or unpleasant they were, even such things as her present horrid condition.

Thinking about that, about names and how they got affixed to things that, of themselves, of course had no names, she recalled longingly the dark wood of forgetfulness, not seen since first seen, if ever (when she asked about it, people said it was only a legend, she must have imagined it, child that she was), a marvelous place where things had no name, and a place wherein she now wished desperately to lose herself. I don't want to be Alice anymore, she whimpered, realizing that in all the hysteria of her encounter with the Knave of Hearts she had apparently wet her drawers again (oh damn! as one of those old gentlemen on the river used to say whenever his pipe went out), and she again began to cry.

"A change like that's not easy, my friend," said a soft delicate voice behind her, "but it can be done. Look at me!"

Behind her, on a gaudily spotted mushroom, perched a beautiful Butterfly with gossamery wings the color of elderberries and orange marmalade, tinged with sugary wisps of silver. Alice wiped the tears from her eyes and squatted down to peer more closely. The mushroom was bloated and venomous looking, but the little Butterfly looked like a picture-book princess with her wings spread regally behind her like a gown flowing in the breeze. "Do I know you?"

"We met some time ago or perhaps in a different place," said the Butterfly in a voice as pretty as her wings. "But I was somewhat otherwise then. Or there. And so were you. You were only three inches tall."

"Ah!" exclaimed Alice. "That surly old blue Caterpillar with the hookah who gave me the magical mushroom! Are you he?"

"I am *not* a he!" snapped the Butterfly, somewhat offended, and she clapped her wings together stiffly, then fluttered them as though shyly batting her eyelashes. "Though once I was."

"But you were so old before, you're so much younger now! And, well, so very different!"

"And beautiful, too! Am I not beautiful?" she cried, preening.

"Exquisitely!" replied Alice, thinking, rather guiltily, how lovely she would look pinned under glass. "*Much* nicer than before!"

"Ah, but the trials of change, my dear! The unspeakable pain and humiliation! The deprivation! It's a terrible thing! And at such a time in one's life! I simply felt like crying all the time!"

"Oh, I know, I know!"

"It was truly an appalling crisis, from which I have only just emerged. I thought it would never end!"

"But it *does* seem to have been worth it," said Alice, feeling just a wee bit envious.

"Oh yes!" exclaimed the Butterfly, her colorful wings trembling with transparent joy and excitement. "Life is going to be so beautiful now! I'm going to enjoy every minute of it!" She flapped her wings more rapidly and rose to hover just above the spotted crown of the mushroom. "Look! I can fly! I shall see the world! Good-bye, dear child!"

"No, wait!" begged Alice. "Before you go, tell me, please! During the worst of it, was there anything, you know, that helped?"

"Only one thing—" said the hovering Butterfly, but just then a Swallow flew past like a flickery gray shadow and snapped her up and that was the end of their conversation. Ah well, thought Alice, staring glumly at the abruptly vacated mushroom. Wonderland.

As she was all alone again in a dead place, far from the party guests, and feeling a bit itchy and leaky once more, she decided to relieve herself while she was still in her squat, so she hiked up her pinafore and skirts and worked her damp drawers down over her knees.

"I've invented a plan," said a voice to her rear, startling her so that, trying to yank her drawers back up, she fell face forward into the desiccated remains of a petunia bed, that part of her which she'd hoped to conceal now most revealed (she seemed to hear a rattle of dry ghostly laughter all about), "by which one might raise and lower one's nether garments by means of pulleys attached to the ears." Ah. It was only her dotty old friend the White Knight. "I've also invented a very clever cure for nettle rash," he added in his kindly voice, and from the sound of it she could tell he was upside-down as usual. "It's made of truffles, boiled ink, and mashed carpet beetles, to be taken in small doses at high tea."

"It's not nettle rash," she said with a shudder, clambering heavily to her feet and lowering her skirts. Her drawers were wet and cold and, though it felt airy, she could not bear anything so unpleasant touching her skin just now, so she kicked them off. "It's more like nappy rash."

"Hm. Just as well, I suppose," he said with a heart-wrenching sigh, "for I have yet to find a sufficient quantity of carpet beetles prepared to devote themselves to medical science."

Alice went over to him where he lay, head downward as she'd supposed, in a ditch. She made no effort to pull him upright for, like one of the antipathies, as she liked to say, he was happier on his head than on his feet or seat. When she first came here, he was more of a grandfather to her; now he was like an addled older brother, but still dearer to her than anyone else in Wonderland. "I see you've fallen down off your wooden horse again."

"Actually, no, dear child, it fell up from under me. A most unreliable beast. But just as well, for, while lying here, I have contrived an ingenious way for someone in my present circumstances to perceive the world aright. As you know, a lens held at a certain distance will turn things upside-down, so one fastened to the toe of my boot would provide me, as I am now, a view of the world right-side-up, which would be very useful if a foe were in the vicinity or if someone were bringing me a present. I could nail a little box to my boot and attach the lens to a cord in it so that whenever I was upended, it would drop out and dangle before my eyes."

"Yes," said Alice, and she smiled down on her gentle foolish half-bald friend in his battered tin armor. Conversation with him always calmed her and held the Jabberwock at bay, if only for a brief time, so even head down, helpless and utterly bonkers, the Knight remained in some sense her protector. "They had such lenses aboveground, I think. They used them for taking pictures."

"*Taking* pictures? Do you mean, stealing them?"

"You might say so. Though, as I recall, I was always a willing victim, in or out of my little frock."

"They stole your frock, too? By my honor!" His mild blue eyes were wide with alarm and perplexity. "Where is this terrible aboveground of yours, pray tell?"

"Up there somewhere, I guess," said Alice gazing into the sky, which was today a shocking shade of paintbox blue. "Above your feet."

"You mean, down there, below my feet."

"If you like. And it was not so bad—having one's picture taken, I mean. It always gave me a kind of thrill. You know. Just to be *looked* at like that."

"I assure you, I *don't* know, my dear!" declared the Knight, trembling inside his tin armor and making it rattle. "It's sounds like a frightful place for little girls! You must promise me never to go there again!"

"That's easy. Unless I can fall up, I don't think I *can* go there again. If there's really a 'there' and it's not just something I dreamt." But it seemed so real. As did her fall, that impulsive leap down the rabbit hole, never once considering how she might get out again, and then the slow weightless plunge, so slow she could catalog the shelves and even practice her curtsey as she dropped. What ecstasy, that sweet dense fall, her whole body embraced by something like liquid yet not liquid! It was probably the last great pleasure she'd had, and the nearest she'd ever come to what she never came to. She often fell asleep thinking about it, her hands between her legs. And now, well... She gazed off into the black shadows of the forest beyond the Knight, where, no doubt, the Jabberwock awaited her, and she knew that she could not avoid it. If she walked toward it she would come to it and if she walked away from it she would come to it and if she remained here in the silent garden she would also come to it.

In fact, she had already come to it, to the edge of it anyway, for the dark forest had risen up before her, menacing, yet beckoning. The White Knight was somewhere far behind her, she was alone. Was this the mysterious wood of forgetfulness for which she longed? Alas, far from it. She saw lichens and ivy and hemlock and the webs of spiders and the spoor of woodland rodents, and knew them to be such and to be called such. She saw a flower and thought: Larkspur. Also known as delphinium. She saw trees and thought: Larch. Flowering chestnut. Copper beech. She saw many other things which did not even belong here, such as a writing desk, white kid gloves, a soup cauldron, a ladder with a snake curled round one rung. Which she could name exactly, if she thought a little harder. No, far from being the wood where things have no name, this was surely the dismaying wood where every name has its thing.

And then she saw, hanging in the air above a pin oak limb, a catless grin. "Hello," she said, and the Cheshire Cat emerged around his toothy smile. "I thought you might be here. You always turn up at the direst moments."

"You are missing your birthday party," said the Cat without moving his lips.

"Well, I am not missing it very much," replied Alice, grateful for a bit of company, even one so ghostly. "And I doubt if it is missing me. Like you, I've become almost invisible here."

"You are hardly invisible," said the Cat with his fixed grin.

"Because I'm so big and floppy? That's just another way to disappear. Did you bring anything to eat?"

"No. But you'll find some mushrooms at the foot of the tree."

"Will any of them make me smaller?" she asked hopefully.

"No. But they may make you feel a little better for a while."

"Why should I want to feel any better? I feel just perfect, if you don't mind."

The Cheshire Cat did not reply, but merely continued to smile down at her enigmatically.

Alice sighed, stuffed her hands into her pinafore pockets. "All right, not *exactly* perfect." As the Cat remained silent, she went on. "It's the Jabberwock, you see. I try to hold it back, but it's stronger than I am and it claws its way inside me somehow and makes me feel like I'm roasting myself, and *that* makes it hard for me to hold my temper. I get all uffish, if that's the word, which gives me headaches and palpitations, and I become dizzy and have a bad tummy and a wretched itching in the worst places, which is there sometimes even after the Jabberwock has gone galumphing off again. It's all very strenuous and cruel and makes me perspire awfully, and that dries my skin out and leaves behind all these *brown* spots and white hairs and loads and loads of ghastly *wrinkles!* I wasn't supposed to *have* wrinkles! How did this *happen?* I *hate* them!" She was beginning to shriek like the Queen of Hearts again, so she paused and took a deep breath, her bosom heaving tremulously. Off with her head! that frumious Queen once screamed, and Alice now feared that that sentence of so long ago was finally being carried out, that she was indeed beginning to lose her head. It was maybe what frightened her most of all at this uncomfortable sort of age. Not to know herself might be even worse than not to be herself. The quizzical Cat meanwhile just grinned expectantly, showing all his teeth. "What else? Oh, I can't sleep, I cry all the time, my teeth hurt, my chest is as crinkly as funeral crêpe, I'm growing a mustache, I can't remember yesterday, I've got little purple doodles all over my legs, I don't see as well as I used to, I can't stop eating, I'm so *very* lonely, I think I'm going to die soon, I'm not at all pretty, nobody loves me, I'm bloated and saggy and red-eyed and ugly and I've had a stupid and useless life and I'm just dreadfully dreadfully depressed." Now she'd begun to cry. "I think I'm even starting to *smell* old," she sobbed, then stopped herself with a little stamp of her foot. It was just too embarrassing really, especially while being stared at with such derision. Which was, as she recalled, along with Ambition, Distraction, and Uglification, one of the branches of the Mock Turtle's Arithmetic, the one that left you with considerably less than what you had before. Another foolish blubberer, that Mock Turtle, and she was behaving just like him. She ought to be ashamed of herself, well schooled as she was in his dead languages of Laughing and Grief wherein one learned, above all, to keep a stiff upper lip. Even if it was puckery and creased and asprout with evil little hairs.

Remembering the Mock Turtle's lessons calmed her some: she hadn't forgotten *everything*. She wiped her nose on the shoulder of her pinafore. It was very quiet here in the wood, and it had grown darker. "Listen," she said, and she tossed her hair to get it out of her eyes in the old way: it made a rasping sound like river rushes in the wind. "Do you hear that? Dry as broomstraw! And it's falling *out*, too! That's right! Keep grinning at me, you loony old thing! I'm sure it's *very* amusing!" The Cat, though still smiling, began to fade a bit, she could see the oak leaves through its haunches, and she was suddenly terrified of being left alone here in the dimming forest. "I'm sorry. Wait! Don't go! I know I'm not as nice as I used to be, but it's not my fault. I'm just not *who*

I used to be. It's a *very* curious sensation. And it has all happened so fast. There was something the Red Queen once told me that I didn't understand at the time. We were racing along, going nowhere, and she said: 'When you're over the hill, you pick up speed.' There, in that flat place, it seemed like complete nonsense, but I know now what she meant." That lady's rival the White Queen was able to make time run backward: How did she do that? Maybe she had one of those watches with a reversal peg. If I could run time backwards, Alice asked herself, would I do it? I would, oh yes, I certainly would. Anything but having to face what's coming.

She looked up at the Cheshire Cat, who was only half there now, and she sighed, having the very strong sensation that she was merely talking to herself again. "All I want is just to be able to go home and be a child again and play with my cats and sisters and get my picture taken. I so loved it up there. It was a place that shaped itself around me and was as much part of me as I was, even if maybe it wasn't completely real. It was much more wonderful than this place, which *thinks* it's so wonderful, but is really very mean and tedious. I hate it here and the way I am now. But, well, you don't have to tell me, I know that's not going to happen, I'm stuck here and as I am and there's nothing to be done about it. After they made me a queen and all the fun was over, though it seemed like more fun for them than it was for me, I kept trying to find the way out. I used to follow the old White Rabbit around, thinking he might lead me back to that long hall with the glass table and cakes which one crawled into by way of a door in a tree. Ancient and feeble as he was, he still moved a lot faster than I could, so I had to follow the little, you know, clues that he dropped. Finally, one day, they did lead me to that little door, but I was too big by then to squeeze through. I could only get my head inside, but far enough to be able to stare up the hole down which I'd fallen, or supposed I had. Oh how I hoped to see something familiar, a face I knew looking down at me maybe, or even my cat Dinah, who was nice and cuddly and never showed her teeth and, if she was real, must have been missing me very much, but as far as I could see there was nothing up there but a terrible black emptiness. I lay there for hours to see if it would change, but it didn't. It gave me a very sinister feeling, and I thought: That's it. There's nothing up there and I am where I am and where I've always been." She shuddered. "And now all that emptiness has somehow got inside. Like whatever *me* was in there has been oozing away with everything else that's been squeezed out by the Jabberwock, leaving just a black empty hole in there. I wake up at night, soaking wet with perspiration, trying to remember who I am or what I am, afraid that Alice isn't going to be Alice any more. It's as though that pretty little girl has gone away and left me and I'm now just another extinct and imbecilic old creature stumbling around crazily in Wonderland." Oh dear, she was crying again. Never mind. Let it come. If she couldn't cut the Jabberwock's head off, maybe she could drown it. "I just have this awful feeling of having lived a life inside an insoluble riddle made up by some mad, savage, unkind child!" she sobbed. "And if that's how this world works, *it's a poor thin way of doing things!*"

The Cat had continued to fade away as though dissolved by her tears, only his grinning head remaining. She envied the Cat, being able to leave his body like that and just be a grin, but talking to him for solace was like quenching one's thirst with a dry biscuit. Even the Mad Hatter was more like company. And then she remembered: reparteed. She'd meant to use it at the re-party, but she'd forgotten. She should have made a note. Now it was too late. It was always too late. She could hear whiffling and burbling sounds deep in the dark wood now. Or maybe she was making those sounds deep in her own body, which had become stranger to her than Wonderland itself. There was a chill wind rising, which she felt particularly as an unpleasant airiness between her legs, and she regretted having kicked her drawers off. The way she'd been lately, it would be wise to carry a second pair in her pinafore pocket. If she was going to die, she'd at least like to have clean drawers on. But she was not going to die, she knew. Not yet. Encounters with the Jabberwock might not leave you feeling like seven years old after, but they were not immediately fatal, or so the old Queens had assured her. After it was all over, there would be more insane tea parties, flamingo croquet, and stupid lobster quadrilles, there was much yet to look forward to. In fact, she realized she'd never really been a Queen, all that was just a pleasant mockery at her expense, it was only now she was truly about to become one.

"Tell me," she asked the Cheshire Cat whose eyes still gazed down at her over the grin, though little else of him could be seen, "am I just an entertainment for everybody else?" He did not reply but his eyes disappeared, leaving only his uncanny grin afloat above the branch. She snuffled and wiped her tears again and felt the Jabberwock's heat rising in her breast. Sweat broke out on her brow. Yes, soon now. And chin up, soon enough all over: snicker-snack. Like everything else. That's time for you. That's glory.

"If a riddle is insoluble," whispered the wicked grin, growing faint as it too faded away, "it is usually because you know the answer but are afraid of it."

"I'm *not* afraid!" Alice shouted out after it into the gathering storm. "I'm just rather *angry* is all! It's all so *unfair!*"

And then a great hot darkness descended upon her or arose within her, blowing in with flapping wings and stirring up a wind as strong as soup. It was not unlike that medium through which she sank when she first fell down the rabbit hole, though much more unpleasant.

"What a thick black cloud that is!" she seemed to hear someone say. It might have been the Cheshire Cat or his toothy grin. Or perhaps that pretty little Alice who once lived inside her. She could hardly breathe. But she would. Even if only for a short time. *"And how fast it comes!"*

THE FALLGUY'S FAITH

FALLING FROM FAVOR, or grace, some high artifice, down he dropped like a discredited predicate through what he called space (sometimes he called it time) and with an earsplitting crack splattered the base earth with his vital attributes. Oh, I've had a great fall, he thought as he lay there, numb with terror, trying desperately to pull himself together again. This time (or space) I've really done it! He had fallen before of course: short of expectations, into bad habits, out with his friends, upon evil days, foul of the law, in and out of love, down in the dumps—indeed, as though egged on by some malevolent metaphor generated by his own condition, he had *always* been falling, had he not?—but this was the most terrible fall of all. It was like the very fall of pride, of stars, of Babylon, of cradles and curtains and angels and rain, like the dread fall of silence, of sparrows, like the fall of doom. It was, in a word, as he knew now, surrendering to the verb of all flesh, the last fall (*his* last anyway: as for the chips, he sighed, releasing them, let them fall where they may)—yet why was it, he wanted to know, why was it that everything that had happened to him had seemed to have happened in language? Even this! Almost as though, without words for it, it might not have happened at all! Had he been nothing more, after all was said and done, than a paraphrastic curiosity, an idle trope, within some vast syntactical flaw of existence? Had he fallen, he worried as he closed his eyes for the last time and consigned his name to history (may it take it or leave it), his juices to the soil (was it soil?), *merely to have it said he had fallen?* Ah! tears tumbled down his cheeks, damply echoing thereby the greater fall, now so ancient that he himself was beginning to forget it (a farther fall perhaps than all the rest, this forgetting: a fall as it were within a fall), and it came to him in these fading moments that it could even be said that, born to fall, he had perhaps fallen simply to be born (birth being less than it was cracked up to be, to coin a phrase)! Yes, yes, it could be said, what can *not* be said, but he didn't quite believe it, didn't quite believe either that accidence held the world together. No, if he had faith in one thing, this fallguy (he came back to this now), it was this: in the beginning was the *gesture*, and that gesture was: he opened his mouth to say it aloud (to prove some point or other?), but too late—his face cracked into a crooked smile and the words died on his lips...

THE RETURN OF THE
DARK CHILDREN

WHEN THE FIRST black rats reappeared, scurrying shadowily along the river's edge and through the back alleyways, many thought the missing children would soon follow. Some believed the rats might *be* the children under a spell, so they were not at first killed, but were fed and pampered, not so much out of parental affection, as out of fear. For, many legends had grown up around the lost generation of children, siphoned from the town by the piper so many years ago. Some thought that the children had, like the rats, been drowned by the piper, and that they now returned from time to time to haunt the town that would not, for parsimony, pay their ransom. Others believed that the children had been bewitched, transformed into elves or werewolves or a kind of living dead. When the wife of one of the town councilors hanged herself, it was rumored it was because she'd been made pregnant by her own small son, appearing to her one night in her sleep as a toothless hollow-eyed incubus. Indeed, all deaths, even those by the most natural of causes, were treated by the citizenry with suspicion, for what could be a more likely cause of heart failure or malfunction of the inner organs than an encounter with one's child as a member of the living dead?

At first, such sinister speculations were rare, heard only among the resentful childless. When the itinerant rat-killer seduced the youngsters away that day with his demonic flute, all the other townsfolk could think about was rescue and revenge. Mothers wept and cried out the names of their children, calling them back, while fathers and grandfathers armed themselves and rushed off into the hills, chasing trills and the echoes of trills. But nothing more substantial was ever found, not even a scrap of clothing or a dropped toy, it was as though they had never been, and as the weeks became months and the months years, hope faded and turned to resentment—so much love misspent!—and then eventually to dread. New children meanwhile were born, replacing the old, it was indeed a time of great fertility for there was a vacuum to be filled, and as these new children grew, a soberer generation than that which preceded it, there was no longer any place, in homes or hearts, for the old ones, nor for their lightsome ways. The new children were, like their predecessors and their elders, plump and happy, much loved, well fed, and overly indulged in all things, but they were more closely watched and there was no singing or dancing. The piper had instilled in the townsfolk a terror of all music, and it was banned forever by decree. All musical instruments had been destroyed. Humming a tune in public was an imprisonable offense and children, rarely spanked, were spanked for it. Always, it was associated with the children who had left and the chilling ungrateful manner of their leaving: they did not even look back. But it was as though they had not really quite gone away after all, for as the new children came along the old ones seemed to return as omnipresent shadows of the new ones, clouding the nursery and playground, stifling laughter and spoiling play, and they became known then, the lost ones, the shadowy ones, as the dark children.

In time, all ills were blamed on them. If an animal sickened and died, if milk soured or a house burned, if a child woke screaming from a nightmare, if the river overflowed its banks, if money went missing from the till or the beer went flat or one's appetite fell off, it was always the curse of the dark children. The new children were warned: Be good or the dark children will get you! They were not always good, and sometimes, as it seemed, the dark children did get them. And now the newest menace: the return of the rats. The diffident pampering of these rapacious creatures soon ceased. As they multiplied, disease broke out, as it had so many years before. The promenade alongside the river that ran through the town, once so popular, now was utterly forsaken except for the infestation of rats, the flower gardens lining the promenade trampled by their little feet and left filthy and untended, for those who loitered there ran the risk of being eaten alive, as happened to the occasional pet gone astray. Their little pellets were everywhere and in everything. Even in one's shoes and bed and tobacco tin. Once again the city fathers gathered in emergency council and declared their determination to exterminate the rats, whether they were bewitched dark children or not; and once again the rats proved too much for them. They were hunted down with guns and poisons and burned in mountainous heaps, their sour ashes blanketing the town, graying the laundry and spoiling the sauces, but their numbers seemed not to diminish. If anything, there were more of them than ever seen before, and they just kept coming. But when one rash councilor joked that it was maybe time to pay the piper, he was beaten and hounded out of town.

For, if the dark children were a curse upon the town, they were still their own, whereas that sorcerer who had lured them away had been like a mysterious force from another world, a diabolical intruder who had forever disturbed the peace of the little community. He was not something to laugh about. The piper, lean and swarthy, had been dressed patchily in too many colors, wore chains and bracelets and earrings, painted his bony face with ghoulish designs, smiled too much and too wickedly and with teeth too white. His language, not of this town, was blunt and uncivil and seemed to come, not from his throat, but from some hollow place inside. Some seemed to remember that he had no eyes, others that he did have eyes but the pupils were golden. He ate sparely, if at all (some claimed to have seen him nibbling at the rats), and, most telling of all, he was never seen to relieve himself. All this in retrospect, of course, for at the time, the townsfolk, vastly comforted by the swift and entertaining eradication of the rats, saw him as merely an amusing street musician to be tolerated and, if not paid all that he impertinently demanded (there had been nothing illegal about this, no contracts had been signed), at least applauded—the elders, like the children, in short, fatally beguiled by the fiend. No, should he return, he would be attacked by all means available, and if possible torn apart, limb from limb, his flute rammed down his throat, the plague of rats be damned. He who placed himself beyond the law would be spared by none.

Left to their own resources, however, the townsfolk were no

match for the rats. For all their heroic dedication, the vermin continued to multiply, the disease spread and grew more virulent, and the sky darkened with the sickening ash, now no longer of rats only, but sometimes of one's neighbors as well, and now and then a child or two. Having lost one generation of children, the citizenry were determined not to lose another, and did all they could to protect the children, their own and others, not only from the rats but also from the rumored dark children, for there had been reported sightings of late, mostly by night, of strange naked creatures with piebald flesh moving on all fours through the hills around. They had the form of children, those who claimed to have seen them said, but they were not children. Some said they had gray fleshy wings and could hover and fly with the darting speed of a dragonfly. Parents now boiled their children's food and sterilized their drink, policed their bedrooms and bathrooms and classrooms, never let them for a single minute be alone. Even so, now and then, one of them would disappear, spreading fear and consternation throughout the town. But now, when a child vanished, no search parties went out looking for it as they'd done the first time, for the child was known to be gone as were the dead gone, all children gone or perished spoken of, not as dead, but taken.

The city elders, meeting in continuous emergency session, debated the building of an impregnable wall around the town to keep the dark children out and hopefully to dam the tide of invading rats as well. This had a certain popular appeal, especially among the parents, but objections were raised. If every ablebodied person in town worked day and night at this task, it was argued, it would still take so long that the children might all be gone before it could be finished: then, they'd just be walling themselves in with the rats. And who knew what made a wall impregnable to the likes of the dark children? Weren't they, if they really existed, more like phantoms than real creatures for whom brick and stone were no obstruction? Moreover, the building of such a wall would drain the town of all its energy and resources and close it off to trade, it would be the end of the era of prosperity, if what they were suffering now could still be called prosperity, and not only the children could be lost but also the battle against the rats which was already proving very taxing for the community. But what else can we do? We must be more vigilant!

And so special volunteer units were created to maintain a twenty-four-hour watch on all children. The playgrounds were walled off and sealed with double locks, a compromise with the proponents of the wall-building, and all the children's spaces were kept brightly lit to chase away the shadows, even as they slept at night. Shadows that seemed to move by themselves were shot at. Some observed that whenever a child disappeared a pipe could be heard, faintly, just before. Whether this was true or not, all rumors of such flaunting of the music laws were pursued with full vigor, and after many false alarms one piper was at last chased down: a little boy of six, one of the new children, blowing on a wooden recorder. He was a charming and dutiful boy, much loved by all, but he had to be treated as the demon he now was, and so, like any diseased animal, he and his pipe were destroyed. His distraught parents admitted to having hidden away the childish recorder as a souvenir at the time of outlawing musical instruments, and the child somehow, inexplicably, found it. The judges did not think it was inexplicable. There were calls for the death penalty, but the city fathers were not cruel or vindictive and understood that the parents had been severely punished by the loss of their child, so they were given lengthy prison sentences instead. No one protested. The prison itself was so rat-infested that even short sentences amounted to the death penalty anyway.

The dark children now were everywhere, or seemed to be. If the reports of the frightened citizenry were to be believed, the hills about now swarmed with the little batlike phantoms and there was daily evidence of their presence in the town itself. Pantries were raided, flour spilled, eggs broken, there was salt in the sugar, urine in the teapot, obscene scribblings on the school chalkboard and on the doors of closed shops whose owners had taken ill or died. Weary parents returned from work and rat-hunting to find all the pictures on their walls tipped at odd angles, bird cages opened, door handles missing. That these sometimes turned out to be pranks by their own mischievous children was not reassuring for one had to assume they'd fallen under the spell of the dark children, something they could not even tell anyone about for fear of losing their children to the severity of the laws of vigilance now in place. Whenever they attempted to punish them, their children would cry out: It's not my fault! The dark children made me do it! All right, all right, but shush now, no talk of that!

There were terrible accidents which were not accidents. A man, socializing with friends, left the bar one night to return home and made a wrong turn, stumbled instead into the ruined gardens along the promenade. One who had seen him passing by said it was as if his arm were being tugged by someone or something unseen, and he looked stricken with terror. His raw carcass was found the next morning at the edge of the river. One rat-hunter vanished as though consumed entirely. Another was shot dead by a fellow hunter, and in two different cases, rat poison, though kept under lock and key, turned up in food; in both instances, a spouse died, but the partners were miraculously spared. When asked if the killing was an accident, the hunter who had shot his companion said it certainly was not, a mysterious force had gripped his rifle barrel and moved it just as he was firing it. And things didn't seem to be where they once were any more. Especially at night. Furniture slid about and knocked one over, walls seemed to swing out and strike one, stair steps dropped away halfway down. Of course, people were drinking a lot more than usual, reports may have been exaggerated, but once-reliable certainties were dissolving.

The dark children remained largely invisible for all that the town felt itself swarming with them, though some people claimed to have seen them running with the rats, swinging on the belfry rope, squatting behind chimney pots on rooftops. With each reported sighting, they acquired new features. They were said to be child-sized but adult in proportions, with long arms they sometimes used while running; they could scramble up walls and hug the ground and disappear right into it. They were gaudily colored and often had luminous eyes. Wings were frequently mentioned, and occasionally tails. Sometimes these were short and furry, other times more long and ratlike. Money from the town treasury disappeared and one of the councilors as well, and his wife, though hysterical with grief and terror, was able to describe in startling detail the bizarre horned and winged creatures who came to rob the town and carry him off. Ah! We didn't know they had horns. Oh yes! With little rings on the tips! Or bells! They were glittery all over as if dressed in jewels! She said she was certain that one of them was her own missing son, stolen away by the piper all those many years ago. I looked into his eyes and pleaded with him not to take his poor father away, she wept, but his eyes had no pupils, only tiny flickering flames where the pupils should be! They asked her to write out a complete profile of the dark children, but then she disappeared, too. When one of the volunteer guards watching children was charged with fondling a little five-year-old girl, he insisted that, no, she was being sexually assaulted by one of the dark children and he was only doing all he could to get the hellish creature off her. The child was confused but seemed to agree with this. But what happened to the dark child? I don't know. The little girl screamed, a crowd came running, the dark child faded away in my grasp. All I managed to hold on to was this, he said, holding up a small gold earring. A common ornament. Most children wear them and lose them daily. I tore it out of his nose, he said. He was found innocent but removed from the unit and put on probation. In his affidavit, he also mentioned horns, and was able to provide a rough sketch of the dark child's genitalia, which resembled those of a goat.

The new children pretended not to see the dark children, or perhaps in their innocence, they didn't see them, yet overheard conversations among them suggested they knew more than they were telling, and when they were silent, they sometimes seemed to be listening intently, smiling faintly. The dark children turned up in their rope-skipping rhymes and childish riddles (When is water not wet? When a dark child's shadow makes it...), and when they chose up sides for games of ball or tag, they tended always to call one of their teams the dark children. The other was usually the hunters. The small children cried if they couldn't be on the dark children's team. When a child was taken, his or her name was whispered among the children like a kind of incantation, which they said was for good luck. The church organist, unemployed since the piper went through and reduced to gravetending, a task that had somewhat maddened him, retained enough presence of mind to notice that the familiar racket of the children's playground games, though still composed of the usual running feet and high-pitched squealing, was beginning to evolve into a peculiar musical pattern, reminiscent of the piper's songs. He transcribed some of this onto paper, which was studied in private chambers by the city council, where, for the first time in many years, surreptitious humming was heard. And at home, in their rooms, when the children played with their dolls and soldiers and toy castles, the dark children with their mysterious ways now always played a part in their little dramas. One could hear them talking to the dark children, the dark children speaking back in funny squeaky voices that quavered like a ghost's. Even if it was entirely invented, an imaginary world made out of scraps overheard from parents and teachers, it was the world they chose to live in now, rather than the one provided by their loving families, which was, their parents often felt, a kind of betrayal, lack of gratitude, lost trust. And, well, just not fair.

One day, one of the rat-hunters, leaning on his rifle after a long day's work and smoking his old black pipe, peered down into the infested river and allowed that it seemed to him that whenever a child vanished or died, the rat population decreased. Those with him stared down into that same river and wondered: Was this possible? A rat census was out of the question, but certain patterns in their movements could be monitored. There was a wooden footbridge, for example, which the rats used for crossing back and forth or just for cavorting on, and one could at any moment make a rough count of the rats on it. At the urging of the hunters, these tabulations were taken by the town clerk at dawn, midday, and twilight for several days, and the figures were found to be quite similar from day to day, no matter how many were killed. Then, a little girl failed to return from a game of hide-and-seek (the law banning this game or any game having to do with concealment was passing through the chambers that very day), and the next day the rat numbers were found to have dropped. Not substantially perhaps, one would not have noticed the change at a glance, but it was enough to make the bridge count mandatory by law. A child, chasing a runaway puppy, fell into the turbulent river and was taken and the numbers dropped again, then or about then. Likewise when another child disappeared (he left a note, saying he was going where the dark children were to ask if they could all be friends) and a fourth died from the diseases brought by the rats.

Another emergency session of the council was called which all adult members of the community were invited to attend. No one stayed away. The choice before them was stark but, being all but unthinkable, was not at first enunciated. The parents, everyone knew, were adamant in not wanting it spoken aloud at all. There were lengthy prolegomena, outlining the history of the troubles from the time of the piper's visit to the present, including reports from the health and hospital services, captains of the rat-hunting teams, the business community, the volunteer vigilance units, school and toilet monitors, the town clerk, and artists who provided composite sketches of the dark children based on reported sightings. They did not look all that much like children of any kind, but that was to be expected. A mathematician was brought in to explain in precise technical detail the ratio between the disappearance or death of children and the decrease in the rat population. He was convincing, though not well understood. Someone suggested a break for tea, but this was voted down. There was a brief flurry of heated discussion when a few parents expressed their doubts as to the dark children's actual existence, suggesting they might merely be the fantasy of an understandably hysterical community. This argument rose and faded quickly, as it had few adherents. Finally, there was nothing to do but confront it: their choice was between letting the children go, or living—and dying—with the rats.

Of course it was unconscionable that the children should be sacrificed to save their elders, or even one another. That was the opinion vehemently expressed by parents, teachers, clergy, and many of the other ordinary townsfolk. This was not a decision one could make for others, and the children were not yet of an age to make it for themselves. The elders nodded solemnly. All had to acknowledge the rightness of this view. Furthermore, the outcome, based on speculative projections from these preliminary observations, was just too uncertain, the admirable mathematics notwithstanding, for measures so merciless and irreversible. A more thorough study was required. As for the bridge counts themselves, seasonal weather changes were proposed as a more likely explanation of the decline in the rat population—if in fact there had been such a decline. The numbers themselves were disputed, and alternative, unofficial, less decisive tabulations made by others, worried parents mostly, were presented to the assembly and duly considered. And even if the official counts were true, a teacher at the school argued, the vermin population was probably decreasing normally, for all such plagues have their tides and ebbs. With patience, it will all be over.

The data, however, did not support this view. Even those

sympathetic with them understood that the parents and teachers were not trying to engage in a reasoned search for truth, but were desperately seeking to persuade. The simple facts were that the town was slowly dying from its infestation of rats, and whenever a child was taken the infestation diminished; everyone knew this, even the parents. The data was admittedly sketchy, but time was short. A prolonged study might be a fatal misjudgment. A doctor described in uncompromising detail the current crisis in the hospitals, their staffs disease-riddled, patients sleeping on the floors, medications depleted, the buildings themselves aswarm with rats, and the hunters reminded the assembly that their own untiring efforts had not been enough alone to get the upper hand against the beasts, though many of them were parents, too, and clearly ambivalent about their testimony. Those who had lost family members to the sickness and risked losing more, their own lives included, spoke bluntly: If the children stay, they will all die of the plague like the rest of us, so it's not as though we would be sacrificing them to a fate worse than they'd suffer here. But if they go, some of us might be saved. A compromise was proposed: Lots could be drawn and the children could be released one by one until the rats disappeared. That way, some might be spared. But that would not be fair, others argued, for why should some parents be deprived of their children when others were not? Wouldn't that divide the community irreparably forever? Anyway, the question might be purely academic. Everyone had noticed during the mathematician's presentation the disconcerting relationship between the rate of decrease of the rat population and the number of children remaining in the town. They want the children, shouted a fierce old man from the back of the hall, so let them have them! We can always make more!

Pandemonium broke out. Shouts and accusations. You think it's so easy! cried one. Where are your own? It's not the making, cried others, it's the raising! They were shouted down and they shouted back. People were called murderers and cowards and egoists, ghouls and nihilists. Parents screamed that if their children had to die they would die with them, and their neighbors yelled: Good riddance! Through it all, there was the steady pounding of the gavel, and finally, when order was restored, the oldest member of the council who was also judged to be the wisest, silent until now, was asked to give his opinion. His chair was wheeled to the illumined center of the little platform at the front of the hall whereon, behind him, the elders sat. He gazed out upon the muttering crowd, his old hands trembling, but his expression calm and benign. Slowly, a hush descended.

There is nothing we can do, he said at last in his feeble old voice. It is the revenge of the dark children. Years ago, we committed a terrible wrong against them and this is their justified reply. He paused, sitting motionlessly in the pale light. We thought that we could simply replace them, he said. But we were wrong. He seemed to be dribbling slightly and he raised one trembling hand to wipe his mouth. I do not know if the dark children really exist, he went on. I myself have never seen them. But, even if they do not, it is the revenge of the dark children just the same. He paused again as if wanting his words to be thoroughly understood before proceeding, or perhaps because his thoughts came slowly to him. I have, however, seen the rats, and even with my failing eyesight, I know that they are real. I also know that the counting of them is real, whether accurate or not, and that your responses to this counting, while contradictory, are also real. Perhaps they are the most real thing of all. He seemed to go adrift for a moment, his head nodding slightly, before continuing: It may be that the diminishing number of rats is due to the day-by-day loss of our children or it may be due to nature's rhythms or to the weather or the success at last of our hunters. It may even be that the numbers are not diminishing, that we are mistaken. It does not matter. The children must go. There was a soft gasp throughout the hall. Because, he said as the gasp died away, we are who we are. The old man gazed out at them for a short time, and each felt singled out, though it was unlikely he could see past the edge of the platform. The children will not go one by one, he went on. They will go all at once and immediately. That is both fair and practical. And, I might add, inevitable. He nodded his head as though agreeing with himself, or perhaps for emphasis. They themselves will be happier together than alone. And if we who remain cannot avoid grief, we can at least share it and comfort one another. Even now, if our humble suggestions are being followed, the children are being gathered together and told to put on their favorite clothes and bring their favorite toys and they are then being brought to the town square outside this building. As parents, turning pale, rose slowly from their seats, he again wiped his mouth with the back of his hand and his expression took on a more sorrowful aspect. I foresee a rather sad future for our town, he said. The rats will finally disappear, for whatever reason, though others of us will yet perish of their loathsome diseases, and our promenade will reopen and trade will resume. Even should we repeal the music laws, however, there will still be little if any singing or dancing here, for there will be no children, only the memory of children. It has not been easy for the town's mothers and fathers to suffer so, twice over, and I feel sorry for them, as I am sure we all do.

We must not ask them to go through all that again. He cocked
his old head slightly. Ah. I can hear the children outside now.
They are being told they are going off to play with the dark children. They will leave happily. You will all have an opportunity to
wave goodbye, but they will probably not even look back. Nor of
course will they ever return. In the shocked pause before the rush
to the exits, he added, speaking up slightly: And now will we at
last be free of the dark children? He sighed and, as his head
dipped to his chest, raised one trembling finger, wagging it
slowly as though in solemn admonishment. No. No. No, my
friends. We will not.

THE PRESIDENTS

THE ELECTORAL SEASON! How delightful is it when the Quadrennium is in bloom and our particolored Presidents arrive to spangle the fields and factory floors! Welcome visitants they always are, low forms of existence though they be. "The Presidents are come!" the children cry and rush out to be hugged and kissed and have their photos taken with these singular creatures, half blind yet sensitive to the least hoot and twitter, elusive yet omnipresent, and, even when repulsive, endowed with such curious instincts and so diverse in form and structure as to attract the attention of the most jaded observer, even if only in self-defense.

"The Presidents are come!" Yes, it sends a thrill through the heart, whether of pleasure or of apprehension, to see, after the long dry years of stagnation and dormancy, the first one of the season sailing in on broad sylphic pinions in the cool slanted

157

beams of a calm autumn morning, or else traversing the surface of the earth by those remarkable leaps and wriggles for which they are renowned. Some are gloriously bedizened, others naked but for a film of gelatinous flesh, so tightly stretched as to be reduced to an invisible tenuity; still others are soft, plump, pale, and woolly, or else a livid gray-green with hideous tail pustules, or tender, white, and tantalizingly delicate, and there are many, more familiar to the electorate perhaps, which are actually capable of altering their external shape and changing their spots and colors even as they busily slither, flutter, and honk.

While it is true that the common consent of mankind regards most of these creatures with revulsion and abhorrence, and not without reason, inasmuch as many of them are more or less noxious, and some of them are terribly fatal to their fellows (monstrosities by excess are not uncommon), being rapacious and vindictive, treacherous and cruel even to their own kind, full of stratagem and artifice, highly venomous, lurking in darkness, endowed with curious instincts, feeding off excreta, and furnished with many accessory means for the capture and destruction of their opponents, it must nevertheless be remembered always that even these vile creatures are the handiwork of Infinite Wisdom, and so worthy of our admiration, however distant and guarded our scrutiny must, for our own safety, be.

Such scrutiny is invariably rewarded, for the Presidents are curious beings in many respects. Though more or less inactive for most of their lives, they are nevertheless very enduring; they respire little, are susceptible of hibernation, and can remain for a considerable time shut up in confinement so restricted as to produce astonishment. In their movements they are lazy and half-torpid, and yet are capable of sudden gestures, short and jerky and all too often lethal, even when perhaps not so meant. When not frightened or running for election or both, they slowly crawl along, with their tails and bellies dragging on the ground. They often stop and doze for a moment, with closed eyes and hind legs spread out. Many of these creatures bear highly curious appendages that resemble trumpets in form, and they emit incessant chattering sounds which simulate speech but which are mostly imitations of the cries of other species. When they take an antipathy to any one, they immediately show it. They suffer no rivals to approach them, but harass them ceaselessly, emitting rank screens of smoke and tearing from them the ballots that are their very sustenance. When a President has glutted itself, its crop, swelled by the votes which it has received, forms a voluminous projection in front of the neck; a fetid humor oozes from its nostrils, and it remains sunk in a state of stupid torpor until the electoral outcome is finally determined, generally at the far end of the alimentary canal.

If we were asked where throughout the world specimens were to be met with, we might reply, almost everywhere, provided only that voters, a necessary nutrient, be present; but even where such prey is scarce Presidents have been detected and have moreover, in their various mutations, thrived. Darwin in his famous voyage on the *Beagle* was much struck by the curious phenomena of distribution and survival which that voyage brought before his eyes, remarking that, while some classes die out as civilization spreads, others, like the Rats, the common Sparrow, the Presidents, the Cockroaches, some parasites, and so on, adjust themselves to the altered conditions, and prosper under civilization as they never did in former days. Warm and temperate regions with abundant moisture are the localities favorable to all the Presidents. They are said to live chiefly in ditches, especially those where stagnant and corrupt water has lain a long time, but they are also found in dung heaps, caves, swamps, and other obscure and fetid locations, choosing secret places wherein to store up all that tempts their cupidity or excites their covetousness, whether in or out of the zoo.

Certainly, wherever else they might be found, they are nowhere more abundant than in America, civilization's gem and Nature's pride, as is widely acknowledged, especially by the gabbling and squawking Presidents themselves and by their keepers. In America, Presidents find a natural habitat, abundant in provender and mud and congenial to their notorious reproductive habits. They are not, here at least, an endangered species. Indeed well over fifty families or subspecies have been recorded, and it is probable that they are even much more numerous than this, as new discoveries are constantly rewarding the close examination of any particular locality with each new Presidential season.

The Prickly, Candescent, Wind-Up, and Comatose Presidents are, for example, well-known, as are the Inflatable President (sometimes referred to, erroneously, as the Bouncing President), the savage Blueballed President, the infamously deviant Quincuncial (or Conical) President, and the nocturnal three-legged Oblique President with its heavily lidded eyes and skin resembling in consistence wetted parchment. Most readers would also recognize the common Abominable President, the Immaculate or Two-Humped President, the cave-dwelling Abstract President, distinguishable by its multiple stomachs, contractile bladder, and abyssal eyes which tend to disappear in thick scaly fleshfolds, and the once-famous Flesh-Colored President from those legendary times when specimens were still found in the wild, only later tamed in the national zoo, and then let loose to reproduce. Now most Presidents, of course, are zoo-born of stocks bred in captivity, and either spend their freed lives in the circus or are kept as domesticated house pets and fed on perks and taxes.

The (possibly mythical) Flesh-Colored Presidents were said to have given birth to the Homuncular, Beggar Tick, and Revolving Presidents, as well as to have sired the predaceous Boundless Presidents, also known as the Join-the-Dots Presidents because of their tendency to lose their outline to their immediate surroundings. It was this asexual yet fecund family of Boundless Presidents in its various evolutionary permutations that gave rise in our own times, not only to the Mechanical, Abridged (or Bedside), Montage, and Cartoon Presidents, but also to the proliferation of multinational gathering and feeding stations and to intergalactic sporogenesis.

None of this, however, has altered for the better their reputation. It is not clear why Presidents should have been considered from the earliest ages as the symbol of stupidity and venality, and branded with a stigma of infamy which will always cast an odium on their name. Many, to be sure, are by nature of a despotic and combative temperament, irascible and quarrelsome, living by plunder and blood-shedding, destruction the sole object of their existence, but the innocent, which arguably outnumber the noxious and are merely ridiculous, share the disrepute, and are unjustly visited with the hatred and aversion due to their malefic fellows. Nor is this popular prejudice against the entire species moderated, alas, by any evidence of natural grace and beauty. It is difficult to comprehend why Nature, while it has been so kind to the related families of Athletes, Gigolos, and Starlets, has stamped the Presidents with so ungainly a form, for most families of Presidents, it must be said, are homely creatures, their physiognomy at once disproportionate and peculiarly threatening, and, from their low facial angle, they do have a singularly witless appearance, making them objects of general repugnance and causing evil properties to be attributed to them.

But these much-despised beings are surely not so universally stupid or voracious as they are commonly said to be. In the present day it is really time to have done with all these timeworn rhetorical fancies which are in continual and complete variance with the results of science and observation, and to cry with the children: "The Presidents are come! Hooray! Don't get too close! But long live the Presidents!"

CHICAGO CRYPTOGRAM

"It is death for souls to become wet."

That's Harry, skunk drunk, pontificating. It's the middle of the century and we're down on State Street, Dee, Anna, Harry, Empty, and me. Xenophanes. Casino, for short. My name for the boozy night, a game we wayward students play. The university's fallen away behind us, the library has. Good riddance, we're out on the town on this desolate blind-eyed night, searching out the elusive Logos in our beer.

"If God had not created beer," I say, paraphrasing my Presocratic of the night, "they would say that piss was drinkable."

Whereupon Anna observes that the beer she's drinking is the material cause for an effect that is overtaking her: She goes off to pee.

Longhaired Empty in his furlined cape gazes down disdainfully on Harry, ogling Annie Axe's butt as she wags it johnward.

163

"Alas, wretched mortal!" he says. Empty, alias Empedocles, flamboyant charlatan, lofty romantic, gay vegetarian, is the brightest and the maddest of us all. For Empty, ardent but gloomy democrat, the Red Scare is real, the Bomb is. "It's a time of increasing Strife," he oft laments.

True, we're mired in evil brawls in which no adventure is, though our student deferments shield us from the worst.

"The present is worse than the past and the future will be worse yet," Empty says, and Dee, our atomist, lifts her glass and laughs. "The goal of life is cheerfulness, so bottoms up!"

Prolific Dee, who began the night as DeMockery, is the atomist among us, her subject much on our minds. Annihilation. The philosopher's nightmare.

"The cosmos as we know it is doomed."

Harry, hand on returned Anaxagoras's behind, is more sanguine. "All things are beautiful and good," he says, "including death and war."

"Fuck you," says Empty.

"Come on, fellow philosophasters, forget the war," complains Anna, and Empty says, "You're not draftbait, kiddo."

"Enough of this malakies," laughs well-traveled Dee, showing off her street Greek. "Stinnyashoo!"

We raise our glasses to toast the fucked-up gods, down drinks, and Harry raises his middle digit like a gnomon to order up another round. Harry's an arrogant antidemocratic asshole, but we love him.

"Harry," I say, "you authored the most poetically enigmatic line of all Presocratic thought."

"I wish to know it," exclaims Anna.

"It lies hidden."

"We can know nothing about anything," Dee declares.

"Is this another bloody cryptogram?" That's disdainful Empty. "Am I a mere emanation of a thinking god?" he groans.

"That's my line," I say.

"As usual, Casino you barbarian, you have probably mistranslated my wisdom for your own nefarious purposes," complains Harry.

"Cease strife," declaims Empty, "and in this joyless place let's resolve enigma and celebrate the bonding force of love!"

Q: What is the line and who is its author?

McDUFF ON
THE MOUND

IT WASN'T MUCH, a feeble blooper over second, call it luck, but it was enough to shake McDuff. He stepped weakly off the left side of the pitcher's mound, relieved to see his catcher Gus take the job of moving down behind the slow runner to back up the throw in to first. Fat Flynn galloped around the bag toward second, crouched apelike on the basepath, waggled his arms, then bounded back to first as the throw came in from short center. McDuff felt lightheaded. Flynn's soft blooper had provoked a total vision that iced his blood. Because the next batter up now was Blake: oh yes, man, it was all too clear. "Today's my day," McDuff told himself, as though taking on the cares of the world. He tucked his glove in his armpit briefly, wiped the sweat from his brow, resettled his cap, thrust his hand back into his glove.

Gus jogged over to the mound before going back behind the plate, running splaylegged around the catcher's guard that padded his belly. McDuff took the toss from first, over Gus's head, stood staring dismally at Flynn, now edging flatfooted away from the bag, his hands making floppy loosewristed swirls at the cuffs of his Mudville knickers. Gus spat, glanced back over his shoulder at first, then squinted up at McDuff. "Whatsa matter, kid?"

McDuff shrugged, licked his dry lips. "I don't know, Gus. I tried to get him." He watched Flynn taunt, flapping his hands like donkey ears, thumbing his nose. Rubbing it in. Did he know? He must. "I really tried." He remembered this nightmare, running around basepaths, unable to stop.

Gus grinned, though, ignoring the obvious: "Nuts, the bum was lucky. C'mon, kid, ya got this game in ya back pocket!" He punched McDuff lightly in the ribs with his stiff platter of a mitt, spat in encouragement, and joggled away in a widelegged trot toward home plate, head cocked warily toward first, where Flynn bounced insolently and made insulting noises. Settling then into his crouch, and before pulling his mask down, Gus jerked his head at the approaching batter and winked out at McDuff. Turkey Blake. Nothing to it. A joke. Maybe Gus is innocent, McDuff thought. Maybe not.

Now, in truth, McDuff was not, by any standard but his own, in real trouble. Here it was, the bottom of the ninth, two away, one more out and the game was over, and he had a fat two-run lead going for him. A lot of the hometown Mudville fans had even given it up for lost and had started shuffling indifferently toward the exits. Or was their shuffle a studied shuffle and itself a cunning taunt? A mocking rite like Flynn's buffoonery at first? Had they shuffled back there in the shadows just to make Flynn's fluke hit sting more? It was more than McDuff could grasp, so he scratched his armpits and tried to get his mind off it. Now, anyway, they were all shuffling back. And did they grin as they shuffled? Too far away to tell. But they probably did, goddamn them. You're making it all up, he said. But he didn't convince himself. And there was Blake. Blake the Turkey. Of course.

Blake was the league clown, the butt. Slopeshouldered, pot-bellied, broadrumped, bandylegged. And a long goiter-studded neck with a small flat head on top, overlarge cap down around the ears. They called him "Turkey," Blake the Turkey. The fans cheered him with a gobbling noise. And that's just what they did now as he stepped up: gobbled and gobbled. McDuff could hardly believe he had been brought to this end, that it was happening to him, even though he had known that sooner or later it must. Blake had three bats. He gave them a swing and went right off his feet. Gobble gobble gobble. Then he got up, picked out two bats, chose one, tossed the other one away, but, as though by mistake, hung on to it, went sailing with it into the bat racks. Splintering crash. Mess of broken bats. Gobble gobble gobble. McDuff, in desperation, pegged the ball to first, but Flynn was sitting on the bag, holding his quaking paunch, didn't even run when the ball got away from the first baseman, just made gob bling noises.

Vaguely, McDuff had seen it coming, but he'd figured on trouble from Cooney and Burroughs right off. A four-to-one lead, last inning, four batters between him and Casey, two tough ones and two fools, it was all falling into place: get the two tying runs on base, then two outs, and bring Casey up. So he'd worked like a bastard on those two guys, trying to head it off. Should've known better, should've seen that would have been two easy, too pat, too painless. McDuff, a practical man with both feet on the ground, had always tried to figure the odds, and that's where he'd gone wrong. But would things have been different if Cooney and Burroughs had hit him? Not substantially maybe, there'd still be much the same situation and Casey yet to face. But the stage wouldn't have been just right, and maybe, because of that, somehow, he'd have got out of it.

Cooney, tall, lean, one of the best percentage hitters in the business: by all odds, see, it should have been him. That's what McDuff had thought, so when he'd sucked old Cooney into pulling into an inside curve and grounding out, third to first, he was really convinced he'd got himself over the hump. Even if Burroughs should hit him, it was only a matter of getting Flynn and Blake out, and they never gave anybody any trouble. And Burroughs *didn't* hit him! Big barrelchested man with a bat no one else in the league could even lift—some said it weighed half a ton—and he'd wasted all that power on a cheap floater, sent it dribbling out to the mound and McDuff himself had tossed him out. Hot damn! he'd cried. Waiting for fat Flynn to enter the batter's box, he'd even caught himself giggling. And then that unbelievable blooper. And—*bling!*—the light.

McDuff glared now at Blake, wincing painfully as though to say: Get serious, man! Blake was trying to knock the dirt out of his spikes. But each time he lifted his foot, he lost his balance and toppled over. Gobble gobble gobble. Finally, there on the ground, teetering on his broad rump, he took a healthy swing with the bat at his foot. There was a bang like a firecracker going off, smoke, and the shoe sailed into the stands. Turkey Blake hobbled around in mock pain (or real pain: who could tell and what did it matter? McDuff's pain was real), trying to grasp his stockinged foot, now smoking faintly, but he was too round in the midriff, too short in the arms, to reach it. Gobble gobble

gobble. Someone tossed the shoe back and it hit him in the head: bonk! Blake toppled stiffly backwards, his short bandy legs up in the air as though he were dead. Gobble gob—

McDuff, impatient, even embittered, for he felt the injury of it, went into his stretch. Blake leaped up, grabbed a bat from the mad heap, came hopping, waddling, bounding, however the hell it was he moved, up to the plate to take his place. It turned out that the bat he'd picked up was one he'd broken in his earlier act. It was only about six inches long, the rest hanging from it as though by a thread. McDuff felt himself at the edge of tears. The crowd gobbled on, obscenely, delightedly. Blake took a preparatory backswing, and the dangling end of the bat arced round and hit him on the back of the head with a hollow exaggerated clunk. He fell across the plate. Even the umpire now was emitting frantic gobbling sounds and holding his trembling sides. Flynn the fat baserunner called time-out and came huffing and puffing in from first to resuscitate his teammate. McDuff, feeling all the strength go out of him, slumped despairingly off the mound. He picked up the resin bag and played with it, an old nervous habit that now did not relieve him.

His catcher Gus came out. "Gobble gobble," he said.

McDuff winced in hurt. "Gus, for God's sake, cut that out!" he cried. Jesus, they were all against him!

Gus laughed. "Whatsa matter, kid? These guys buggin' ya?" He glanced back toward the plate, where Flynn was practicing artificial respiration on Blake's ass-end, sitting on Blake's small head. "It's all in the game, buddy. Don't forget: Gobble and the world gobbles with ya! Yak yak!" McDuff bit his lip. Past happy Gus, he could see Flynn listening to Blake's butt for a breath of life.

"Play baseball and you play with yourself," McDuff said sourly, completing Gus's impromptu aphorism.

"Yeah, you *got* it, kid!" howled Gus, jabbing McDuff in the ribs with his mitt, then rolling onto the grass in front of the mound, holding his sides, giddy tears springing from his eyes, tobacco juice oozing down his chin.

There was a loud moist sound at the plate, like air escaping a toy balloon, and it was greeted by huzzahs and imitative noises from the stands. Flynn jumped up, lifted one of Blake's feet high in the air in triumph, and planted his fallen baseball cap in the clown's crotch, making Blake a parody of Blake, were such a thing absurdly possible. Cheers and courteous gobbling. Blake popped up out of the dust, swung at Flynn, hit the ump instead.

"Why don't they knock it off?" McDuff complained.

"Whaddaya mean?" asked Gus, now sober at his side.

"Why don't they just bring on Casey now and let me get it over with? Why do they have to shove my nose in it first?"

"Casey!" Gus laughed loosely. "Never happen, kid. Blake puts on a big show, but he'd never hit you, baby, take it from old Gus. You'll get him and the game's over. Nothin' to it." Gus winked reassuringly, but McDuff didn't believe it. He no longer believed Gus was so goddamn innocent either.

Flynn was bounding now, in his apelike fashion, toward first base, but Blake had a grip on his suspenders. Flynn's short fat legs kept churning away and the dust rose, but he was getting nowhere. Then Blake let go—*whap!*—and Flynn blimped non-stop out to deep right field. Gobble gobble gobble. While Flynn was cavorting back in toward first, Blake, unable to find his own hat, stole the umpire's. It completely covered his small flat head, down to the goiter, and Blake staggered around blind, bumping into things. The ump grabbed up Blake's cap from where it had fallen and planted it defiantly on his own head. A couple of gallons of water flooded out and drenched him. Blake tripped over home plate and crashed facefirst to the dirt again. The hat fell off. The umpire took off his shoes and poured the water out. A fish jumped out of one of them. Blake spied his own hat on the umpire's soggy head and went for it. The ump relinquished it willingly, in exchange for his own. The ump was wary now, however, and inspected the hat carefully before putting it back on his head. He turned it inside out, thumped it, ran his finger around the lining. Satisfied at last, he put the hat on his head and a couple of gallons of water flooded out on him. Gobble gobble, said the crowd, and the umpire said: "PLAY BALL!"

Flynn was more or less on first, Blake in the box, the broken bat over his shoulder. McDuff glanced over toward the empty batter-up circle, then toward the Mudville dugout. Casey had not come out. Casey's style. And why should he? After all, Blake hadn't had a hit all season. Maybe in all history. He was a joke. McDuff considered walking Blake and getting it over with. Or was there any hope of that: of "getting it over with"? Anyway, maybe that's just what they wanted him to do, maybe it was how they meant to break him. No, he was a man meant to play this game, McDuff was, and play it, by God, he would. He stretched, glanced at first, studied Gus's signal, glared at Turkey Blake. The broken end of the bat hung down Blake's sunken back and tapped his bulbous rump. He twitched as though shooing a fly, finally turned around to see who or what was back there, feigned great surprise at finding no one. Gobble gobble. He resumed his batter's stance. McDuff protested the broken bat on the grounds that it was a distraction and a danger to the other players. The umpire grumbled, consulted his rulebook. Gus showed shock. He came out to the mound and asked: "Why make it any easier for him, kid?"

"I'm not, Gus. I'm making it easier for myself." That seemed true, but McDuff knew Gus wouldn't like it.

"You are nuts, kid. Lemme tell ya. Plain nuts. I don't folla ya at all!" Blake was still trying to find out who or what was behind him. He poised very still, then spun around—the bat swung and cracked his nose: loud honking noise, chirping of birds, as Blake staggered around behind home plate holding his nose and splattering catsup all around. Gobble gobble gobble. Gus watched and grinned.

"I mean, a guy who can't hit with a good bat might get lucky with a broken one," McDuff said. He didn't mean that at all, but he knew Gus would like it better.

"Oh, I getcha." Gus spat pensively. "Yeah, ya right." The old catcher went back to the plate, showed the ump the proper ruling, and the umpire ordered Blake to get a new bat. Gus was effective like that when he wanted to be. Why not all the time then? It made McDuff wonder.

Blake returned to the plate dragging Burroughs's half-ton bat behind him. He tried to get it on his shoulder, grunted, strained, but he couldn't even get the end of it off the ground. He sat down under it, then tried to stand. Steam whistled out his nose and ears and a great wrenching sound was heard, but the bat stayed where it was. While the happy crowd once more lifted its humiliating chorus, Flynn called time-out and came waddling in from first to help. The umpire, too, lent a hand. Together, they got it up about as high as Blake's knees, then had to drop it. Exaggerated thud. Blake yelped, hobbled around grotesquely, pointing down at the one foot still shoed. The toe of it began to swell. The seams of the shoe split. A red bubble emerged, expanded threateningly: the size of a plum, a crimson baseball, grapefruit, cannonball, a red pumpkin. Larger and larger it grew. Soon it was nearly as big as Blake himself. Everyone held his ears. The umpire crawled down behind Flynn and then Flynn tried to crawl behind the umpire. It stretched, quivered. Strained. Flynn dashed over and, reaching into Blake's behind, seemed to pull something out. Sound of a cork popping from a bottle. The red balloon-like thing collapsed with a sigh. Laughter and relieved gobbling. Blake bent over to inspect his toe. Enormous explosion, blackening Blake's face. Screams and laughter.

Then Burroughs himself came out and lifted the half-ton bat onto Blake's shoulder for him. What shoulder he had collapsed and the bat slid off, upending Blake momentarily, so Burroughs next set it on Blake's head. The head was flat and, though precariously, held it. Burroughs lifted Blake up and set him, bat on head, in the batter's box. Blake under his burden could not turn his head to see McDuff's pitch. He just crossed his eyes and looked up at the bat. Gus crouched and signaled. McDuff, through bitter sweaty tears, saw that Flynn was still not back on first, but he didn't care. He stretched, kicked, pitched. Blake leaned forward. McDuff couldn't tell if he hit the ball with the bat or his head. But hit it he did, as McDuff knew he would. It looked like an easy pop-up to the mound, and McDuff, almost unbelieving, waited for it. But what he caught was only the cover of the ball. The ball itself was out of sight far beyond the mowed grass of left-center field, way back in the high weeds of the neighboring acreage.

McDuff, watching then for Casey to emerge from the Mudville dugout, failed at first to notice the hubbub going on around the plate. It seemed that the ump had called the hit a home run, and Gus was arguing that there were no official limits to the Mudville outfield and thus no automatic homers. "You mean," the umpire cried, "if someone knocked the ball clean to Gehenny, it still wouldn't be considered outa the park? I can't believe that!" Gus and the umpire fought over the rulebook, trying to find the right page. The three outfielders were all out there in the next acreage, nearly out of sight, hunting for the ball in the tall grass. "I can't believe that!" the umpire bellowed, and tore pages from the rulebook in his haste. Flynn and Blake now clowned with chocolate pies and water pistols.

"Listen," said McDuff irritably, "whether it's an automatic home run or not, they still have to run the bases, so why don't they just do that, and then it won't matter."

Gus's head snapped up from his search in the rule book like he'd been stabbed. He glared fiercely at McDuff, grabbed his arm, pushed him roughly back toward the mound. "Whatsa matter with you?" he growled.

"Lissen! I ain't runnin' off nowheres I ain't got to!" Flynn hollered, sitting down on a three-legged stool which Blake was pulling out from under him. "If it's automanic, I'll by gum walk my last mile at my own dadblamed ease, thank ya, ma'am!" He sprawled.

"Of *course* it ain't automatic," Gus was whispering to McDuff. "You know that as well as I do, Mac. If we can just get that ball in from the outfield while they're screwin' around, we'll tag *both* of 'em for good measure and get outa this friggin' game!"

McDuff knew this was impossible, he even believed that

Gus was pulling his leg, yet, goddamn it, he couldn't help but share Gus's hopes. Why not? Anyway, he had to try. He turned to the shortstop and sent him out there with orders: *"Go bring that ball in!"*

The rule book was shot. Pages everywhere, some tumbling along the ground, others blowing in the wind like confetti. The umpire, on hands and knees, was trying to put it all back together again. Gus held up a page, winked at McDuff, stuffed the page in his back pocket. Flynn and Blake used other pages to light cigars that kept blowing up in their faces. That does it, thought McDuff.

He looked out onto the horizon and saw the shortstop and the outfielders jumping up and down, holding something aloft. And then the shortstop started running in. Yet, so distant was he, he seemed not to be moving.

At home plate, the umpire had somehow discovered the page in Gus's back pocket, and he was saying: "I just can't believe it!" He read it aloud: "'Mudville's field is open-ended. Nothing is automatic here, in spite of appearances. A ball driven even unto Gehenna is not necessarily a home run. In short, anything can happen in Mudville, even though most things are highly improbable. Blake, for example, has never had a hit, nor has Casey yet struck out.' And et cetera!" The crowd dutifully applauded the reading of the rule book. The umpire shook his head. "All the way to Gehenny!" he muttered.

The baserunners, meanwhile, had taken off, and Turkey Blake was flapping around third on his way home, when he suddenly noticed that fat Flynn, who should be preceding him, was still grunting and groaning down the basepath toward first.

The shortstop was running in from the next acreage with the ball.

Blake galloped around the bases in reverse, meeting Flynn head-on with a resounding thud at first. Dazed, Flynn headed back toward home, but Blake set him aright on the route to second, pushed him on with kicks and swats, threw firecrackers at his feet. The fans chanted: "*Go! Go! Go!*"

The shortstop had reached the mowed edge of the outfield. McDuff hustled back off the mound, moved toward short to receive the throw, excitement grabbing at him in spite of himself.

Flynn fell in front of second, and Blake rolled over him. Blake jumped up and stood on Flynn's head. Honking noise. Flynn somersaulted and kicked Blake in the teeth. Musical chimes.

The shortstop was running in from deep left-center."*Throw it!!*" McDuff screamed, but the shortstop didn't seem to hear him. He ran, holding the ball high like a torch.

Flynn had Blake in a crushing bearhug at second base, while Blake was clipping Flynn's suspenders. Blake stamped on Flynn's feet—sound of wood being crushed to pulp—and Flynn yowled, let go. Blake produced an enormous rocket. Flynn in a funk fled toward third, but his pants fell down, and he tripped.

The shortstop was still running in from the outfield. McDuff was shouting himself hoarse, but the guy wouldn't throw the goddamn ball. McDuff's heart was pounding and he was angry at himself for finding himself so caught up in it all.

Flynn had pulled up his pants and Blake was chasing him with the rocket. They crashed into McDuff. He felt trampled and heard hooting and gobbling sounds. When the dust had cleared, McDuff found himself wearing Flynn's pants, ten sizes too large for him, and Blake's cap, ten sizes too small, and holding a gigantic rocket whose fuse was lit. Flynn, in the confusion, had gone to second and Blake to third. The fuse burned to the end, there was a little pop, the end of the rocket opened, and a little bird flew out.

The shortstop was running in, eyes rolled back, tongue lolling, drenched in sweat, holding the ball aloft.

Flynn and Blake discovered their error, that they'd ended up on the wrong bases, came running toward each other again. McDuff, foreseeing the inevitable, stepped aside to allow them to collide. Instead, they pulled up short and exchanged niceties.

"After *you*," said Blake, bowing deeply.

"No, no, dear fellow," insisted Flynn with an answering bow, "after *you!*"

The shortstop stumbled and fell, crawled ahead.

Flynn and Blake were waltzing around and around, saying things like "Age before beauty!" and "Be my guest!" and "Hope springs eternal in the human breast!," wound up with a chorus of "Take Me Out to the Ballgame!" with all the fans in the stands joining in.

The shortstop staggered to his feet, plunged, gasping, forward.

The umpire came out and made McDuff give Flynn his pants back. He took Blake's cap off McDuff's head, looked at it suspiciously, held it over his own head, and was promptly drenched by a couple of gallons of water that came flooding out.

McDuff felt someone hanging limply on his elbow. It was the shortstop. Feebly, but proudly, he held up the baseball. Blake, of course, was safe on second, and Flynn was hugging third. The trouble is, thought McDuff, you mustn't get taken in. You mustn't think you've got a chance. That's when they really kill you. "All right," he said to Blake and Flynn, his voice choking up and sounding all too much like a turkey's squawk, "screw you guys!" They grinned blankly and there was a last dying ripple of mocking gobbling in the stands. Then: silence. Into it, McDuff dropped Blake's giant rocket. No matter what he might have hoped, it didn't go off. Then he turned to face the Man.

And now, it was true about the holler that came from the maddened thousands, true about how it thundered on the mountaintop and recoiled upon the flat, and so on. And it was true about Casey's manner, the maddening composure with which he came out to take his turn at bat. Or was that so, was it true at that? McDuff, mouth dry, mind awhirl, could not pin down his doubt. "Quit!" he said, but he couldn't, he knew, not till the side was out.

And Casey: who *was* Casey? A Hero, to be sure. A Giant. A figure of grace and power, yes, but wasn't he more than that? He was tall and mighty (omnipotent, some claimed, though perhaps, like all fans, they'd got a bit carried away), with a great mustache and a merry knowing twinkle in his eye. Was he, as had been suggested, the One True Thing? McDuff shook to watch him. He was ageless, older than Mudville certainly, though Mudville claimed him as their own. Some believed that "Casey" was a transliteration of the initials "K. C." and stood for King Christ. Others, of a similar but simpler school, opted for King Corn, while another group believed it to be a barbarism for Krishna. Some, rightly observing that "case" meant "event," pursued this reasoning back to its primitive root, "to fall," and thus saw in Casey (for a case was also a container) the whole history and condition of man, a history perhaps as yet incomplete. On the other hand, a case was also an oddity, was it not, and a medical patient, and maybe, said some, mighty Casey was the sickest of them all.

Yet a case was an example, cried others, plight, the actual state of things, while a good many thought all such mystification was so much crap, and Casey was simply a good ballplayer. Certainly, it was true, he could belt the hell out of a baseball. All the way to Gehenny, as the umpire liked to put it. Anyway, McDuff knew none of this. He only knew that here he was, that here was Casey, and the stage was set. He didn't need to know the rest. Just that was enough to shake any man.

Gus walked out to talk to McDuff, while the first baseman covered home plate. Gus kept a nervous eye on Flynn and Blake. "How the hell'd you let that bum hit ya, Mac?"

"Listen, I'm gonna walk Casey," McDuff said. Gus looked pained. "First base is open, Gus. It's playing percentages."

"You and ya goddamn percentages!" snorted Gus. "Ya dumb or somethin', kid? Dontcha know this guy's secret?" Gus wasn't innocent, after all. Maybe nobody was.

"Yeah, I know it, Gus." McDuff sighed, swallowed. Knew all along he'd never walk him. Just stalling.

"Well, then, *kill* him, kid! You can do it! It's the only way!" Gus punctuated his peptalk with stiff jabs to McDuff's ribs. At the plate, Casey, responding to the thunderous ovation, lightly doffed his hat. They were tearing the stands down.

"But all these people, Gus—"

"Don't let the noise fool ya. It's the way they want it, kid."

Casey reached down, bat in armpit, picked up a handfull of dust, rubbed it on his hands, then wiped his hands on his shirt. Every motion brought on a new burst of enraptured veneration.

McDuff licked his dry lips, ground the baseball into his hip. "Do you really think—?"

"Take it from old Gus," said his catcher gently. "They're all leanin' on ya." Gus clapped him on the shoulder, cast a professional glance over toward third, then jogged splaylegged back to the plate, motioning the man there back to first.

Gus crouched, spat, lowered his mask; Casey swung his bat in short choppy cuts to loosen up; the umpire hovered. McDuff stretched, looked back at Blake on second, Flynn on third. Must be getting dark. Couldn't see their faces. They stood on the bags like totems. Okay, thought McDuff, I'll leave it up to Casey. I'm just not gonna sweat it (though in fact he had not stopped sweating, and even now it was cold in his armpits and trickling down his back). What's another ballgame? Let him take it or leave it. And without further wind-up, he served Casey a nice fat pitch gently down the slot, a little outside to give Casey plenty of room to swing.

Casey ignored it, stepped back out of the box, flicked a gnat off his bat.

"*Strike one!*" the umpire said.

Bottles and pillows flew and angry voices stirred the troubled air. The masses rose within the shadows of the stands, and maybe they'd have leapt the fences, had not Casey raised his hand. A charitable smile, a tip of the cap, a twirl of the great mustache. For the people, a pacifying gesture with a couple of mighty fingers; for the umpire, an apologetic nod. And for McDuff: a strange sly smile and flick of the bat, as though to say... everything. McDuff read whole books into it, and knew he wasn't far from wrong.

This is it, Case, said McDuff to himself. We're here. And he fingered the resin bag and wiped the sweat and pretended he gave a damn about the runners on second and third and stretched and lifted his left leg, then came down on it easily and offered

Casey the sweetest, fattest, purest pitch he'd ever shown a man. Not even in batting practice had he ever given a hitter more to swing at.

Casey only smiled.

And the umpire said: "*Strike two!*"

The crowd let loose a terrible wrathful roar, and the umpire cowered as gunfire cracked and whined, and a great darkness rose up and all the faces fell in shadows, and even Gus had lost his smile, nor did he wink at McDuff.

But Casey drew himself up with a mighty intake of breath, turned on the crowd as fierce as a tiger, ordered the umpire to stand like a man, and then even, with the sudden hush that fell, the sun came out again. And Casey's muscles rippled as he exercised his bat, and Casey's teeth were clenched as he tugged upon his hat, and Casey's brows were darkened as he gazed out on McDuff, and now the fun was done because Casey'd had enough.

McDuff, on the other hand, hadn't felt better all day. Now that the preliminaries were over, now that he'd done all he could and it was on him, now that everybody else had got serious, McDuff suddenly found it was all just a gas and he couldn't give a damn. You're getting delirious, he cautioned himself, but his caution did no good. He giggled furtively: there's always something richly ludicrous about extremity, he decided. He stepped up on the rubber, went right into his stretch. Didn't bother looking at second and third: irrelevant now. And it was so ironically simple: all he had to do was put it down the middle. With a lot of stuff, of course, but he had the stuff. He nearly laughed out loud. He reared back, kicking high with his left, then hurtled forward, sent the ball humming like a shot right down the middle.

Casey's mighty cut split the air in two—*WHEEEEP!*—and

when the vacuum filled, there was a terrible thunderclap, and some saw light, and some screamed, and rain fell on the world.

Casey, in the dirt, stared in openjawed wonderment at his bat.

Gus plucked the ball gingerly out of his mitt, fingered it unbelievingly.

Flynn and Blake stood as though forever rooted at third and second, static parts of a final fieldwide tableau.

And forget what Gus said. No one cheered McDuff in Mudville when he struck Casey out.

loss of childhood
self-
not sexual —

separation/physical
experience
thinking

GRANDMOTHER'S NOSE

SHE HAD ONLY just begun to think about the world around her.
Until this summer, she and the world had been much the same
thing, a sweet seamless blur of life in life. But now it had broken
away from her and become, not herself, but the place her self
resided in, a sometimes strange and ominous other that must for
one's own sake be studied, be read like a book, like the books
she'd begun to read at the same time the world receded. Or
maybe it was her reading that had made the world step back.
Things that had once been alive and talked to her because part of
her—doll, house, cloud, well— were silent now, and apart, and
things that lived still on their own—flower, butterfly, mother,
grandmother—she now knew also died, another kind of distance.
This dying saddened her, though she understood it but dimly
(it had little to do with her, only with the inconstant world she
lived in), and it caused her to feel sorry for these ill-fated things.

She used to think it was funny when her mother chopped the head off a chicken and it ran crazily around the garden; now she didn't. She no longer squashed ants and beetles under foot or pulled the wings off flies and butterflies, and she watched old things precious to her, like her mother, with some anxiety, frightened by the possibility of their sudden absence. Since dying was a bad thing, she associated it with being bad, and so was good, at least as good as she could be: she wanted to keep her mother with her. If her mother asked her to do something, she did it. Which was why she was here.

She also associated dying with silence, for that was what it seemed to come to. So she chattered and sang the day through to chase the silence away. A futile endeavor, she knew (she somehow had this knowledge, perhaps it was something her grandmother taught her or showed her in a book), but she kept it up, doing her small part to hold back the end of things, cheerfully conversing with any creature who would stop to talk with her. This brought smiles to most faces (she was their little heroine), though her mother sometimes scolded her: Don't speak with strangers, she would say. Well, the whole world was somewhat strange to her, even her mother sometimes, it was talk to it or let the fearful stillness reign.

Though the world was less easy to live in than before, it was more intriguing. She looked at things more closely than she had when looking at the world was like looking in at herself, her eyes, then liquid mirrors in a liquid world, now more like windows, she poised behind them, staring out, big with purpose. To be at one with things was once enough, sameness then a comfort like a fragrant kitchen or a warm bath. Now, it was difference that gave her pleasure: feathers (she had no feathers), petals, wrinkles, shells, brook water's murmuring trickle over stones, not one alike, her mother's teeth (she hadn't even seen them there in her mouth before), the way a door is made, and steps, and shoes. She thought about words like dog, log, and fog, and how unalike these things were that sounded so like cousins, and she peered intensely at everything, seeking out the mystery in the busyness of ants, the odd veiny shape of leaves, the way fire burned, the skins of things.

And now it was her grandmother's nose. It was a hideous thing to see, but for that reason alone aroused her curiosity. It was much longer and darker than she remembered, creased and hairy and swollen with her illness. She knew she ought not stare at it— poor Grandma!—but fascination gripped her. Such a nose! It was as if some creature had got inside her grandmother's face and was trying to get out. She wished to touch the nose to see if it were hot or cold (Grandma lay so still! it was frightening); she touched her own instead. Yes, dying, she thought (though her own nose reassured her), must be a horrid thing.

The rest of Grandma had been affected, too. Though she was mostly covered up under nightcap, gown, and heaped-up bed-clothes as though perhaps to hide the shame of her disease, it was clear from what could be glimpsed that the dark hairy swelling had spread to other parts, and she longed—not without a little shudder of dread—to see them, to know better what dying was like. But what could not be hidden was the nose: a dark bristly outcropping, poking out of the downy bedding like the toe of a dirty black boot from a cloud bank, or from snow. Plain, as her grandmother liked to say, as the nose on your face. Only a soft snort betrayed the life still in it. Grandma also liked to say that the nose was invented for old people to hang their spectacles on

(Grandma's spectacles were on the table beside her bed, perched on a closed book), but the truth was, eyes were probably invented to show the nose where to go. The nose sat in the very middle of one's face for all to see, no matter how old one was, and it led the way, first to go wherever the rest went, pointing the direction. When she'd complained that she'd forgotten the way to Grandma's house, her mother had said: Oh, just follow your nose. And she had done that and here she was. Nose to nose with Grandma.

Her grandmother opened one rheumy eye under the frill of her nightcap and stared gloomily at her as though not quite recognizing her. She backed away. She really didn't know what to do. It was very quiet. Perhaps she should sing a song. I've brought you some biscuits and butter, Grandma, she said at last, her voice a timid whisper. Her grandmother closed her eye again and from under her nose let loose a deep growly burp. A nose was also for smelling things. And Grandma did not smell very nice. On the way I also picked some herbs for tea. Shall I put some on? Tea might do you good.

No, just set those things on the table, little girl, her grandmother said without opening her lidded eye, and come get into bed with me. Her voice was hoarse and raw. Maybe it was a bad cold she was dying of.

I'd rather not, Grandma. She didn't want to hurt her grandmother's feelings, but she did not want to get close to her either, not the way she looked and smelled. She seemed to be scratching herself under the bedding. It's... not time for bed.

Her grandmother opened her near eye again and studied her a moment before emitting a mournful grunt and closing it again. All right then, she mumbled. Forget it. Do as you damned well please. Oh dear, she'd hurt her feelings anyway. Her grandmother burped sourly again and a big red tongue flopped out below her swollen nose and dangled like a dry rag on a line, or her own cap hanging there.

I'm sorry, Grandma. It's just that it scares me the way you look now.

However I look, she groaned, it can't be half so bad as how I feel. Her grandmother gaped her mouth hugely and ran her long dry tongue around the edges. It must have been—*fooshh!*— something I ate.

She felt an urge to remark on her grandmother's big toothy mouth which was quite shocking to see when it opened all the way (so unlike her mother's mouth), but thought better of it. It would just make her grandmother even sadder. She'd said too much already, and once she started to ask questions, the list could get pretty long, not even counting the parts she couldn't see. Her big ears for example, not quite hidden by the nightcap. She remembered a story her grandmother told her about a little boy who was born with donkey ears. And all the rest was donkey, too. It was a sad story that ended happily when the donkey boy got into bed with a princess. She began to regret not having crawled into bed with her poor grandmother when she begged it of her. If she asked again, she would do it. Hold her breath and do it. Isn't there some way I can help, Grandma?

The only thing you're good for, child, would just make things worse. Her grandmother lapped at her nose with her long tongue, making an ominous scratchy sound. Woof. I'm really not feeling well.

I'm sorry...

And so you should be. It's your fault, you know.

Oh! Was it something I brought you that made you sick?

No, she snapped crossly, but you led me to it.

Did I? I didn't mean to.

Bah. Innocence. I eat up innocence. Grandma gnashed her teeth and another rumble rolled up from deep inside and escaped her. When I'm able to eat anything at all... foo... She opened her eye and squinted it at her. What big eyes you have, young lady. What are you staring at?

Your... your nose, Grandma.

What's the matter with it? Her grandmother reached one hand out from under the bedding to touch it. Her hand was black and hairy like her nose and her fingernails had curled to ugly claws.

Oh, it's a very *nice* nose, but... it's so... Are you dying, Grandma? she blurted out at last.

There was a grumpy pause, filled only with a snort or two. Then her grandmother sighed morosely and grunted. Looks like it. Worse luck. Not what I had in mind at all. She turned her head to scowl at her with both dark eyes, the frill of the nightcap down over her thick brows giving her a clownish cross-eyed look. She had to smile, she couldn't stop herself. Hey, smartypants, what's funny? You're going to die, too, you know, you're not getting out of this.

I suppose so. But not now.

Her grandmother glared at her for a moment, quite ferociously, then turned her head away and closed her eyes once more. No, she said. Not now. And she lapped scratchily at her nose again. In a story she'd read in a book, there was a woman whose nose got turned into a long blood sausage because of a bad wish, and the way her grandmother tongued her black nose made her think of it.

Did her grandmother wish for something she shouldn't have?

I sort of know what dying is, Grandma. I had a bird with a broken wing and it died and turned cold and didn't do anything after that. And living, well, that's like every day. Mostly I like it. But what's the point if you just have to die and not be and forget everything?

How should I know what the damned point is, her grandmother growled. She lay there in the heaped bedding, nose high, her red tongue dangling once more below it. She didn't move. It was very quiet. Was she already dead? Or just thinking? Appetite, her grandmother said finally, breaking the silence. And the end of appetite. That's it.

That was more like the Grandma she knew. She had lots of stories about being hungry or about eating too much or the wrong things. Like the one about the little girl whose father ate her brother. He liked it so much he sucked every bone (now every time she ate a chicken wing, she thought of that father). The little girl gathered all the bones he threw under the table and put them together and her brother became a boy again. Grandma often told stories about naughty boys and cruel fathers, but the little boy in this story was nice and the father was quite nice, too, even if he did sometimes eat children.

Her grandmother popped her eye open suddenly and barked in her deep raspy voice: Don't look too closely! It scared her and made her jump back. She'd been leaning in, trying to see the color of the skin under the black hairs. It was a color something like that of old driftwood. Look too closely at anything, her grandmother said, letting the dark lid fall over her eye once more and tilting her nose toward the ceiling, and what you'll see is nothing. And then you'll see it everywhere, you won't be able to see anything else. She gaped her jaws and burped grandly. Big mistake, she growled.

The thing about her grandmother's nose, so different from her own, or from anyone's she knew, she thought as she put the kettle on for tea, was that it seemed to say so much more to her than her grandmother did. Her nose was big and rough, but at the same time it looked so naked and sad and kind of embarrassing. She couldn't figure out exactly *what* she thought about it. Grandma's talk was blunt and plain and meant just what it said, no more. The nose was more mysterious and seemed to be saying several things to her at once. It was like reading a story about putting a brother back together with his licked bones and discovering later it was really about squashing bad ladies, one meaning hidden under another one, like bugs under a stone. With a pestle, she ground some of the herbs she'd brought in a mortar, then climbed up on a chair to get a cup down from the cupboard. Her grandmother's nose was both funny and frightening at the same time, and hinted at worlds beyond her imagination. Worlds, maybe, she didn't really want to live in. If you die, Grandma, she said, crawling down from the chair, I'll save all your bones.

To chew on, I hope, her grandmother snapped, sinking deeper into the bedding. Which reminds me, she added, somewhat more lugubriously. One thing your grandmother said, as I now recall, was: Don't bite off more than you can chew.

Yes. But *you're* my grandmother.

That's right. Well—*wuurpp!*—don't forget it. Now go away. Leave me alone. Before I bite your head off just to shut you up.

This dying was surely a hard thing that her grandmother was going through, one had to expect a little bad temper. Even her grandmother's nose seemed grayer than it had been before, her

tongue more rag-like in its lifeless dangle, her stomach rum-
blings more dangerously eruptive. It was like she had some wild
angry beast inside her. It made her shudder. Dying was definitely
not something to look forward to. The kettle was boiling so she
scraped the mortar grindings into the cup and filled it full of hot
water, set the cup on the table beside the bed. Here, Grandma.
This will make you feel better. Her grandmother only snarled
peevishly.

Later, when she got home, her mother asked her how
Grandma was feeling. Not very well, she said. A wolf had eaten
her and got into bed in Grandma's nightclothes and he asked me
to get in bed with him. Did you do that? No, I sort of wanted to.
But then some men came in and chopped the wolf's head off and
cut his tummy open to get Grandma out again. I didn't stay but
I think Grandma was pretty upset. Her mother smiled, showing
her teeth, and told her it was time for bed.

Was that what really happened? Maybe, maybe not, she
wasn't sure. But it was a way of remembering it, even if it was
perhaps not the best way to remember poor Grandma (that nose!),
though Grandma was dying or was already dead, so it didn't
really matter. She crawled into her bed, a place not so friendly as
once it was, but first she touched her bedstead, the book beside
it (Grandma gave it to her), her pillow, doll, felt the floorboards
under her feet, convincing herself of the reality of all that, because
some things today had caused her doubt. No sooner had her feet
left the floor, however, than there was nothing left of that sensation except her memory of it, and that, she knew, would soon be
gone, and the memory of her grandmother, too, and some day the
memory of her, and she knew then that her grandmother's warning about the way she looked at things had come too late.

Each puzzle piece represents a character, as defined by relationships and personalities. When identified, their names spell out an acrostic.

SUBURBAN JIGSAW

LUCILLE IS OBSESSED with love's great mystery. When she and Larry first moved to this pretty neighborhood, her notion of love was inextricably tied up with marriage and family. Larry, whose business career had taken off when he'd cornered the market on disposable wearables, was feeling ecstatically full of himself (Top of the world, Ma! he liked to exclaim, rearing high above her, when about to have his orgasm, which was always a thrilling moment for her as well, and brought on an orgasm of her own, or something like one), and their lovemaking was delightfully spontaneous and lighthearted. One of the products he had in his portfolio was candy panties of which he got sent samples, and not only did he like to eat them off her, he also wore them (he was so cute in those thin little things!) and let her do the same. They tasted like cotton candy and licking them off seemed both very sophisticated and like being a child again at the circus. They simply had fun and, almost as an afterthought, had children, whom they also loved, and she thought this was how it would be until they got old and loved each other in another, quieter way, and devoted themselves to their grandchildren.

But then she met Pavel the handyman. He came to clean out their gutters, and he quite bluntly, and quite excitingly, said he'd like to clean out hers. She became flustered and resisted, this would not do at all, but the next thing she knew she was into something quite different from anything she had ever experienced before. She doesn't even know if she should still call it love. It is certainly full of passion and desire and is incredibly erotic but there's not much of simple fun or tenderness in it. It's closer to the bone than that, an expression that, when she used it, made Pavel laugh. Pavel calls what they do fucking, a word she has never used before, not out loud, but that's just what it is, something that brings out the animal in her, overriding mind and heart. And conscience. And good taste. Vulgar, yes, it is. Though she knows it is wrong and dangerous and has tried to stop it, she can't. He feels like a giant in her, whichever way he takes her, he completely fills her up, and now she knows what an orgasm really is, and she suffers from an insatiable desire for more and more. Pavel teases her about this as she invents job after job for him to do, and he often takes off his pants while he does the jobs and makes her wait and wait, staring at his big hammer, as he calls it, and his strong handsome bottom, while he changes a washer or paints a patch of ceiling or gets down on his hands and knees to rewire a wall plug.

This mad obsession with the handyman has caused a great deal of turmoil and remorse in Lucille, for she loves Larry and the little family they have made together and she knows he is true to her and worth all the Pavels in the world and she really doesn't want to hurt him, while at the same time the fun they were having in bed together isn't really all that much fun any more. She is talking about this in a somewhat coded way (she pretends to be talking about a book she has read) one afternoon in the local bookstore coffee lounge with her young friend Rick from the neighborhood literary society, a gentle fellow who works in the bookstore and writes poems about the sadness of life for the Sunday supplement of the city newspaper. He reminds her of several books they have read together in the literary society which celebrate love in all its varieties from the merely physical to the most pure and transcendent and he gets down a copy of *Madame Bovary* and reads a passage from it to her, and while he is doing that, he takes her hands in his and interrupts his reading to tell her that he adores her, he has since the moment he saw her when she first came to one of their Tuesday night meetings when they were discussing *Women in Love*. When I saw you, it was like a miracle, he says. And so, well, something else gets started, and again it is something quite different.

Lucille's husband Larry is also suffering pangs of turmoil and guilt, though they don't show on his face because he is by nature such a happy fellow. Larry's success in life, as in business, has been due to his singular focus, which was how he cornered the market on disposable wearables and made his fortune. When Larry sets his mind on something he sticks to it and stays by it, and that includes his relationship with Lucille, who is his sexy loving helpmeet and the mother of his children. He knows that such lifelong relationships risk being stifled by routine, so he works hard at enlivening theirs with novelty and romantic surprise. But Larry is also a kind and generous man, touched by the pain and sorrow of others, so when their neighbor Opal, a demure widow living alone since the tragic highway death of her husband (the perils of commuting!), asked him for help in opening a stuck window in her bedroom, and then fell into his arms sobbing, he felt somehow humanly obliged to help her alleviate her terrible loneliness. After all, what did it cost him? Another disposable. And she was so profoundly grateful, weeping afterwards like a happy child and holding him tight and saying he was the loveliest man she had ever known. She has often had things that needed fixing since then, and Larry has found much gratification in being of service to a fellow being in need, but also a certain anguish. He is not a man who keeps secrets well, and fears for the moment when dear faithful Lucille finds out. Already, he is practicing what he might say to her should that happen.

Victor, who lives on the other side of the widow's house with his little homebody wife Evelyn, has fewer scruples. When the widow asked him for help with a stuck window, he didn't even bother to take his tools with him, other than the one he knew she really wanted. She was passionate and tender and grateful if somewhat straitlaced (there are many things she hasn't done and won't do), but it was better than fucking a prostitute, which, since he has moved here at his boss's urging (a good place to raise children, he said with a smirk around his bobbing cigar), has been his usual fare, other than Evelyn who seems to get little pleasure out of it and gives little. Victor, though frustrated by the widow's entrenched naiveté, is also grateful and takes what she offers him, treating her like the proper lady she is. Victor is a top-rank insurance salesman who has known many women in his day, though he has found himself somewhat cut off from the action in this neighborhood, so he is glad at least the widow is available, and when he's not been sent off traveling by his boss, which is all too often these days, he visits her at least once a week to unstick her windows. At one point Victor met with his boss to ask about cutting back on the travels, it was taking the starch out of him, and he wasn't seeing enough of his kids, but his boss said he was doing a great job, raised his pay, and sent him out on the road again. Victor knows there's a lot going on out here in the suburbs, there always is, these places are made for it, just a matter of getting your tab in the right hole, but he and Evelyn are apparently living on the wrong street. His boss is a generous guy to work for, but he is a fat ugly old fart who is reduced to fucking whores (he passed on a phone number to Victor) and no longer appreciates the subtler things in life. Victor keeps his eye on the housing ads and stays in touch by phone with Homer, a local real estate agent with the style of a fagged-out undertaker. Victor has told him what he's looking for, but the dismal creep never seems to get the picture.

He is a creep, but Irene is attracted to horny melancholic losers like Homer, as long as they are not married (married guys are a pushover but always have the same irritating hang-ups); they are fun to seduce and, because they have no wills of their own, they are usually ready to play any game she proposes. For Irene, love is exciting only when it's theatrical and transgressive. Her unsuspecting lovers are really supporting actors in a licentious drama of sexual outlawry, starring Irene. Sometimes quite literally: she has videocams mounted in her bedroom, where there is only a big black mat on the floor, and she has hired professional photographers and filmmakers to follow her on some of her public escapades, posting the results on the Internet. She hangs out in the corner bar where she picks up her costars, as she calls them, and one night she picked up Homer in there. She sat down beside him at the bar, and started talking with him about the utter madness of the so-called civilized world, striking a chord with Homer, and pretty soon she had his pants open and his sex in her hand, thumbing him off. She spun him on his stool to send his spunk flying into the midst of the patrons standing around the bar, with the consequence that they dragged Homer off his stool in disgust and thumped the daylights out of him, while Irene sat watching from her perch, clutching herself between her legs with both hands, dizzy with ecstasy and trying not to fall off her stool.

Homer had had a few that night and was never quite sure what happened or how, except that he remembered thinking when she pulled his dick out that it was both completely insane and the most glorious thing that had happened to him since he got dumped out of puberty. The end result was seriously depressing, but then so was much of his life, so he hasn't been able completely to disavow it, even though it cost him a tooth and a shiner. When Homer is down in the dumps, which is most of the time, he tries to look up cheerful Lily with the golden curls, who will sleep with just about anybody in the neighborhood, even a fucked-up depressive like himself, the only problem being to catch her when she's free. He had her to himself for awhile when she was house-hunting, a lost golden age he mourns. They tried out every place he took her to, sometimes on kitchen counters or the odd carpeted floor, mostly standing up on bare boards against a freshly painted wall beside curtainless windows (once he saw crazy beautiful Irene passing by, dressed only in a wide-brimmed fluorescent orange hat with green flowers and purple stilettos: did she know he was in there?), and whenever possible in front of fitted mirrors. Lily's desire, not his. Homer never looks at one of the damned things, for he is never cheered by what he sees there. Lily had been recently divorced and said she wanted to be in the middle of the social whirl, and eventually he found her the perfect place, complete with pool and bedrooms with mirrored ceilings, and though they had a lot of fun when they found it, it was really bad luck, because that ended his exclusive rights. In fact, since moving in, she has seemed only to be tolerating him, so even the occasional happy moment with her is cause for further gloom. Homer knows what Victor is looking for, and has a line on a property that might work for him, but he really doesn't want more competition for Lily's time. He has other options, though even more depressing—he can let Irene mess him up again, for example—and there are always fresh clients coming along who are excited by the glamour of empty rooms and good for a quick one-off. But Lily is the only one who can lift him out of himself, and he needs her from time to time as a junkie needs a fix.

The property that Homer has in mind for Victor belongs to a gynecologist named Oscar, who is thinking of selling up and changing neighborhoods while he still has a reputation and a practice left, and before some husband shoots him. He knows the real estate agent is somewhat enthralled by that wiry exhibitionist who is often seen, out on the street or in the corner bar, as stitchless as the women in his private examination room, and admittedly there is something electric about the little sprite, but though intense perverse women appeal to him, the kicks she delivers are not really where Oscar's appetites lie. Oscar needs physical pain, not mere humiliation. The lash arouses him, giving or receiving, bondage does. The apparati of dominatrices give him an erotic charge, and he keeps his own doctor's office stocked with exotic toys. He takes his punishment from professionals, deals it out to willing submissive women. Of whom, never few. He is not cruel, he is a healer, after all, and in fact the threat of pain, especially when one is helpless, is always more stimulating than pain itself, as his women all agree, no matter their predilections, but there has to be real pain from time to time to make the threat of pain more than a game of make-believe. It was Sheila who taught him that principle by strapping him over a velvet horsing stool the first time he consulted her, and whipping him till he screamed. Now just the strapping, the feel of velvet against his groin, the sight and sound of the whip, do it for him. Her foot between his shoulderblades, her heated curling iron. He will miss Sheila if he leaves the neighborhood.

As will Wanda miss her doctor if he goes. She went to him for a checkup, fearful she might have caught something from a casual, almost accidental fling with a sad sack who came to give an estimate on their home at a time when her husband was worried his bank might be transferring him to another branch. She was right, she has had to go back every week for further treatment. Call it that. It's pretty awesome. Getting a dose was maybe the most interesting thing that has ever happened to her, if she really did, and he didn't just make it up to keep her coming back. Whatever, no matter. On her first visit the doctor asked her to strip down completely and he buckled her to an examining table with her legs spread apart and her knees up. She had left her socks on, and he peeled them away slowly, one by one, as if skinning her, making her more naked than she ever thought she could be, all the while watching her somberly through his thick glasses as she went wet between the legs. Then he put little clamps on her to open her up and poked all sorts of things up her, including his whole hand, his fingers pushing and probing. It hurt and she knew he was trying to hurt her, but his crisp white jacket was open and she could see he was enormously excited and there was a kind of fire in his goggly eyes, and that excited her, too. Her total helplessness did. It was like being trapped in somebody else's nightmare, terrifying but excitingly vivid. He could kill her, she knew, and she could do nothing about it. She was at his mercy, and he doesn't seem to have a lot of that. It is being what he wants her to be that protects her.

Sheila also hopes the doctor will stay. He is one of her most responsive and malleable clients, and he pays well. Love doesn't factor into it, never does. If anything, Sheila has the corner of her eye on Odette. Most of Sheila's men are pathetic little self-hating wimps, which is to say they are also in love with themselves; they often like to watch their punishment in mirrors. She hates them and finds a certain satisfaction in castigating their flabby suburban souls and corrupt pallid flesh, but no pleasure. Igor is by nature a tougher sort, though still a narcissist, one of those pompous self made men these neighborhoods are always full of, but he only wants to be tied up in leather thongs and paddled from time to time. He says it reminds him of his school days and makes him feel a kid again. He really doesn't have a clue about the true nature of her art. Which is about progression, not regression. It takes an unusual imagination to be able to grasp that and go with it, and the doctor is so endowed. Not only has she been able to push him into greater and greater depths of depravity and pain (which is Sheila's definition of growing up), she finds she is learning from him as she goes, not about technique but about the deeper meaning of her art. Which, at some level, is about love, after all.

Odette, like big Sheila, who frightens her with her strange

sideways glances, is also a businesswoman, but she has much less personally at stake. It's just a job. Art she doesn't know, though skills, yes. She is good at her work and, in this expensive neighborhood, well paid for it. No one has ever complained and they keep asking for her services. In fact, she makes more money than the guy she lives with, which helps keep the arrogant pig in his place. Mostly it's just the old slap and tickle with a few toys of the trade thrown in, but she has her inevitable share of perverts, too, and can roll with that, though she has her limits. Fantasy's okay, dressing up is, if guys want to wear panties and high heels, fine, and she lets her clients choose their favorite orifices, it's all the same to her. She even tolerates the old guy with the handlebars who tries to sell her insurance on her asshole while buggering her (she also services his subordinate, who is a regular guy who only wants to get his rocks off, and she figures, if she could talk them into it, she could take both of them on at once and make double the pay). But Odette hates pain of any kind and doesn't understand how people can be turned on by it. Some guy smacks her bottom, that sucker is out of there and he's not coming back. Pinches, love bites, bruising, same thing. House rules. Dishing it out is not fun for her either, for she has a tender heart, but she has a customer who wants it that way and she submits to the idea only because it's part of the profession and he's a big spender. He likes her to wear a riding helmet and boots and get on his fat hairy back and swat his withers with a riding crop. Odette imagines him to be the thug she lives with and is able to lay it on him with vindictive vigor, at least for a stroke or two, but then she just gets bored and is reduced to draping him over her lap and, while examining her nails, stubbing out cigarette butts on his behind.

Lily shares a lot of Odette's aptitudes and attitudes (she doesn't know this; they have seen each other at a distance, shopping in the neighborhood boutiques, but have never spoken), though she would never think of charging money for any of it and, in fact, often helps out her lovers, especially quality studs like the guy who comes to fix her plumbing and clean her pool or the sweet melancholic boy from the bookstore who brings her books she never reads and adores her madly, or so he says. And why not? She is indeed adorable. Not all her lovers are so desirable and, once they've had a little fun together, some of these guys seem to think they own her and are hard to get rid of. That bluesy dork who sold her her house, for example, worse than her ex-husband. She should probably be more discriminating, but it's really not in her nature. As for the neighborhood doctor, Lily also hopes he'll stay. He's a beastly sonuvabitch and has truly weird ideas (she'll never forget the time she went to him for an examination when she thought she was pregnant! it's a good thing she wasn't!), and she likes pain even less than Odette, taking just about everything there is for it, even when she's not suffering any. But the doctor makes up for the rough stuff by providing her with all the painkillers, antibiotics, amphetamines, tranquilizers, and contraceptives she wants, and he just fills out the pattern of the neighborhood somehow. She's not sure she'd be who she is if he left. Everything happens around Lily and her swimming pool and he is something of what happens and, now that she has located herself here and is happy, she wants everything to stay that way.

If Lily is surrounded by lovers and admirers, no one even notices Evelyn. Sometimes, when she can get a babysitter, she goes to the Tuesday night literary society meetings and sits in the back of the room and they don't even know she is there. Shop clerks look right through her. She could walk down the street in her birthday suit like that wild little girl on the other side of the neighborhood, and people would not even tip their hat. Not that she ever would do that. She is happy being nondescript and unnoticed. It was she who chose this house, far from the center of things, even though it's not the nicest part of town. She stays at home and keeps house and makes fruit jellies and feeds the children when they come home from school and tends the back garden and watches television and waits for Victor, who is gone a lot of the time now, to return from his travels. So, just how she ended up in bed in the middle of one morning with her husband's boss, Evelyn is not sure. It is not the sort of thing that ever happens to her, but then, no one has ever asked before, so maybe it might have happened all the time. It began almost as soon as they moved in, on the day Victor left on one of his sales trips, it was like he was there waiting for her. He was very persuasive and somehow she felt cornered. Didn't she want to help her husband, she was asked, and wasn't this the easiest way to do it? It's true, Victor has kept getting raises ever since, though she has seen less and less of him. Not that she misses him all that much. When he is home, he complains all the time about all the traveling he is being asked to do, about the stupid street they live on, and about that nuisance of a widow next door who doesn't seem to be able to change a lightbulb for herself. And then, he is no sooner here than gone, and even as his car is pulling out of the drive, there's her husband's boss back in her bed again, puffing on one of his big brown cigars, letting the ash fall where it may and mostly on her chenille bedspread. He likes to do dirty things, but then so does Victor. Evelyn has always had the feeling she has never met the right man in her life.

Lucille is one of those who has failed to notice Evelyn at the literary society meetings, but then she fails to notice just about anyone there other than her beautiful young poet who conducts the meetings. Lucille, at a time in her life when she thought romance was a thing of the past, has found herself quite astonishingly head over heels in love. It is a love unlike any she has ever known before, so profound and moving it almost makes her bones ache. They just fit in all ways, and he adores her as she adores him. But it is also an ill-fated love for it has no logical outcome: she is a happily married woman with children (whom she has been neglecting, she knows, dropping them off at nursery schools or with babysitters, she must do something about that) and sooner or later they will have to bring this divine madness to an end. But not now, not now, it would break her heart; and his. Of late at the society, they have been discussing a book by a Russian, and Lucille has wanted to protest that she doesn't think that an older man seducing a child is very nice, but then she realizes that her relationship with Rick is not much different and she has no right to be critical. Rick is so tender about her age, much nicer than the girl in the novel. He kisses her wherever time has made its mark and gasps with wistful joy when he fondles her breasts, which in truth have seen better days. When they first made love and he was so eager to see everything, she worried about her stretch marks, but he wrote a poem about them which was the sweetest thing. It was just for her, he didn't publish it in the Sunday supplement, thank goodness. She still finds jobs for Pavel to do but that's like a separate part of her life, somewhere she goes from time to time like to the movies—or, better said, to the library, for her time with the handyman amounts to a kind of self-study and search for the true breadth and meaning of love, while she is still young enough (she feels so young!) to do so. Lucille thought she was tired of her body, but suddenly she just loves it.

Pavel is in great demand in the little community, a craftsman much appreciated who can crack any problem, but when he doesn't have jobs to do and his woman is plying her trade and he can't go back to the house, he often goes for a swim in Lily's pool. Provided that Lily, the hottest piece in the neighborhood, is not entertaining some other guy. Pavel likes to swim bare-ass, watched admiringly by the divorcee, also in the altogether, which she wears well. He has often told her she could make a killing on the game, but she only smiles and says she has enough money and doesn't like the business world. Sometimes she jumps in the pool with him and they thrash around a bit in the way kids do, but mostly she just squats at the edge of the pool with her drink in one hand and his in the other, and he comes by from time to time to give her a lick to salt his drink and tell her what a princess she is and what a sweet coozie she has. The handyman follows the old rule of love, treating sluts like ladies and ladies like sluts, and, though he doesn't succeed too well at the first part, he is a master of the second. And anyway it works with Lily either way, she's a happy girl. She likes it all ways when it comes to the main feature, but above all, after a cool hit or two (she has her own steady supplier, which Pavel taps into indirectly), on her big round satin-sheeted bed under the ceiling mirror.

Rick has been there, gazing up through Lily's thighs at himself, what he could see of himself, his hands squeezing the cheeks of her bottom, her head, with its tight blond curls matching those now scuffing his chin, bobbing away between his raised knees, like a—what? like an animated merkin, a word he has discovered in a book he's reading and hopes he's using correctly. It was a dazzling sight and he felt like he sometimes feels sitting beside her pool, gazing into its cerulean depths: like he is being sucked down (or up) into the vortex of... of... what did that Norwegian writer call it? a maelstrom. The dizzying maelstrom of love. From which there is no escape, only surrender. When Lily walked into the bookstore and went straight to the back where they keep the more salacious material, he fell immediately in love with her and told her he adored her and the next thing he knew, there he was, under the mirror. Of course his true love is Lucille, with her he feels like Lancelot with Queen Guinevere; it is a noble passion that lifts him above himself and he is utterly devoted to her and will love her forever. Even if forever, as he knows, is merely a literary convention. Her fading beauty breaks his heart. Sometimes, gazing at her during an embrace, while kissing away her worry lines, tears come to his eyes. Lily he thought of at first as just a kind of adventure on the side, a bit of casual sallying forth of the errant sort, but he underestimated love's overmastering force, as so many characters in novels do, usually to their regret, for in spite of himself he has come to love her madly, adoring her with all his heart as she adores him. She quite literally lifts his spirits, not only with the little pills she gives him (so you won't be so sad, she says), but also with her lightness of being, her sweet vulnerability, her tender incarnation of impermanence, ephemerality, the phantom self, the human tragedy.

Not all love is so ennobling or inspiring. Rick knows this. He has read a lot of books about the perverse side of love, its depravities and obsessions, and so he was not completely surprised when he also fell under the spell of a strange wild enchantress in the bar on the corner by the bookstore. Rick often stops in the bar for a few drinks after work to meditate on the puzzle of life, that grand enigma, trying to put the pieces together, as one might say, and one night, one thing following upon another, he found himself making mad passionate love to the frenetic creature in the lit street window of his bookstore, right in the middle of a display of popular books on religion and mysticism, before a fascinated audience out in the street, an audience which eventually included the police. He was arrested and lost his job at the bookstore, but he got it back again when Lily talked to the owners and bought a thousand dollars worth of cookbooks. That should have been the end of it, especially when he discovered the entire display window episode out on the Internet (his face is thankfully somewhat obscured, Lucille may not recognize him and probably knows nothing about computers anyway), but, even though the bewitching nymph is dragging him down into the baser side of himself and into further danger, he has kept going back to the bar, he can't stop himself. He is completely in her power. She is a veritable spider woman, a Circe, a voracious Lorelei (he has written a prose poem called "The Succulent Succubus," but the Sunday supplement has not yet accepted it). And the terrible truth is he loves her no less than any of the others, and has told her so, choking up with the emotion of it even as she tied him naked to the lamppost, and he fears there might be no end to his capacity for that notorious and enigmatic affection. He feels like an unhappy character in a postmodern novel, condemned to live forever inside a form he cannot escape. A man by love possessed.

Wanda is also a prisoner of strange love, but what or who she is in love with, she can't quite say. It is not exactly the doctor, who is not even attractive and has very hairy hands, but more like some kind of terrible compelling power that is inside him like a demon and that overwhelms her and makes her feel like she is melting. Each time she has been back for a checkup, he has found new things to do with wires and big steel things and clamps and needles and a little stiff whip like a magician's wand that he uses on her when giving her hot enemas, and even before the straps are buckled she is already having the most ferocious orgasms and at the same time peeing herself in terror. She has never known anything like it. Her husband will make love only if she works at arousing him, and then always passively, with her on top doing everything, it's hardly worth it. It's like he's never got over his nursemaid giving him his baths and pinching his little nipples. The doctor won't let her touch him—in fact she can't, locked down like that—but sometimes he gets too excited, especially when she starts to cry, and he has to excuse himself for a minute. After which, he is always crueler than ever. It is a quirky sort of love; they never talk about what they are doing, they just silently play their parts—her shameful sickness, his furious treatments like naughty little kids playing doctor.

Though his wife ridicules his passivity, Alan has also learned about love through play-acting. In fact, it might be said he seeks Wanda's ridicule, for that was always part of his nursemaid's games as well, she heaping playful scorn upon him even as she dallied with him, insisting always that he lie utterly still and be completely silent or she won't play with him any more. All of this happened long ago in his parents' house far away in the center of the city, but he has tried to re-create something of that house in his own little corner of the world, even down to the old-fashioned bathroom fixtures and the children's book illustrations of dying maidens and wounded knights on the bedroom walls.

His upbringing has made him a circumspect and courteous person, and so has served to raise his prestige at the bank (he is the quiet wise man to whom one comes for advice), while at the same time depriving him of any ambition, making advancement seem a kind of vague threat to his tranquility. When it is offered, he always, politely but resolutely, turns it down. Which also provokes his wife's derision, in spite of all the expensive gifts he buys her. She is not Alan's first wife, of course. They come and go, claiming mental cruelty and taking away substantial portions of his wealth, and Wanda will no doubt soon follow. She has been ill of late, though ominously she won't say of what, and has become quite distracted, unwilling or unable to play their little games or even to give him his baths, so, for lack of any other outlet (he is attracted to the pretty young divorcée who has recently moved into the neighborhood, but he could never approach her, much less touch her), he has taken to visiting a professional lady in the neighborhood who specializes in various forms of humiliation. What he asks of her is so little it is no doubt an insult to her talents, and she clearly despises him for it (he watches her in the mirrors, not himself), but it is that loathing perhaps more than the punishment or simple humiliation that he seeks.

Lucille, sitting in the bookstore coffee lounge with her young lover, has finally decided she must put her life in order and bring an end to her adultery (even the word shocks her, often as she has seen it written), which threatens, she knows, to destroy her marriage. She has already canceled Pavel's next visit and got the name of a new handyman who is said to be old and fat, and she has booked a day at the zoo with the children (she feels like she hardly knows them!), a day previously devoted each week to Rick. This is a nice community, full of bankers and lawyers and

doctors and business executives and real estate brokers, and she
worries that her behavior will become known and embarrass her
husband and turn the happy life she and Larry have created for
themselves into a kind of French-novel nightmare. She also worries that Larry might already have guessed something of what
was happening, perhaps sensing her infidelity in the diminishing
intensity of their own romance, for the normally high-spirited
fellow has acquired a certain tender wistful demeanor (which is
attractive to her, even though she feels accused by it), and she
almost wishes he might have an affair and so make her feel less
guilty about her own. While trying to get up the courage to tell
Rick (how lovely he is! how she adores him!) that it's over, she
sips her cappuccino and listens to him explain his theories about
the neighborhood. Certainly he knows a lot about the place just
from the books that people are reading, and it is his belief, he
says, that something is being spelled out and he has been trying
to piece it all together. You're Lucille and I'm Rick, he says.
That's important. Of course it is, she smiles, touched. No, I
mean, it wouldn't work if it was the other way around. Goodness,
I can't even imagine it! No, he says, and he smiles, I can't either.
I only meant... well, it may be something significant or it may
not, but it doesn't matter. Life like literature, he says, taking her
hands in his, is often quite frivolous. She finds his theories amus-
ingly paranoid, reminiscent of a contemporary writer they have
been discussing in the literary society, and is about to say so when
a girl comes in wearing only a short, nearly transparent nightie.
Maybe that sort of thing is the fashion nowadays, but it doesn't
belong in this neighborhood, and it has poor Rick, who has let
go of her hands and sprung to his feet, completely flustered. The
girl, after taking in blushing Rick, turns and gives Lucille the

most wicked grin as though she knows everything and Lucille is suddenly afraid it's already too late. Are those cameras? It is a moment when Lucille has a sudden understanding of the phrase: my heart stood still! The girl has an arm around Rick, winking at Lucille over his shoulder, and seems to be taking his trousers down. Lucille doesn't know whether to rush over and defend her lover (her ex-lover, she is already thinking) from this scandalous attack, or to flee, her research project concluded.

Larry is home alone, just removing a reheated cup of coffee from the microwave, Lucille having left for her usual afternoon of shopping and browsing in the bookstore, when the widow from next door turns up, bursting in through his kitchen door with a somewhat desperate look on her face. Larry, whose changed demeanor has in truth been due to an unwonted commingling of pleasure and regret, has been staying away from the widow of late, fearful that Lucille might get suspicious. Lucille is a good reader and his face, he knows, is an open book. Moreover, he has no doubt been seen going in and out of Opal's house rather too often, and this is the sort of neighborhood where any sort of irregular romantic behavior would naturally be frowned upon, even if it had to do with being of assistance to a poor lonely widow who deserved everyone's sympathy. Opal says now that she is afraid there might be a mouse behind the refrigerator and she is terrified and needs his help and why hasn't he been by recently? He tries to explain but she breaks into tears and falls weakly against his chest with her arms around him as though unable to stand without him. Such a soft willowy creature, he cannot find it in his heart to be cruel to her. I'm so sorry, she whispers. I'm such a slut, I know it. I just want to fuck all the time and blow people's cocks off, and, well, whatever, you name it, I don't care what you do! Even as she says these outrageous things, Opal somehow sounds as demure and innocent as ever. Where, Larry wonders, as the widow undoes his belt buckle, did she learn such language? She must have had other visitors. She has also learned some new things she never did before. Which is how it is that he's standing in the kitchen with a cup of luke-warm coffee in his hand, his pants around his ankles, and his penis in Opal's mouth, thinking that life is amazing and completely inscrutable, when he hears his wife come in through the front door. He tries to remember what it was he'd planned to say if ever he had to explain things to her, but his mind is a complete blank.

Capricious. Malicious. Vicious. Delicious. Perverse. Curse. Verse. Or worse. Gross. Eros. Is that a rhyme? Hmm. A dose is. Verbose. No, she is not verbose. She's ribald. He scribbled. Improper. A showstopper. A whirly girly. Illicit. So, kiss it. Don't miss it. Obscene Irene. Lean and mean. She's offbeat. Indiscreet. Street meat in heat. Rick is sitting all alone beside Lily's pool like the period at the end of a sentence, tripping (ripping? flipping?) on her little pills and searching for the right words (it's easy, they're flying all about him) to describe the crazy creature from the corner bar for a lyric he is writing, probably not for the Sunday supplement. In fact, he is entering a new phase of his poetical career, to which he is at the moment able to devote himself full-time, and the Sunday supplement is probably not part of it. He is in the diabolic frolic phase, writing his exciting bizarre memoir, searching for the absurd furred bird word. Oh man! It has been an amazing day! He has lost his job again, but Lily, who is off to the doctor to restock her medications (that's right, the doctor restocked her; he unlocked her, shocked her, mocked her, rocked her—Rick is on a roll, he has never felt so creative or so wise, for he's got the picture now, he has put it all together, he can read the neighborhood), promises to get his job back for him, one way or another. As Lily says, they need him to run the literary society, he makes them a lot of money, getting all those ladies in the neighborhood to buy new books each week, and thanks to Irene he even has a certain celebrity status now as a kind of Internet amateur porn star that makes it difficult for them to ignore him. They have no choice. And that's not all that's illumined his day. Even as his pants came down in front of Irene's camera crew, his true love and muse suddenly called off their romance to return to her husband, which was terribly distressing in the midst of all his other troubles, and he thought that Irene had spoiled things forever with Lucille, but then fifteen minutes later his dearly beloved was back again and dragging him into the stock room for the most beautiful time they have ever had together. She was really fired up (love's great mystery, what can he say, that old cliché, the poet's métier), and they'd be locked up in there still if she hadn't had to go home to get her gutters cleaned.

STICK MAN

THE STICK MAN is gazing out upon the horizon. Wistfully perhaps, it's hard to be certain. Even he is not sure what he is feeling or ought to be feeling. The horizon is a mere line, but as always he fills it in with a landscape of his imagination. He does this simply by announcing it: e.g., the Stick Man is standing in the Garden of Paradise. And, with that, so he is. This is usually rewarding and satisfies him. He lives a rich and complex life and is rarely not satisfied. Today, however, the Garden of Paradise seems a bit tatty. Trampled. Gone to seed.

Perhaps he has been too long inactive. Standing limbs akimbo in the same place inventing landscapes. Straightening up from time to time when pleased or displeased with his mental transformations of the horizon line, otherwise motionless. So he puts himself through some exercises. He lifts his stick hands above his head. He bends over and touches the ends of his stick feet. He squats. He sits. He lies down. That's better. He lies there for awhile on the featureless plain, inventing activities appropriate to this position. The Stick Man meditates on the ontology of being. The Stick Man digests. The Stick Man gazes at the stars (it is night now). The Stick Man watches the clouds roll by, changing their shapes (it is day). The Stick Man waits in vain for a revelation to descend. The Stick Man wonders if he can get up again. The Stick Man attempts a sit-up. Abandons it. The Stick Man rests.

It is in the prone position that he has his best ideas, and his idea now is to make love to the Stick Woman. He often does this when he's feeling a bit low or his imagination goes flat. To have the idea is to bring her to his side. She is identical to him in every way—the same empty circle for a head, the same straight spine, crossed by a shoulder bar and a hip bar at the base, with the four trisected limbs hanging off the bar ends—except that she has a notch in the bottom of the hip bar where he has a tab, which is something like a comma except when making love. Even then, actually. A thing of naught. The Stick Woman calls it his tendril. Always hopeful. When their sticks are heaped together, they make a pretty picture, as of secret hieroglyphs.

After making love, he does feel better and he thanks the Stick Woman for it, but his creative appetite remains unaroused. The Stick Man reinvents the universe, he announces. But in fact he continues to lie there in the inert postcoital position. Perhaps he should visit the human world again. The Stick Woman reminds him that in the past these visits have not been very successful. That's right, he had forgotten. Or, rather, he had not forgotten, but he had not wanted to remember. No, he tells the Stick Woman, they have not, but they give me fresh ideas. Help me get up.

The horizon line has vanished and all visible space in all possible directions is filled with human activity. The Stick Man is standing in the middle of it, more or less erect, his limbs slightly akimbo: he wants to appear relaxed. But he is not relaxed and anyone can see that. He looks desperately out of place and all too aware that he looks out of place. These humans would look out of place in his stick world, too, he knows that, but they are not in his world, nor are they likely to go there; he is in their world. Where he is unwanted. He remembers now that the last time he was here they tried to dismantle him and use his head for a manhole cover. People are uncomfortable around someone without facial features of any kind. Not to mention someone without clothing, however simple and innocent may be his poor figure. On this occasion, a crowd gathers around him, pointing and staring. They do not seem hostile. Or merely hostile. They seem prepared to give him a chance. But a chance at what? Perhaps they think he is a street performer. In order to try to please them, he does a little dance. It is a very elaborate dance, as he thinks of it, balletic and energetic (e.g., the Stick Man attempts a flying *pas de chat*), but to the humans it probably appears that he is standing still. At most, twitching slightly. They grow restless. Someone speaks of building a bonfire and cigarette lighters are produced. Humans are a hard lot. The Stick Man is standing in the Garden of Paradise, he announces resolutely; it worked before, more or less, but it doesn't work now. He's in the wrong world. And it's closing in on him. The Stick Man runs like a bat out of hell, he announces, but that doesn't work either. His knees bend slightly. More in dismay probably than in flight.

Just when all seems lost, a Cartoon Man flies in from overhead and the humans fall back. Leave him alone, you racist assholes, the

Cartoon Man shouts, or prepare to die! He looks rather out of place, too, with his bright colored body suit and sketchy features, and he seems anything but threatening, even somewhat undersized, they could probably tear him apart, but they do as they are told. Maybe it's the surprise factor. Or maybe it's the intimidating way the Cartoon Man speaks, as if in capitals and bold type like a billboard. It's okay now, he says to the Stick Man, lowering his booming voice. Let's go throw back a snort.

In the bar, they are drinking and telling each other their life stories. The Cartoon Man is soaking up glass after glass of whiskey, with beer chasers. I can't get enough of this swill, he says, pouring another glassful down his cartoon gullet. Not that it does much for me, he adds with a belch so powerful it makes the bottles tinkle on the shelves behind the bar. I seem to have a hard time getting a buzz on, but when I do, boy, watch out! The Stick Man is not actually having a drink in human terms, because they won't serve him. The Cartoon Man made a loud fuss about this, springing up and down so he could see over the bar, banging his fist on it as he leapt and speaking in huge jagged capitals, but the Stick Man told him not to bother, he prefers having a drink his own Stick Man way. To demonstrate this, he bends one arm at the elbow and holds his stick hand near his tipped "O" of a head, and announces: The Stick Man tastes a glass of wine. He makes a scuffing noise, which might be the sound of him sniffing or that of his knees brushing together. Hmm, he says. Complex bouquet of black currant, green olive, and cedarwood, faintly herbaceous, reminiscent of bell peppers. Promising. He tips his head back; the movement is almost imperceptible. Harmonious flavors, deep and long-lasting, with a noble balance of fruit, alcohol, tannin, and acid. It's a classic from the best vintage of the decade. Beautiful. And it's opening up nicely. I think I'll have another. And he does.

That's pretty good, says the Cartoon Man. Me, I couldn't tell a bell pepper from a stale armpit. We're not very big on taste and smell in the cartoon world. Mostly we're into low comedy and killing people. A lot of people. Fighting evil, man, it's fucking endless. He shakes his cartoon head sadly, his eyes and nose seeming to move about on his face as he does so, and throws down another tumbler of whiskey. The Stick Man thinks about evil. Perhaps for the first time. He realizes it has caused him to bend over slightly as if he has taken up a sack of potatoes. But tell me, Stick Man, what brings you to this shapeless shithole? These humans'll snuff you, you know. You're a fucking insult to their world.

I come to watch them, and when I see them do something interesting, I remember it and take it back to my stick world and do it there. In truth, I can't imagine my own world except in relation to theirs, though of course mine's superior. To walk on water or fall off a building is not the same in my world as it is here. There's so little in my world, there's room for everything, all I have to do is think of it, but theirs is so cluttered and congested, and, well, so obvious. In your face, as they like to say. If you have one, that is.

Yeah, I know what you mean, Stick Man, this bloated meat farm dumps a streamlined heavy action guy like me straight into snore mode. Five minutes and out come the Z's. A bore to the core, show me the door. Don't know why they love it so. Just goddamn stupid, I guess. It's not like where I come from. We got the best of their world in ours, all the sex and violence, tears and laughter, but speeded up with none of the dull sweaty bits. The

Stick Man disagrees with this, the cartoon world just makes the obvious more obvious, painting it, as one might say, in primary colors, but out of politeness does not say so. He tilts his shoulder bar in sympathy, though perhaps a little too far. The Stick Man expresses empathy should perhaps read: The Stick Man expresses inebriation. Shouldn't have had that second one. No tolerance. Delicious, though. Listen, come on back with me to my strip, Stick Man. We'll go on a toot, tear up the fucking frame. I got a set of wheels you won't believe. We'll pick up some hot dames. I know a couple of doozies who'll blow your pants off. Loosely speaking, I mean.

Thanks. But I've been there. I get treated as a handicapped person. Or else I'm just laughed at.

I know, it's that kind of place, they'll laugh at anything, they can't help themselves. But, hey, this time you'll be with me, man. I'm a superhero, they don't mess with me. I catch anyone even smirking, he's a dead man. Or woman. I'm evenhanded on that score. Whaddaya say?

It's very kind. But, well, I have a doozie back in the stick world, and I miss her. Maybe that's what he's expressing in his drunken tilt: the Stick Man remembers his absent lover. The tilt deepens. But you could come with me to the stick world.

Nah. Too square for me. So goddamn flat and colorless. Whaddaya got? A straight line and a few sticks to play with. No wonder you come slumming here. Mix it up with a little push and shove, get your feet in the paint, pick up the tempo for a change. Must be a drag to hang out in all that emptiness for long.

No. Not for stick people. It's exciting, really. It's got everything. For it's always just what we imagine it to be.

Yeah? Listen, tell me, do you really get your rocks off with your little doozie, Stick Man, or do you just imagine that, too?

Well. I guess in my world, it's sort of the same thing.

That's what I thought, says the Cartoon Man, throwing down another tumblerful. I'll stick with what I got. I don't want to have to think it up. I love to get hit by surprises. Even bad ones. Especially bad ones. I love the danger, the speed, the contact, the whole wild toot and scramble. Bif! Boff! He drives his free fist into the bar. I need adversaries!

As if on cue, a group of humans come in, shoulders squared, looking threatening. There he is! The Stick Man! The Cartoon Man tosses his empty glass over the bar, causing an explosive crash that makes the humans stagger back a step, and prepares to defend them both. They'll never take us alive, Stick Man!

No, wait, says one of the humans. We are here on a peaceful diplomatic mission.

Bullshit! Take another step, you treacherous scumbags, and I'll peaceful mission your ass! His head's down and his legs are churning. He seems about to fly forward and head-butt them all. Don't trust those shifty meatsacks, Stick Man! You know what they're like! Let's kill them!

Tell him to calm down, Stick Man. And to stop using such appalling language. We are here to speak about large and serious matters.

And we do quite a lot of killing in the human world, too, Cartoon Man, so you better cool it!

The Stick Man assumes a posture of conciliation, something he learned on previous visits here. We should hear what they have to say, he says, but be prepared. Also something learned. Not sure what it means, but it's effective.

Stick Man, we realize that—excuse me, but am I looking at

your face or—? never mind, I shouldn't have asked—we realize that, as a people, we have not always received you here with the dignity and respect properly due you and, well, your kind. But now, on behalf of the entire human world, or at least that part of it which is empowered to establish committees such as ours, we are calling upon you henceforth to represent officially for us the human condition, as we understand it. We feel somehow you can encapsulate it in economical ways difficult to achieve for those of us with a, what can one say, a more complex personal architecture.

The Stick Man's posture of conciliation shifts slightly to express the humility he feels in the face of such an unexpected honor and, at the same time, the anxiety aroused by its implicit obligations which may include having to remain in the human world, and he knows that he is already, in exhibiting this struggle with ambivalence, exercising his new office.

We have prepared a stage, Stick Man, that captures the essence of your world, which is to say, imitates it exactly, for you have nothing but essence there. We will provide the text each day; you will, so to speak, illustrate it.

I have always made my own announcements, he says, letting his turned-out elbows suggest modesty and apology.

We know that, but that's in the stick world. This is the human world. We do things differently here.

We hope you'll accept our offer, Stick Man.

And anyway you have no alternative. We always get what we want.

You going along with this horseshit? the Cartoon Man asks at his elbow.

It appears I have no choice.

I could kill them all if you want me to. Wham! Ker-splat!

No. I'll do as they ask. It should be fun. He expresses this with a lighthearted disposition of his limbs and tilt of his head, though he recognizes (and probably reveals this to a careful observer) that a certain dissimulating artifice has crept into his demeanor, for he does not feel at all lighthearted, and he wonders if he has caught some baneful human infection. The Stick Woman was probably right. He shouldn't have come here.

Well then, I'm popping back to the strip to get in a few frames of the old down-and-dirty. Pow! Whop! Blam! I can use a workout. But if you need me, pal, just blow your horn.

Wait a minute, says the bartender. Who's paying for all this broken glass?

Do not complain, says the leader of the humans. History has been made in here today. By next week, this will be a famous tourist attraction. You can sell the broken glass as souvenirs. In fact, you'd be doing yourself a favor to smash a few more things.

When the Stick Man takes the oath of office on his little stage, he bends one of his stick arms at the elbow and raises his stick hand. It is the wrong arm, the left one, but no one objects, given the solemnity of the occasion. There are vast multitudes gathered to witness this oath and his premier performance, which can begin only after elaborate ceremonies and a great many lengthy orations of the sort that humans seem to require. Perhaps because their other means of expression are so limited and so occluded by their clumsy fragile integument. Or perhaps because they can never say one thing alone or directly, but must always, as if by nature, flesh out the bare bones of their simple little thoughts. He warms up for his new role by acting out the successive lines of the orations, but he is all too aware of what his posture really expresses: The Stick Man is bored to tears.

Commingled with: the Stick Man is homesick. He hopes that no one perceives this, but that they all assume instead that he is responding dutifully to the text provided by the committee for the occasion: the Stick Man receives with a mixture of pride and humility the adulation of the masses.

They do seem to have warmed to him. The speeches are flattering and enthusiastically applauded, and his every gesture brings on wild cheering. Here you see him in all his suchness, in all his plenitude! declares one speaker, and everyone claps and huzzahs. His more or less rectilinear, geniculate, and symmetrical frame is utterly without habiliment, and yet it cannot be said the Stick Man is standing here before us in the buff, for he has no buff either! Whistles and applause. He has no pelt or epidermis, no casing, sheath, or rind, no fell, fur, leather, fleece, husk, or pericarp! No *flesh!* Cheers and whoops of friendly laughter. Which is why his expression of our existential situation is so vivid! So transparent! He shows us the naked truth! He continues to receive the feverish adulation of the masses. He has nothing extraneous! Not even a face! Just a head that says "O!" A head wide open to all experience! What is his age? He can be—and is—a baby, child, adult, and ancient, all at once, or in any order as he pleases! Most persons are less within than they seem on the surface, the Stick Man is more! Watch him now as he ponders infinity! As he demonstrates that it is better to sit still than to rise and fall! As he counts his blessings! As he decries disorder! As he admires the perfect beauty of the human world!

And so, at the inauguration ceremony and during the weeks that follow, he does these things and to great acclaim, not only from the crowds who gather daily before his stage, but also from the vast television audiences throughout the human world, for his every move and position are captured by the cameras and shown live every hour on the news and each evening on prime time in an edited version. He is, as the humans say, hot. A celebrity. Presidents, kings, and movie stars send their greetings and felicitations, ordinary people their gratitude and suggestions for further aspects of the human condition he might take on, professors critical disquisitions for him to comment upon by word or gesture, human women love letters. Though he would be hard pressed to respond to the latter in the ordinary way, even his ordinary way which is not theirs. The committee members who appointed him to this office were greatly disturbed by his tab, feeling that it marred the purity of his representations, sprouting there on the stick between his legs like an unruly twig, a kind of obscene error of punctuation, as one of them said, and they considered shaving it off, but they were a bit queasy about handling it, so they accepted the idea that it could be taped to the back of his hip bar with black electrical tape, provided the Stick Man kept it taped and out of sight at all times, though they do, being realists, permit him, as an official act, to meditate from time to time upon the mind-body paradox, to the delight, as with all else, of his fans.

The committee is well pleased with his success, and on the whole they treat him kindly and with consideration, but they turn a deaf ear to his expressed wish to return home, if only for a visit, believing that their world is so vastly superior to his, he should be grateful to be allowed to live in it and should desire no other. And so he goes on, though with increasing sorrow in his heart, performing in his Stick Man way the texts that they provide: The Stick Man demonstrates that good service is a great enchantment. The Stick Man recalls the joys of childhood. The

Stick Man bears with equanimity the malice of others, while anticipating always their kindness. The Stick Man laughs at adversity. The Stick Man goes shopping. He takes up positions reflecting grand themes like good and evil, illusion and reality, money (his illustration of the ancient human proverb that a man without money is like a bow without an arrow, is particularly successful), religion, politics, work, and the arts of success, but also lesser elements of the human condition like desire, knowledge, manners, the digestive processes, the fine arts, and so on, as well as certain negative aspects thought to be exemplary: The Stick Man wrestles with his guilty conscience. The Stick Man is embarrassed by his bodily parts. The Stick Man is envious of the success of others. The Stick Man is obsessed by the memory of his mother. The Stick Man is afraid of heights. The Stick Man fails to understand the meaning of the universe. Of course, he's just acting. He is not embarrassed, envious, or afraid, and he does understand the meaning of the universe, at least in Stick Man terms. It's quite simple, but not really relevant to the human world. But he understands why they are asking him to do this. He is not illustrating their condition merely, he is also absorbing it. Sucking it up into his rectilinear and geniculate frame. The Stick Man fully recognizes that the humans hope that his taking on the human condition will free them from it. And he knows that they will be frustrated in their hope.

As happens. After he represents the human condition, it is still theirs, not his, and the crowds begin to drift away, burdened as before. The hourly news dispatches end and The Stick Man Show moves out of prime time into the latenight comedy and extended news hour. There are no more love letters. Many do still come to see him, especially groups on package tours sold during the height of his popularity, but the expressions of excitement and delight which had previously confronted him now give way to ones of disappointment, perplexity, and even revulsion. Which he reads, of course, as self-revulsion and -disappointment, for he is only reminding them of their own condition. The Stick Man contemplates the sadness of the human enterprise: a position he takes up on his own without informing the committee, his posture in effect imitating that of most of his audience, a posture appropriate as well to his stick condition, for he longs only to be back in his stick world again and with his Stick Woman and his tab untaped. He has often imagined her, when making love, in a shape the human world would call voluptuous, but he realizes, far from her, he loves her just as she is, her simple notched frame now dearer to him than anything in this world or any other.

The committee, for its part, works hard to revive interest in him, evidently having considerable personal investment in the success of his office, as created by them. Aware that illustrated texts of edifying moral uplift are failing to attract audiences, they impose upon him the darker aspects of the human condition: The Stick Man suffers from an inferiority complex. The Stick Man tells a lie and is empowered by it. The Stick Man shows the ill effect of trying to live on hope alone. The Stick Man feels like a worm and behaves like one. The Stick Man emits a bad odor. The Stick Man fears death. Now he no longer suffers neglect. He suffers rejection. Hostility. The Stick Man is shunned as the bearer of ill tidings. Those who come to his performances do so only to insult him (Sick Sticks, they call him) and throw things at him. Their enmity worries him less than the possibility that he might be acquiring the fears and complexes that he is asked to represent. If left alone, these ideas might never have occurred to him, and he is afraid that he will contaminate the stick world with them, should he ever be able to return. The Stick Man peers into an open grave, displaying a distasteful morbidity. The Stick Man lusts after a small child. The Stick Man considers poisoning his neighbor's dog. The Stick Man ridicules the human condition. The Stick Man betrays his best friend. He remains a celebrity, but in the way that serial killers are celebrities. There are protests and The Stick Man Show is taken off the air.

Desperate, the committee decides to untape his tab and let it, as they say in their world, all hang out. They run electric billboard advertisements of his forthcoming texts: The Stick Man exposes his private parts, heretofore concealed. The Stick Man admires his backside in the mirror. The Stick Man goes to the bathroom standing up. The Stick Man goes to the bathroom sitting down. The Stick Man wishes someone would lick his tab. He becomes fair game for the human comedians and his ratings rise, but this is not his office as originally defined. The Stick Man laments his unhappy fate: this is the position he would assume were he not obliged to assume so many others, mostly related to his tab. The Stick Man, stroking himself, thinks of his beloved. The Stick Man attempts an act of autofellatio. The Stick Man suffers from castration anxiety. He is a celebrity again, but the committee members themselves are wrangling about ends and means. The Stick Man suggests it might be time for him to return quietly to the stick world. They don't listen. It's as though he's not even there. When he timidly repeats his suggestion, they throw up a new text—the Stick Man scratches his hemorrhoids—and tell him to get to it, while they continue their deliberations.

In the end, though some of the more sober and idealistic

committee members resign in disgust, the decision of those remaining (they speak vaguely of the educational aspect) is to introduce the Stick Woman into the act, and an expedition is mounted to capture her and bring her back to the human world. The Stick Man is both elated and fearful, for the Stick Woman has never been to the human world, nor ever wished to be. Far less restless than he, she has always been happy in the stick world and unhappy whenever he left it. She arrives, chained and manacled, desperately relieved to see him again but terrified by her ordeal (she resisted her captors and now has a second elbow on her right arm), his worst fears realized. The Stick Man tenderly embraces his loved one. As officially announced. She melts into his arms. Also. The crowds have returned. Some of the delight. The cameras. She does not see them. She sees only him. She clings to him. He was not really afraid before, but now, for her, he is. They are encouraged to enjoy each other in the classical manner, and they do, though more in a consolatory fashion than a passionate one, for they are well aware that their trials are not concluded. After the initial surprise of this newest innovation has worn off, they are obliged to perform all the positions known to the human world, which they do, but, by unspoken agreement, they do not reveal those intimacies peculiar to their stick world. The Stick Man Show returns to the networks during the afternoon hours of the soap operas.

Stick person sex is different and has a certain appeal of the sort described by the orator on the day of the Stick Man's inauguration, namely, its naked and exemplary transparency, but in the end it cannot compete in the human world with fleshy sex. Even the simple stroking of human skin—a knee, say, or a fat bottom, a tear-stained cheek—seems to have more appeal to humans than the Stick Man and Stick Woman attempting exotic positions like the wheelbarrow or the triple X, especially given the subdued nature of their performances. The show's ratings, at first promising, drop off again. The committee, what's left of it, feels the act has to be more extreme, there's no other way. Animals are ruled out. There are no available stick animals. Likewise, third or fourth parties. They decide on violence. Rape. Whips. Bondage. Torture. Disfigurement. Hammers and nails.

The Stick Man refuses. His imagination is vast, but hurting the Stick Woman is beyond it. They have reached a point of no return. The committee meets in emergency session. It is clear to them that the show must end. But it is still in their power to decide how it will end and what they can extract from it. They consider the possibility of destroying the Stick Woman, reducing her to a heap of broken sticks, her facial platter shattered as a mirror might be, all of her remains dumped on the stage in front of the Stick Man to see what he will do. Text: The Stick Man throws up. The Stick Man mourns his beloved. The Stick Man goes berserk. But then what would they do with the Stick Man? He'd be useless but still here. He'd probably have to be destroyed, too. So they decide to get rid of them both at the same time. A lovers' tragedy. But it makes for better television if they can create a plot around the killings and delay over a few weeks the final denouement to lure the audiences back. They find the perfect solution: Let the audience kill them.

First, they must begin a rumor campaign against them. They must be utterly reviled. Later, it will be seen that they were only misunderstood, but only after they no longer exist. Then it will be a sad story. Songs will be written and so on. There will edited reruns. For now, by way of letters to the editor, graffiti, anonymous advertisements, phone calls pretending to be from poll takers, dirty jokes, leaked "disclosures," they are decried as deserters, traitors, perverts, racketeers, revolutionary anarchists, scofflaws, thieves, sex fiends, mercenaries, atheists, dangerous aliens. The crowds begin to gather once more. They are increasingly hostile. Weapons appear. Guns and knives are temptingly displayed in shop windows. The gathered multitudes shout out positions the Stick Man and Stick Women are to take, but they have stopped performing and simply cling to one another. It is not clear whether their circle heads are looking out upon the crowd or at each other. Either way, they make a good target. Down on your knees! the mob shouts. Eat shit, Stick Man! Say your prayers! It is happening faster than the committee has expected but it is too dangerous to try to do anything about it. They watch the proceedings from the safety of a television studio. It becomes apparent to them that many in the crowd must have hankered to do this since the day of the Stick Man's inauguration. They have not aroused them so much as released them, a lesson to be learned. Thus, they tell themselves they are not responsible for what happens next.

What happens next, however, could not have been anticipated. The Cartoon Man swoops down, snatches up the Stick Man and Stick Woman, and flies them back to their stick world. They are shot at as they lift away, but without consequence; tragedies only happen in the human world and they are soon out of it. How did you know we were in trouble? I saw it on television. In the cartoon world? We get the same programs. The Stick Man feels like weeping when he sees the stick world again, though he never wept before; something the humans taught him. Many things will be different now. Expressing his gratitude, he remarks that the Cartoon Man has served as a kind of miraculous deus ex machina. I'm not a fucking deus of any kind, man, replies the Cartoon Man. I'm just a superhero. It's what I do. It gives me a surge. They invite the Cartoon Man to stay for supper in the stick world, but the Cartoon Man declines, saying the place makes him itchy. I need a place I can sink my teeth into, as you might say. Let me know, though, the next time you're back in the neighborhood. Not soon, says the Stick Woman, having locked her double-elbowed arm around the Stick Man.

When the Cartoon Man has gone and the Stick Man and Stick Woman are embracing once more, tab to slot, in the old stick world way, the Stick Man sighs and says: A little while ago I decided to imagine the Garden of Paradise. Just to feel like I was home again. And I did, but it was darker than I remembered, and I saw that dangers lurked there, and I was afraid. In the past I have, whenever I wished, imagined fear, but now it's inside me without my imagining it and I know it will never go away. It is the darkness of the human world, says the Stick Woman. We have brought it back with us like a kind of shadow. We never had shadows before. Yes, but I don't think that's what I'm afraid of. I've always known the human world was a sad place where lives are short and meaningless and mostly wasted, and where the fear of death drives humans either to madness or despair unless they find some means of distracting themselves, which, if it's not lethal, is a kind of benign madness. That's what they call the human comedy. In fact, it's their gentle crazed distractions that I have mostly taken pleasure in expressing here in the stick world, and it has often made it beautiful. The humans really only asked me to do what I've been doing all along, though they made me take up many aspects of their lives I had never imagined before. Some of them left me very sore at heart. And the trouble is, now that I have lived in their world, truly lived there, I don't really like it any more. And if I don't like it, how can I find pleasure in imagining it? The darkness I saw in the Garden of Paradise was an omen of an absolute darkness setting in. And when it does, then what? That's what I'm afraid of. The Stick Woman grips his hip bar tenderly, her round head on his shoulder bar. We need another world, she says. Yes. But there is no other.

THE LAST ONE

THIS ONE ASKS at breakfast about the first one. My impertinent bride. Impertinent and imprudent (I tell her so and a gentle blush colors her cheeks and her lashes blink away a dewy mist, though her adoring gaze does not waver). Of course she will go the way of all the others. Perhaps before the day is over. Such a pity. But she is young and beautiful, not yet seventeen, and I indulge her. She was young and beautiful, I say, no older than you, and I indulged her in everything. But she did not respect my wishes.

Are your wishes so terrible then? she asks. There is a hint of a smile on her soft unrouged lips. Is she flirting with me?

Not at all, I say with an answering halfsmile. You will find me a devoted, attentive, and considerate husband, demanding almost nothing of you and desiring only to enrich your young life with all the means at my disposal.

Then I shall have to invent your demands that I might please you, she says, putting down her golden fork and fondly covering my hand with hers, for I am like that, too, and truly love you with all my heart. Her touch seems to find its way directly to my loins as if her sweet hand held me there and I am deliciously aroused, but I am also overswept by a sudden sorrow, for, though I have loved and miss them all, I know I shall miss this one more than any other. Indeed, I am already missing her. I shall begin by learning prudence and discretion, she adds, and her lips seem to draw together as though to form a kiss. She lets go my hand and reaches out to touch my blue beard with her fingertips. You are so beautiful! she sighs.

I know that I am not, I reply with a melancholic smile, recalling her ingenuous endearments of the night before, but I love your innocent love and wish that it might last forever.

And so it shall, she says. Why should it not? I am here to serve you in all ways that you might wish until death do us part, exactly as I promised and as is my one desire.

Alas, that's just short of forever, my dear, but I understand your loving intent. So now, to serve me well, please state your other, more intimate desires, that I might have the pleasure of fulfilling them. My entire wealth is at your disposal.

Oh, as your wife, of course, I can and do demand nothing, for that would be an impertinence worse than any other.

You have not a single favor to ask?

No. Well… No…

Please. Name it. It's yours.

I hope it's not impertinent, too. She lowers her head, peering modestly down into her lap where one hand now enfolds the other. As she does so, she exposes her alluring young nape with its delicate spinal knuckles and skin like silk. It is unutterably precious to me and begs a kiss, not of my ruthless blade (which regretfully I must sharpen before I leave), but of my worshipful lips, and it receives one. But... well... the nursery...

Yes? Inwardly, I am delighted—and flattered—that the thoughts of this playful and sensuous child have been so quickly drawn to aspirations of such maturity, however unlikely it is they can ever be realized. You wish it to be redecorated perhaps? A more cheerful color, a bit more light—?

No, no, it's lovely! It's only... well... She lifts her head to gaze wistfully up at me, and her soft bosom into which I am peering heaves with a tremulous sigh, and I think: Though I shall leave her today and test her as I always do—and must—we shall perhaps first taste the fruits of love once more... It's just that I sometimes feel so lost and inadequate in this grand world of yours, I need a quiet little place all my own to which I might retire to gather my poor childish wits about me and recover my composure. A place where I can be just by myself to reflect upon my love for you and upon ways that I might better please you. The nursery next to our bed chamber is as yet unoccupied—and here she blushes becomingly, and casts her eyes down once again, then timorously looks back up at me—and I feel at home in it, perhaps because I've not been long away from one. Might it just be mine, until... until we... you know,..?

This is not the request that I have anticipated, but it befits her modesty and I recall that when she first arrived she brought with her all her childhood toys— as familiar company for her in this strange place, as she said, begging my pardon for her inability as yet to leave her past behind entirely. I've only brought the little things, she said. Granted, I say now, roguishly arching my brow and taking her hands to draw her up from her chair, provided I might now occupy for a short time that lovely place where I have so come to feel at home.

It is yours to possess without provision, she responds with a shy but welcoming smile.

She is of course vastly disappointed and not a little alarmed when later, clasped still in her arms, I inform her that I must undertake a sudden journey and leave her here to tend the castle while I am gone. We dress and I show her through those parts she has not yet visited, keeping my instructions to a minimum, assuring her that the staff is well-trained and accustomed to my frequent absences, providing her with keys to all my strongboxes and personal wealth and all the castle's rooms, including the blue room with the blue door, which I tell her, as I have told them all, she is not on any condition to enter. I add that she is not even to put the key in the lock, for if she does so she might expect the most dreadful of punishments, but though I tell her this with my sword at the whetstone, she seems hardly to be listening, fascinated instead by a pair of songbirds in a gilded cage. When they stroke each other with their bills, she laughs and claps her hands and says: I'm not afraid! I know you will come back to me! Of course I will, I say. You can count on it. And which one of these unlocks the nursery door? she asks.

My invented travels take me, as they always do, to a small inn on a lake nearby, known for the quality of its food and wine, and for its privacy and discretion. I order a platter of succulent plump partridges with wild mushrooms, braised onions, and roasted aubergines and peppers, together with an opulent red wine, perfectly aged, from the north, but I find my appetite has failed me. I have known brief moments of the most intense pleasure and beauty, but my life has not on the whole been a happy one, and on this day I am as unhappy as I have ever been. I am utterly smitten by this pretty child, and I do not want to lose her, although no doubt I shall. I will return and find the bloodstained key and she will lose her head, as have the countless others, and I will lose a wife I dearly love, as I have loved them all. I am reminded in particular on this gray day of a lovely auburn-haired bride, a few years older than the present one, wilier perhaps, and wittier, yet delightfully fresh and childlike in her ways, who tried to stay my hand with story. Her tale, as she knelt there at the chopping block, was of a room with many doors, the rooms beyond them inhabited more by ghostly concepts than by persons and enmazed into a pretty riddle, whose solution, I supposed (we never got that far), was wisdom, or what passes for it in tales like these. Just for a moment I was enthralled and paused, her conjured room or rooms more real to me than my own, and had she not smiled to see me so and so unmasked my passing weakness, she might still wear her comely head. Alas. And it is not obedience I seek, but mere respect. I am a reasonable man, generous to a fault, demanding only this one small thing: that there be no intrusions upon my private quarters. Which, once upon a time, was what the blue room was for me, though now I dread to enter it myself, such a reeking charnel house it has become. So what am I defending? A principle, I suppose, as dead as the heap of headless corpses it has produced and now contains. And yet I can do no other. It is who I am, it is the bleak lot cast for me and for those I love; to do otherwise than as I must would be an act of the most abject cowardice and self-betrayal. I know that (I accept a truffled chocolate from a proffered tray, my appetite somewhat, if only faintly, revived by my recovered resolution).

But oh how I long for a wife I might keep with her head on for more than a day or two! I think that I deserve as much.

I return by surprise and am surprised. My bride emerges from the nursery with tears of happiness in her eyes to see me, the blue room has not been entered, the golden key is immaculate, she has not even remembered that I asked her not to go there. She chatters on about her day, the games she's played and how she's missed me, and we enjoy another night together more delightful than the night before, if that is possible. Perhaps at last! I think, and fall asleep with my loved one securely in my arms, her sweet breath (she is alive! alive!) upon my breast.

I am tempted on the morrow to let the matter of the blue room rest. Has she not already proven that she is different from all the others? No, not yet, for she would not be the first to pass the first day's test, only to fall upon the second, and I know that I must do as I have always done. To honor the dead, if for no other reason. So once again I announce my abrupt departure, once again we walk the premises, opening and closing doors, visiting all the treasures of the castle, and once again I show her the key to the blue room and admonish her never to go there. Be not too curious, I say, and she replies, with barely a glance at the forbidden door, Do you know that, when you are being stern, a tiny furrow appears between your brows, exactly like the one that appears there when we are making love? And she pulls my head down with both her hands and kisses it. I love you so! she sighs.

My appetite this second day is much improved, and at the inn I order a handsome fish plucked fresh from the lake, beheaded, gutted, stuffed, and baked, with saffron rice on the side and tender wild asparagus. I am feeling elated. I am convinced I have found a love at last that I may keep. I sip the rich straw-colored wine that I have chosen, served precisely at the temperature of the lake itself, and allow myself to contemplate a future quite unlike my ensanguined past. I often use these mock journeys to seek out and woo a possible future bride, knowing that I must soon lose the one I have, but on this day my thoughts are wholly upon the castle I have left behind and the beautiful and obedient child who awaits me there, more mine than I am mine. Today I have even forgotten, I realize with a pained smile, to hone my monstrous blade. Well, perhaps it will join the mounted antlers, portraits, historic tapestries, and the other useless relics upon the walls. I replay the events of the day before, satisfied that she has satisfied me in all particulars. Excepting perhaps that when she returned the keys the one to the nursery was not among them. But, then, I told her the room was solely hers, did I not, she committed no infraction, broke no command, and I feel certain she will not again today, and so order up a bowl of tiny wild strawberries in a delicate liqueur, brushed with mint, to complete in festive manner my lakeside repast.

I am right. My surprise return does not even wholly surprise her. The blue room has not been invaded, the key's unstained. My bride has spent the day in the nursery, playing with her toys, she explains when she emerges from the room and locks it, and then she throws her arms around me and hugs me with such warm passion, my whole body feels like love's erected organ. Don't go away again! she whispers. Stay here with me always! We spend the rest of the dying day in bed and servants later bring us cheese and wine and fresh fruit, peeled and quartered. She tells me about the serving girl she had to scold for failing to remove the night-cloth from the songbirds' cage (You see, I can be useful to you when you're gone, she exclaims with a teasing smile and plucks a fishbone from my beard) and I provide her a fictitious account of my luncheon visit to a neighboring castellan to discuss proposed changes in the game laws. He is widowed yet again, I say, and is looking for a new young bride, both virtuous and beautiful. I told him to resign himself to cease his search. There was only one such left in the whole world and she is mine.

That night my dreams are free for once of severed heads, fountaining blood, eyes popping with terror from their sockets, and I am returned instead to the happier days of my all-but-forgotten childhood. My dream companion, though also a mere infant, is not unlike my present wife and we play games alone in some wild place that end in shy caresses. I awake in a state of profound joy and gratitude, as though some terrible burden has been lifted, receiving in reality the tender caresses of which I have been dreaming. But then later, after breakfast, when my bride has withdrawn to dress herself for the out of doors (It's a beautiful day! Let's walk the castle grounds! she exclaimed happily, and how could I refuse her, recalling, as I was, a certain sunny wild-flowered meadow where we might at midday lie?), my waking joy fades to despair, for I know that I must test her one more time, a third time, I can do no other, and I fear this day will be the one to break my heart.

Of course she is tearfully disappointed and clings to me, pleading with me not to go, and for a moment my resolution wavers—why must I torture myself this way?—but in the end I do, as I always do, what I must do. I explain: an urgent message, a friend in need, I must leave immediately and am not sure when I might return. We tour the castle and its wealth as before, I warn her about the blue room, I give her the keys. She accepts them without so much as a glance, throws herself into my arms, then tears herself away and runs weeping into the nursery. What have I done? I am weeping, too, unable to stay, unable to leave, wringing my hands, pulling at my beard, pacing the castle corridors. No, I shall not go! And yet I must! I do remember this time to sharpen my sword, not because I wish to use it—oh no, please no!—but because, if I must use it, I wish it to be mercifully swift in its barbarous labors. And perhaps because it gives me something more to do, to delay a departure I am so loathe to make. As the whetstone sings its shrieking song, I think: Of course I must go, this trial is not over and must as always be concluded, but need it be today? Another message might arrive: Stay, my friend. Come tomorrow if you can. Why not? Even should she fail me this third time, we would at least have this last day and night together.

I sheathe my sword and hurry to the nursery to tell her so. It is locked. I lift my hand to knock but am stopped by the sound of voices within, her voice at least. Are you lonely? she is asking. Are you in need of company? Probably she is talking to herself in the mirror. Or to her toys. Yet I am troubled by it, and quietly withdraw. I go outside to peer in through the window, but the drapes are drawn. Now, why would she do that on such a lovely day as this? I ask myself, feeling my suspicions rise, and then as quickly ask: And what am I doing prowling around here outside her window like a common thief, a lowly peeper? I reject my behavior as improper and ungallant—as for the darkened room, she is mourning my departure, after all—and I decide to continue on my way as first announced. It is time to bring this sorry business to an end.

Before I reach the inn, however, I turn back. Was hers the only voice I heard? Almost certainly, and yet... I approach the castle from a stand of trees and watch awhile from there. What do I expect to see? I do not know, though disturbing thoughts race through my head and my perspiring hand is on my sword. Of course, nothing happens. Why should it? I begin to feel a fool, all the more so for having passed up that innocent frolic on the meadow, in exchange for such base misery as this, unworthy of my age and of my station. I decide to return immediately: My friend is well, his problem solved, a messenger met me on the way.

My bride greets me as before, throwing herself tearfully into my arms with abject delight as if I've been absent for many days. I try to peek past her shoulder into the nursery, but the door is closed. Locked, no doubt. She strips my shirt away to nuzzle my bare chest as she is wont to do when making love, then tugs me toward our bed chamber, whispering her maidenly endearments. I long for the pleasure that she offers, but am too agitated to perform my part or even to think of doing so. I suggest instead the stroll through the castle grounds we had originally planned and gaily—Oh yes! she cries—she hurries off to the kitchen to arrange a basket lunch. The nursery door is indeed locked, I discover, and I recall now that she has left my side from time to time at night to visit there. A restless sleeper lonely for her lost past? Or...? I put my ear to the door. Nothing. Of course, nothing. What's the matter with me? Standing there, leaning against the locked nursery door with my shirttails dangling like drooping pennants, I suddenly feel desperately old and world-weary, and I know that our walk will not revive my spirits.

It does not. The meadow is there, just as I have remembered it, with its downy bed of soft grasses and silken petals, and naked upon it in the sunlight under the blue breezeless sky, my young bride is a most voluptuous sight, but I am as unaroused as before,

and turn quite irritable when she tries to be of help to me. Where
has she learned such things? I do not ask her that of course, but
complain instead that I feel unwell and fear I may have caught a
fever. She could not be more solicitous, insisting that we return
to the castle immediately where I shall spend the rest of the day
in bed, and she will care for me, and bring me tea and read to me
and with her own gentle hands rub all the aches away, but that
too, inexplicably, causes my choler to rise and I must bite my
beard to refrain from bellowing something at her I would afterwards regret.

Only much later, after she has left me, presumably sleeping
peacefully following her wifely ministrations, to return to her
precious nursery, do I realize I have forgotten to check the blue
room key (I do: no stains), that's not the point any longer.
Stealthily, I creep once more to that door between us and press
my ear against it: She is singing to herself in there, or humming,
a kind of marching tune—Step lively now! she says—and now
and then a happy little laugh escapes her, a girlish giggle. That
she can enjoy such carefree play all by herself, if she is by herself,
when I am ill, or presumably ill—I might be dying for all she
knows—also stirs my fury and resentment, and to calm myself (I
fully intend now to visit the nursery, with or without her invitation, and regardless of any promises to the contrary, but only
when in full control of my emotions, now in such turmoil) I take
the keys and pace the castle corridors in my nightshirt, counting
by candlelight, it would seem to anyone who saw me, my possessions, one madness thus (my possessions are uncountable) con-
cealing another.

At some point in my midnight wanderings, I find myself in
front of the infamous blue door, the room beyond it once the very

locus of my honor and my integrity, and I wonder at the life that I have made. A man of my wealth and power has certain obligations, of course, but I never meant to be cruel, my intentions always noble and instructive, no matter how my actions may appear. I enter it (the nursery key is missing) but am immediately driven out by the stench within: there are rotting heads and bodies and mutilated limbs everywhere and the floor is covered with clotted blood, the horrid proofs of my severe and lonely existence. I have lived, without remorse, a principled life, and I must be resolutely who I am, else I am no one at all—and yet... Well... Such a sickening mess here at the center! Even I am excluded from what might be called the very heart of my own being!

This encounter with the ghastly carnage of my past has a sobering and calmative effect, and I return much subdued to our room wherein my bride lies sleeping now, determined that on the morrow I shall seal that fatal chamber up forever and throw away the key, not so much for her sake, or any who might follow, as for my own. My beloved sleeps there peacefully upon her back, herself toylike in her pretty stillness, the faintest traces of a smile upon her lips, as though her dreams were sweet and pleasing her. That I somewhat shape those dreams I know and know that I must treat her always with tolerance and loving kindness, and beware my volcanic temper. I have heard her, alone, secluded, give vent to the loneliness she suffers in my absence and as well to her more playful whims, which in my preceptive solemnity beyond the nursery I have perhaps unwittingly suppressed, and maybe she meant for me to overhear these things that I might learn to remain always by her side and to join her games, however lightsome, with an open and willing heart. To do so is anyway now my firm resolve, and I slip into the bed beside her full of affection and tenderness and easefully enter her and, at peace with myself at last, fall asleep in our locked embrace.

I wake at dawn to an empty bed and think I hear her in the nursery again. I smile sleepily, imagining her there in all her loveliness, surrounded by her little things, and I close my eyes again and think: Let her be. But even as this thought drifts benignly through my mind, I find myself at the door once more, my ear pressed against it, my hand testing the handle. Did I hear a sound within? No, it's someone coming down the corridor! I leap back into bed and pull the covers up just as she enters cheerfully with a breakfast tray. Good morning, my sweet love! I've brought you all your favorite things! I want to make you well again!

I'm much improved, I say, and I rub my eyes and scratch my beard, which I know amuses her. Your kisses have quite revived me, though I think I may require yet another dosage or two.

I am not well trained in the healing arts, she replies with a twinkling smile, setting the breakfast tray aside and crawling in beside me, but you will find me a quick and eager pupil.

I decide to pass the day in bed, close to the nursery door, and I ask my chamberlain to bring me my accounts that I might go over them there, suggesting to my bride that she is free to do as she pleases while I am working. I assume that she will return to the nursery, but she chooses instead to acquaint herself more thoroughly with the running of the castle that she might, as she says, better serve it as its new mistress. Sometimes I hear noises in there, or think I do, and I hurry over to hear what I can hear, but these excursions are often as not interrupted by her sudden arrival from the hallway, and I must make clumsy excuses about a fallen pen or a troublesome insect or a cramp in my leg: Oh let me squeeze the hurt away! she exclaims, and I must feign an appetite, quite vanished suddenly, for her amorous attentions.

Finally there is nothing for it but to arrange her longer absence somehow that I might, leisurely and unobserved, examine her retreat. And so my illness worsens. She must take the carriage and go visit the doctor, some miles hence, and deliver to him the sealed letter which I place into her hands, then bring back to me the potion I request therein. She protests, she cannot bear to leave me alone in my suffering, let a manservant go, she will stay and care for me. Servants are a meddlesome and unreliable lot, I say. A sealed letter is like an open invitation. I trust only you.

She kisses me passionately, almost tearfully. Don't even move till I return! she cries and, hastily tossing a silken shawl over her shoulders for the journey, she dashes away.

I watch the gilded carriage careen at full gallop out of the yard, then try the nursery door. It is locked, as I have supposed, and its key is missing from the ring, also as I have supposed. What surprises me is that my old master key does not work either. I have a drawerful of ancient keys and think to try them, though it means another visit to the stomach-turning horrors of the blue room. They are equally useless, that hellish errand in vain, and I heave the lot across the room, my frustration mounting. Outside, the window is also locked, or stuck. What's worse, there are fresh boot tracks out there, both coming and going, and my mind is suddenly awhirl with the most abominable imaginings. Of course I myself was standing there only yesterday, those tracks are no doubt mine: I try to calm myself. I drop the brick I might in my madness have heaved through the window, without regard for the stories I would have had to invent thereafter, and I return to my bed chamber, now truly ill.

I prepare to *retire* once more, perhaps this time with a glass
of wine, something noble, complex, engaging, that I might free
my thoughts from the intolerable virulence that has invaded
them, but just as I am about to ring for a servant, I hear whispering inside the nursery. A man! Or men! My worst fears are justified! I try to force the door without success, my fever raging
now, but it will not give way. I rush out to get my sword and as
I'm hurriedly sharpening its blade, I hear the carriage returning
to the yard. There is no time to lose! I am back at the nursery
door, hacking wildly at it, when I hear her enter the castle,
breathlessly calling out my name: I am here, dear love! I have
returned! And, as I break through at last, she appears behind me.
Oh my, she says. Whatever are you doing?

Inside the room, her toys are neatly spread about: a miniature
roofless castle, richly appointed, set upon parklike grounds made
of a green blanket and pebbles from the garden for the drives on
which tiny horsedrawn carriages are placed, a mirror for a pond,
twisted yarn for trees and shrubs, porcelain figurines standing as
statues on wooden blocks, and pillows heaped about to represent
the surrounding hills. The rooms inside the toy castle are ele-
gantly carpeted and hung with tapestries and damask, the chairs
and sofas are covered with silks and velvet and fringed with gold,
the tiny carved dining table set with branched candlesticks and
a golden dinner service, and full-length looking-glasses with
gilded frames have been mounted in the corridors and private
chambers. In one of the these there is a small sign which reads:
THE REWARD OF DISOBEDIENCE AND IMPRUDENT CURIOSITY, and
the dolls that populate it, all little bearded men, are alive, even
the ones whose heads have been taken off and mounted on the
walls. Do you like them, my little toys? my bride asks from

behind my shoulder. She is smiling tenderly but somewhat wistfully down upon me, and I am touched for a moment by the mystery of her and of all the brides before her. You promised, she says
without reproach, though not without a trace of regret, and I feel
the withering power of her affectionate disappointment. You
were so lovely, she sighs. I so much wished you might at last be
the one that I could keep. And she picks me up by my head and
sets me inside the castle with the others.

AESOP'S FOREST

1

DEEP IN THE GLOOM of the forest, the old lion lies dying in his cave. His ancient hide drapes the royal bones like a worn blanket, rheum clots his warm nose, his eyes are dimmed with cataracts. Yet, even in such decline, the familiar hungers stir in him still, rippling in tremors across his body from time to time like mice scurrying under a tattered carpet, his appetite for power outlasting his power to move, his need for raw flesh biting deeper than his decaying teeth. "I would be king!" he rumbles wheezily, his roar muddied with catarrh.

"Eh? Eh?" asks the fox insolently from the mouth of the cave.

"Damn your eyes. Bring me meat."

He does not trust the fox, of course, but on the other hand he has never trusted anyone, and the fox at least is useful. It is a wise policy, he knows, to keep potential enemies where you can either watch them or eat them. Unfortunately, that now means keeping them pretty close (even now, though the mouth of the cave seems empty of his scrawny silhouette, he cannot be sure the devil's gone) and so, fearing seditious alliances just beyond the reach of his shriveling senses, he has reduced his court to one, this fox, whose very notoriety for wiliness has isolated the wretch from any serious contenders for his power. The fox, a likely victim of any new regime, serves him because it is in the fox's own best interest to do so, though such bitter truths—and his helpless reliance on them—sadden the old lion. He has roared against them all his life, knowing that some truths are just not worth having, and now they have returned to haunt him, as though the instinct for survival were itself the ultimate disgrace. A sigh rips through him like the windy echo of some half-remembered rage: his hatred of duplicity.

There was a time when such treacherous lickspits, leading him to trapped prey, would have served him as prior savories: dispassionately he would have slit their bellies with his fierce claws, nuzzled in the hot wound as though to caress them with their own culpability, and, staring resolutely into their craven eyes already glazing over, his cool majestic gaze the last thing on this earth their fading sight would see, would have eaten their still-pulsing hearts, just appetizers for the feast to follow, juicy morals for the hunchback's fables. He who plots against another, the fabler would say then, plots his own destruction, and if this was a truth the world felt it could depend upon, it was a truth founded upon his own powerful claws and sharp white teeth, his incorruptible detachment. It is this—his sovereign independence, his lonely freedom—that he now misses most. As must all. For if he was once the source of all their truths, now, crippled, sinking into

dry rot, reduced to begging from a thieving liar, he still is: it is
truth itself that is changing. Yes, yes, he thinks, we take *every-thing* with us when we go.

"Who, *what—?!*" Ah. That dumb stag. Vainglory in the
flesh. The more or less succulent flesh. The old king, tired eyes
asquint, lies low, settling his jowls behind his paws. He's seen
this one before, smelled him before. That funk: the poor fool
must still have his stripes, and yet here he is, serving himself up
again, will wonders never cease. "I tell you, when he caught hold
of your ear last time," he hears the fox whispering, nudging the
stag forward, "it was to give you his last advice before he died."
Such big eyes he has: eyes for looking where forbidden… "It is
you he wants as our next king: your horns scare the snakes, he
told me so!" Inwardly, waiting patiently, the old lion grins. Have
to admire the sly bastard: in his way, he's an artist. "You see? He's
smiling! He's pleased you're here! Now lean forward and tell him
that you accept your great responsibilities!"

2

Death is everywhere in Aesop's dark forest. Asses are drowning
under sodden loads, vixens are being torn to pieces by maddened
dogs, swans sacrificed for the sake of their songs. Cats are eating
cocks. Kites frogs. "What an unexpected treat has come our
way!" they cry, descending. All have butcher's work to do. Eagles
and vixens devour each other's young, newborn apes are mur-
dered by their mothers, hens by serpents they themselves have
hatched. Partridges, goats, doves betray their own to preying
men, nannies are butchered to doctor asses. At the request of
horses, boars are slaughtered: yet happiness is elusive. Snakes are
driven to suicide by the stinging of wasps, elephants by gnats in

their ears, hares by their own weariness, as though it were time's way of solving difficult problems. "The moral is that it is too late to be sorry after you have let things go wrong," the fabler explains, but the fact is it is always too late. Lambs are being devoured by wolves, mice by weasels, fawns by bears, nightingales by hawks, and all by the patient intransigent vultures. Even lions. The news of the old despot's decline, spread by the fox, stirs ambition in some (a lot of emptyheaded people rejoice over the wrong things, needless to say), but provokes skepticism in most: with that fox things are not always what they seem, most here in the forest know that all too well, having learned from painful experience, once bitten and all that, no, seeing is believing. Not too close, though: there are a lot of bones around the cave mouth, and tracks leading up but none leading away.

3

The fabler watches the watchers watch. It is comforting to the wretched, he knows, to see others worse off than themselves. The victor vanquished, the mighty fallen—it's a kind of narcotic, this pageant, numbing for the cowardly their common wound of mortality. The fabler envies them this easy consolation. In him, something more fundamental is dying with the dying lion, and just when he needs it most, his own death approaching inexorably and apace. Not so much the courage, no, for though his is not so lofty perhaps, being that bitter grit of the misfit, the freak, the taunted cripple, it is no less mettlesome. Not the fabled power either, far from it, he has often reveled in forcing humiliating compromise upon the old tyrant, throwing him into bad company, jamming thorns in his paws and enfeebling love in his heart, snatching him up in nets and cages to spoil his appetite

with a moral lesson or two, chiding him with avarice and bru-
tality. Sour grapes? Perhaps, especially now at life's and wit's end
when he could use a little last-minute clout, but political power
as such has never held the fabler's fancy. Hasn't he turned his
crooked back on it all his life, abandoning the court life again and
again for his dark uncivil forest? Yes, freedom has been his one
desire, freedom and—and this is what the old lion's death means
to him, this is what he fears to lose, even as he's losing it—his
ruthless solitude.

As though to dramatize his sense of loss, the fox, that cart-
load of mischief, emerges from the cavemouth now, swaggering
presumptuously, his red tail on high, a bloody heart between his
jaws. Not the lion's heart, of course—a consumptive rumble from
the cave behind the charlatan attests irritably to that—yet it
might as well be. That lion's kingly roar once caused havoc at
three hundred miles, women miscarried, men's teeth fell out;
now it flutters thinly from the cavemouth like wisps of dirty
fleece. In the end, crushed by fortune, even the strongest become
the playthings of cowards: this is the message of the dripping
heart in the fox's grinning jaws. And it enrages him. Not the
message, but the grin. It is his, the fabler's, own.

4

There is a grisly tension building in the forest, he can feel it as
he stalks the cave mouth, the stag's heart in his jowls like a gag,
bitter foretaste of the impending disaster. Well, foretasted, fore-
armed, he reminds himself with a giddiness that brings a grimace
to his clamped jaws—for how *does* one arm himself against the
sort of nightmare about to descend here? Eyes blink and glitter
behind tree trunks, clumps of grass, leaves, heavy stones: in them

he sees avarice, panic, vanity, distrust, lust for glory and for flesh, hatred, hope, all the fabled terrors and appetites of the mortal condition, drawn together here now for one last demented frolic. The louring forest is literally atwinkle with that madness that attends despair.

Two eyes in particular absorb his gaze: the dark squinty lop-sided orbs of the little brown humpback, come to hurl himself like a clown into the final horror—for isn't it the cripple who always wants to lead off the dance? The grotesque grotesqued. That loathsome monstrosity now huddles swarthily behind a pale boulder, hugging it as if afraid it might fly away from him, his knee-knobs stuck out like a locust's. A turnip with teeth, he's been fairly called, a misshapen pisspot. His hump rises behind his flapping ears like a second head, but one stripped of its sens-es as though struck mute and blind with terror. Or wisdom, same thing. What that snubnosed bandylegged piece of human garbage has never appreciated is how much they're two of a kind, and how much the fraud owes him for his bloated reputation. The fox has been the butt of too many horseshit anecdotes not to have grasped a moral the fabler seems to have missed: that we ridicule in others what we most despise in ourselves.

The humpback lets go the boulder now and hops, toadlike, behind a stunted laurel. Headed this way, it seems. Can't leave well enough alone. Or ill enough. Perhaps he dreams still of some last-minute escape from the calamity that awaits him, awaits them all in this airless stinkhole of a so-called forest. Well, if he hopes for help from the sorehead behind him, still grumbling in his tubercular senility about the missing heart ("You can stop looking, he didn't have one," he'd told the motheaten old geezer, talking with his mouth full, "anybody who'd come twice into a lion's den and within reach of his paws has to be ninety percent asshole, and that's what you just ate..."), then the fool's in for a bitter experience.

5

As the fabler advances through the penumbral forest, creeping, bounding, stumbling over roots, crouching under bushes, zigging and zagging in the general direction of the lion's den, he stirs a wide commotion. There are scurryings, flutterings, rustlings all around. Twigs pop, pebbles scatter, leaves and feathers float on the air like the tatters of muffled rumors, stifled panic, as though the forest were beset on all sides—and from within as well—by strange and unexpected dangers. Wild rumors. Hopes. Mad ambitions.

Much of this the fabler reads in all the shit he squats and tumbles in: the hard nuggets of avidity and pride, puddled funk, noisome pretense, the frantic scatter of droppings unloosed on the run in uncertainty and confusion—that eloquent text of the forest floor. He knows it well, he's had his nose in it since the day he was born. "Has he lost something?" people would ask. "He's like a hog rooting in mud." He was pretending to be studying the ground, of course, in order to pretend he could straighten up if he wanted to, an impostor twice over. But out of adversity, wisdom. Once a famous Hellenic philosopher, his master in the dark days of his enslaved youth, had asked him why it was, when we shat, we so often turned around to examine our own turds, and he'd told that great sage the story of the king's loose-living son who one day, purging his belly, passed his own wits, inducing a like fear in all men since. "But you don't have to worry, sire," he'd added, "you've no wit to shit." Well, cost him a beating, but it was worth it, even if it was all a lie. For the real reason we look back of course is to gaze for a moment in awe and wonder at what we've made—it's the closest we ever come to being at one with the gods.

Now what he reads in this analecta of turds is rampant disharmony and anxiety: it's almost suffocating. Boundaries are breaking down: eagles are shitting with serpents, monkeys with dolphins, kites with horses, fleas with crayfish, it's as though there were some mad violent effort here to link the unlinkable, cross impossible abysses. And there's some dejecta he's not sure he even recognizes. That foul mound could be the movement of a hippogriff, for example, this slime that of a basilisk or a harpy. His own bowels, convulsed by all this ripe disorder, fill suddenly with a plunging weight, as though heart, hump, and all might have just descended there: he squats hastily, breeches down (well, Zeus sent Modesty in through the asshole, so may she exit there as well), to leave his own urgent message on the forest floor. Ah! yes! a man must put his hand to his wealth and use it, example is—grunt!—better than precept. Just so... But quality, not quantity. Inconsistency is harmful in everything, though no fore-thought, of course, can prevail against destiny. Oof! Easy. Accomplishments are not judged by speed but by completeness. With what measure you mete shall it be measured to you again, and so on. That's better. He wipes himself with his soiled breeches, leaves them behind. Doesn't need them here anyway. When in Delphi, as they say...

6

Not all here in Aesop's troubled forest are pleased, of course, to have their miserable excrement read so explicitly. It makes many

of them feel vulnerable and exposed, especially at a time when all
the comforting old covenants are dissolving, and no one knows
for certain who they are anymore, or who they're supposed to
fuck or eat. Can one not even take a homely shit without worry-
ing about the consequences, they ask, are there no limits? But of
course that's just the point, there *are* no limits any longer, that's
the message of the old king's desperate condition, this pointy-
headed freak's intrusion here, his frantic bare-ass bob through
these dark brambly thickets at the core. Though he talks wolfy
enough at times, he rarely comes this deep, skirting the edges
mostly where the shepherds keep their sheep, plummeting in
here only when lust or terror overtakes him. What beast here
wouldn't raise its tail for the hunchback, painful as the experience can be, if that's all it would take to resume the old peaceful
carnage? But, alas, it's plain to see it's not rut that's brought the
fabler back—that heavy wattle he's dragging through the pine
needles and dead leaves between his crooked shanks is, by itself
in its gross wilt, cause enough for panic here.

So it is that birds screech, beetles scurry, moles burrow in
blind desperation, as Aesop makes his way toward the lion's den.
Stupidity, fear, deceit, carnality, treason break out in the forest
like scabies. There is the sharpening of tusks, the popping of
toads, breath-sucking, the casting of long shadows. Suicidal hares
and frogs hurl themselves out of their element, elephants eat
their own testicles, worms blind themselves so as not to see the
approaching catastrophe. As Aesop reaches the cave mouth, the
fox slinks aside, lips curled back, baring his teeth above the stag's
heart cradled bloodily in his paws. He snarls. Clouds of fleas,
gnats, lice, mosquitos explode from foul-smelling holes in the
forest floor like a sudden pestilence. Wells clog with bewildered

beasts fallen they know not where. Storms rumble and winds
whistle. Flames lap at an eagle's nest. And from high in the sky,
a frightened humpbacked tortoise falls.

7

The fox lies stretched out across the cave mouth, as though to
define certain boundaries, or invent them, gnawing, ears perked,
at the stag's heart. Inside, the fabler squats in the dirt, his hump
resting against the cavewall, gazing morosely at the dying lion, a
much sorrier sight than he'd anticipated. "It stinks in here," he
says. The lion snorts sourly, cocks one rheumy eye above his paw.
"Nothing's so perfect," he grumbles, "that it's not subject to
some pisant's criticism." In the old days he'd have simply stepped
on him, popped the runt like a blister. Now he's not even sure he
sees him. "Misfortune stinks, crookback. Dying stinks. If you
don't like it, why do you wallow in it?"

"That's not why I'm here." He stares out past the fox at the
dusky forest, which seems to have brightened slightly, as seen
from within this dreary cave. An illusion, like hope itself. It's
darkening by the second out there. "How is it you've taken up
with this miserable blot on creation?"

"Expediency."

"I expected more from you."

"Our expectations are often deceived."

He accepts this continuous mockery though it pains him.
Somewhere just below the hump, in fact. What is he doing here
in this shithole, taking this kind of abuse? And from an old
friend once honored above all others—even his shabby new
alliance with the fox is a kind of taunt, a way of rubbing the
fabler's nose in his most craven cynicism, just when he needed

something nobler than that. Courage, in a word. Proud example. "I've been condemned."

The fox seems to snicker at this. The lion too would appear to have a grin on his face. The floor of the cave is rough and damp, reassuring in its rude discomfort, but somewhere water is dripping, echoing cavernously as though there might be a leak in the remote recesses of his own skull. He shudders as if to shake himself out of here, but he knows he can never leave again. They'll have to come and kill him in this place. Mangy and decrepit as it's become. Sometimes in the past he has managed to stay away from his forest for days on end, imagining himself a man like any other, yet even then these creatures had a way of haunting his consciousness, lingering just beneath it like stars behind the light of the sun, visible only from the bottom of a well. That well he's always dumping them down as a cushion against his own clumsiness. His own attraction to abysses. "Which flap," the lion rumbles wheezily, "were you wagging this time?"

He shrugs his hump. "Sin against Apollo." This time the fox does snicker, standing to scratch a flea behind his ear, or pretending to. "Go have a fit and tumble in a hole," the vicious schemer once said, all too prophetically. His fate now, by decree, he the fabler become his own goat. "I told them the truth, they called it sacrilege."

"Same old story," sighs the lion.

"Same old story."

"Natures never change. You're a meddlesome foul-mouthed stiff-necked exhibitionist. You remind me of that story of yours about the wild ass and the tame ass."

"Well, but the real moral of that one was—"

"The real moral was they were *both* asses, just the same. What did you think you'd gain by taunting fools?"

"I don't know. A laugh or two?" What does he have left, if not the truth? It has shaped, shaped by his misshapen body, his entire life. One thing about being a monster, it puts you in touch with the cosmos, biggest humpback of all. "I wanted to make the truth so transparent even these pigheaded provincials could see it, that's all." He liked to think of it as a kind of remembering, as though all men were animals in some way, or had been.

"Yes, and turtles want to fly, too," the old king rumbles. "There's only one truth, my friend. If you've forgotten what it is, come a little closer and let me give you a few pointed reminders." A mere reflex. The old fellow hasn't eaten the garbage he's lying in. He laps his jowls with a tongue so dry it sounds like the spreading of sand on stone.

Anyway, it's... "Impossible. There's a barrier..." At least there was... Has it somehow been breached?

"If there's a moral to be had, fabler, it can be done..."

He'd always thought of that distance between them as onto-logical and absolute, but now—he stirs uncomfortably. He's rarely come this deep before. The fox seems to have let one, his own commentary on the truth no doubt. He bats the air irritably, his hump scraping the wall behind: "Filthy bastard!"

"He does that from time to time just to let me know he's still ᷃ere," the lion grumbles drowsily. "You get used to it. ᷃amiliarity, as they say..."

Not they. He. The rich man and the tanner. Or better yet: the ᷃x and the lion, almost forgot that one. Yet now, these words, ᷃o: only an echo... He realizes he hasn't told many fables on the ᷃vanescence of truth, brain-rot as the universal achievement. The

old lion snorts ruefully. He seems to be drifting off. The hunchback trembles. They'll be here soon. He got away from them
once, but they'll find him. Even from inside the cave, he can hear
the turbulence out at the edge. He squeezes shut his eyes.
Sometimes it feels almost like a dream. As though he might still
be back on Samos, living with that fatheaded philosopher and his
lascivious slave-fucking wife, the one who liked to say that even
her arse had eyes. Any minute, he thinks, I might wake up to a
beating or a bath…

8

The tortoise, tumbling through the air, wags his arms frantically.
If he just works at this hard enough, he knows, he can do it, per-
sistence has paid off before, he's famous for it. In order to try to
free his mind from extraneous matters, such as the rising panic
which is threatening to freeze him up entirely and stop his
wings, as they should perhaps now be called, from functioning
at all, he tries to concentrate on the splendid view he has from
up here of the forest, a view few of its inhabitants have been priv-
ileged to enjoy, and one he himself will probably forego in the
future, even if he does manage to get the hang of this flying
thing on this one occasion. Like he told Zeus, meaning no
offense, though unfortunately that's how it was taken, there's no
place like home. If you don't get there too fast. But his effort to
concentrate is frustrated somewhat by the way the forest keeps
looping around him, appearing over his head one moment,
beneath his tail the next: probably this has something to do with
his flying problem.

Why did he want to get up here in the first place? A question he might well ponder, since the second place, rushing up at

him like the moral to a foreshortened fable, is all but imponderable. He always tries to judge every situation from its outcome, not its beginning, though each, as he knows, flapping wildly, contains the other, ambition being both goal and goad. But what *was* that ambition? Was it aesthetic? Philosophical? The pursuit of some sort of absolute worldview (already slipping away from him, he notes, as the forest loops by again, losing now in structural clarity what it is rapidly gaining in detail)? A moral imperative? The spirit of rivalry? A rebellion against boundaries? The desire for travel? Who knows? Why anything? Why is the pig's belly bare or the magpie bald? Why does the crab have its eyes behind? Why does the lizard nod its head or the dying swan sing? Who gives a bloody shit? Should *he* be singing? Why are turtles dumb? Why are their heads flat and their shells hard? But not hard enough? Why has that goddamn eagle left him up here—flap! flap! flap!—*all alone?*

9

When Aesop opens his eyes, he finds himself lying under a tree in a green, peaceful field, where all kinds of flowers bloom amid the green grass and where a little stream wanders among the neighboring trees. The most savage thing in sight is a grazing cow. A gentle zephyr blows and the leaves of the trees around about are stirred and exhale a sweet and soothing breath: he draws in a deep lungful, as a great relief sweeps over him. What a terrible dream I was having, he thinks. Those shits were going to kill me! He still feels vaguely troubled (it seemed so real!), but the stream is whispering, the cicadas are humming from the branches, the song of birds of many kinds and many haunts can be heard, the nightingale prolongs her plaintive song, the branches murmur musically in a sympathetic refrain, on the slenderest branch of a pine tree the stirring of the breeze mocks the blackbird's call, and mingling with it all in harmony, Echo, the mother of mimesis, utters her answering cries, all of it resolving into a kind of rhythmic tinkle, reassuring in its simplicity like the drip of rainwater after a shower. Better a servant in safety, he reminds himself, than a master in danger, though at first this comes out, better a savory never than born a masker in a manger. Which doesn't make much sense. Is it some kind of oracle? And why is that cow standing there with her teats in the fire and plucked crows in her antlers with meat in their beaks? The trees' breath, he now notices, is not as sweet as he'd thought at first, and what the stream is whispering (how is it he fell asleep out here in this open field with his breeches off?) seems to be some suggestion about staying in line or alive, or playing the—

"What? What— ?!" He starts up in alarm, opens his eyes a second time. Ah, it is the fox, that treacherous foulmouth, whispering something in his ear about flaying the lion and wearing his hide as a disguise. "Don't wait until danger is at hand!" He turns his head away. He must have dozed off. But it seemed so *real!* "Fuck these useless shows of strength, humpback! Remember the fable of the hunting dog! Use your wits!"

Perhaps a *third* time, he thinks, straining to pop his eyes wider open. He uses his fingers to press his lids apart. But they *are* apart. Is he dreaming that he's pressing his fingers to his lids? Alas... "It's been tried," he mumbles, trying his voice out.

"Only by asses. The morals of those stories are stay out of the wind and keep your mouth shut."

Would it work? Not likely. He can already hear his pursuers. "We were told to get the one in the lionskin," they'd be saying.

"Why am I even listening to a doublecrossing liar like you?"

"Because we understand each other. I wouldn't even be here without you, I know that, even if the others don't. You think I'd want to shit you now? Anyway, it's impossible. Think about it."

"He'd betray himself if he could figure out how to do it and profit by it at the same time," the lion growls from inside his paws. "Get back to your post, stinkbreath, before I decide to tear that red tail off at the root and sweep out this stinking boghouse with it!" He watches the miserable beggar slink, smirking no doubt (can't see a damned thing), back to the cave mouth. The hunchback stands to piss against the wall, at least that's what it sounds like. "And don't be fooled, fabler. Wit will *not* get the better of strength. Ever. That's just a fairytale for weaklings. Helps them die easier."

"But I can't outrun them and I can't eat them," the dwarf whines from the other side of his hump as he splashes against the wall. "What am I going to *do?*"

"What you can. There's an inscription here..." The old lion knows, in the end, he is going to have to abide by it himself. If puffed-up toads and flying turtles are ridiculous, humble lions are worse. He shakes his mane. If he could just lift his jaws up off the floor. "...At the oracle..."

"I've seen it." The hunchback is wiping that monstrous engine of his on his shirt. "But I don't know who I am and I don't know where to start."

"You know more than you know," the lion rumbles solemnly, and the fox snarls: "There he is!"

"What—?! *Who?*" squeaks the fabler, shrinking back against the wall he's just fouled.

"It's for me," says the lion, rearing his head up at last. It sways a bit like an old drunk's, but he holds it up there. This is not going to be easy, he thinks. But had he ever supposed it would be? "My herald, as you might say. My advice to you is to take a long walk."

"But—!"

"*GET OUT!*" he roars, and the hunchback, in panic, goes lurching out on all fours, nipped mischievously in the tail by the fox as he scrambles past. "Now come here, slyboots, I want to show you something. We're going to let you play the hero."

10

A plaintive ascendant whine silences the unruly forest. Flappings, snortings, rustlings, scurryings cease. The black-hooded magpie, death's acknowledged messenger, lowers his gaping beak and from his perch above the cave mouth shrieks: "*The king is dying! The king is dying!* Scrawk! *Long live the king!*" A kind of communal gasp sweeps through the forest like a sudden brief gust of wind, then dies away. The magpie hacks raucously as though trying to spit. "*Miserable morsels*- -*harck!* tweet!—*mortals who, like leaves, at one moment*- -whawk!—*flame with life and at another weakly*- -prreet! crawl—*perish down the drain of Eternity in the mighty whirl of dust, the hour of*—wheep!- -*equal portions has ARRIVED!*" A furtive scrabbling and fluttering ripples now through the forest like gathering applause, from the outside in, rushing toward the center as though beaters were assaulting the periphery. Though only the magpie is visible (even the fox has disappeared), the area around the cave mouth seems suddenly congested, aquiver with terror and anticipation. And appetite. "*Cree! Cree! Creatures of a day, be quiet and have patience, not even the gods fright*- -purrr-wheet!—*fight against the child within us! We go our*—

WARRCKK!—ways in the same honor already for—caw! caw!—*forfeit!*" The magpie's long bright tail drops like a falling axe. Is it over? Is the tyrant already dead? Heads peek out from behind foliage. Insects hover nervously. Monkeys swing closer, swing back again. A snake uncoils from a limb. A boar in the underbrush snorts and paws the ground. A crab sallies forth, eyes to the rear. "*Either death is a state of nothingness and utter*—kwok!—*or better never to have been born!*" the oracular magpie cries, and parrots, cats, crickets and hermaphroditic hyenas scream their assent. The entire twilit forest is alive with beasts surging furtively toward the dying lion's cave. "*Must not all things be swallowed up in*—shreek!—*a single night? Just SO! Crrrr-AWKK!*" As though in fear of being left behind, the animals at this signal burst from their hiding places and rush, squealing and bawling, toward the cave mouth—but just as suddenly pull up short. The old king stands there in the fading light, muscles rippling, fiery mane blowing in the breeze, eyes feverish with fury. With fierce deliberation, he steps forward, his teeth bared. Has this been a trap? "Only one!" shrieks the magpie. Ah. But a lion...

11

We found the fabulist at last in the Temple of the Muses, clearly deranged, howling about "death in the forest" and "the revenge of dungbeetles," and bounding around arse-high with his nose to the stone floor like a toad looking for water. After having abused us earlier, while still in prison, with filthy tales about the rape of widows and children ("A man put it in me with a long sinewy red thing that ran in and out," he'd leered: had he been trying to seduce us with these simpering obscenities?) as well as racist slurs, insults against our fathers, and seditious threats to revenge himself upon us, even after he was dead, this grotesque little Egyptian, or Babylonian, was now, in one of our own temples, berating us with sacrilege, shrieking something truly offensive about "God with shit in his eye!" It was almost, we thought, as though he'd come here to our city *seeking* to die.

He was not easy to catch or, once caught, to subdue. As we chased him about the temple, wrestling with him, losing him, catching him again, he kept making brutish noises, now squawking, now roaring, now barking or bleating or braying, as though he were all these beasts at once, or thought himself to be, and at times we did feel somewhat like Menelaus grappling with the inconstant and malodorous Proteus. His stunted limbs were too rubbery to hold, his pot too sleek—finally we caught him by the ears (his Achilles' heel, as it were) and, twisting them, extracted from him a more human howl.

As we dragged him toward his site of execution, his madness took on a subtler, yet no less bizarre form. He grew suddenly serene, almost flaccid in our many-handed grip, and commenced to lecture us on the evils we were presumably bringing upon ourselves with this action. "Not much time will be gained, O Delphians," he proclaimed shrilly, as his pointed head bounced along on the uneven ground, "in return for the evil name which you will get from the detractors of the city, who will say that you killed Aesop, a wise man; for it will be said of me, that I never did any wrong, never gave any ill advice to any man, but that I labored all my life long to excite to virtue those who frequented me." Such pomposities, emerging reedily from that twisted liver-lipped mouth with its scattered teeth, under the squashed-up nose and squinty eyes, neither of which ever seemed to be looking at the same thing at the same time, struck us as so ludicrous we were all driven to fits of convulsive laughter, and nearly lost our grip on him again. "Fancy such a warty little thing as you making such a big noise!" we hooted.

"I prophesy to you who are my murderers, that immediately after my departure punishment far heavier than that you have inflicted on me will surely await you!" he squealed then, and we reminded him, laughing, that braggarts are easily silenced, as he was about to discover. "People who brag to those who know them must expect to be laughed at, 'gypsie, evil tricks don't fool honest men! Such playacting has cost many a man his life, you will not be the first or last to perish of it!" We hauled the droll little monster up to the edge of the cliff and prepared to heave him over. Some of us had his arms, some his horny feet. "Destiny is not to be interfered with, melonhead—if you had any real wisdom you'd know that! A man should courageously face whatever is going to happen to him and not try to be clever, for he will— ha ha!—not escape it!"

"Wait!" he begged, gigantic tears rolling down the bumps of his temples and off his earflaps. He seemed prepared to recant at last and, though it wouldn't save his life, right his wrongs against us before he died. We set him on his bandy legs and stepped back, blocking any possible escape. He cocked his head impudently to one side. "Let me tell you a story," he said. Ye gods, the little freak was incorrigible. It has been wisely observed, natures remain just as they first appear. When you do a bad man a service, some sage has said, all you can hope for is that he will not add injury to ingratitude, but even this hope was to prove in vain. "There was this old farmer," he piped, "who had never seen the city and decided to hitch up the donkeys and go see it before he died. But a storm came up and they got lost among the cliffs. 'Oh

God, what have I done to die like this,' he wept (and here *he* wept mockingly), 'in the company of these miserable jackasses?'" We rushed at him, enraged at such impiety, but he stopped us again with a wild bewitching screech, lurching forward as though stabbed from behind, and we fell back, momentarily startled. "A man once fell in love with his own daughter," he wailed as though in great pain, rolling his lopsided eyes, and pointing at all of us—what?! what was he saying? "So he shipped his old lady off to the country and forced himself on his daughter. She said, as I say to you, men of Delphi: 'This is an unholy thing you are doing! I would rather have submitted to a hundred good men than be fucked by you!'" We flung ourselves at this loathsome obscenity, but before we could reach him, he hurled himself, cackling derisively, off the cliff, flapping his stunted little arms as though the fool thought he might fall up instead of down.

12

He has just, with what dignity remains, his knees weak and threatening to buckle, stepped forth from the cave mouth to confront his erstwhile citizenry, when something whistles past his ear and explodes—*SPLAT!*—beside him, startling him just enough to tip him over. What an irony, he muses, shrugging tortoise shell out of his ear, nearly got him before he could even get started. As it is, his jaw is back on the ground again, his paws trapped under his belly. His rear legs seemed to have held, but he is not sure what overall impression this position makes. Perhaps they will think he is crouching, preparing to spring. More likely not.

Though he cannot see them, they are all out there, he knows, all the rejected, the trod-upon, the bitten and the stung, the ridiculed, the overladen, all of God's spittle, lusting now for this compensatory kill. The great equalizer that makes their own poor lives and deaths less odious. Let them come. He will have one last glorious fray, one final sinking of tooth and claw into palpating flesh and gut, a great screaming music of rage and terror, before he dies. If he can just get his feet under him again. How was it he used to do that? He can feel his rump begin to sway, can hear them start to shift and mumble in the clearing down below. His aide-de-camp has slipped out of sight, of course. He has instructed the fox in how to kill him quickly when the time comes, when he's too weak to fight on. He doesn't want to die slowly, or ignobly. Or seem to. He has appealed to the fox's own ambition: let the opposition cut itself up, and then, when he gets the nod, move in as the decisive and heroic liberator. The wily bastard actually seemed moved: perhaps there's hope for him yet.

The sullen hesitant hush is shattered suddenly by another long shrieking whine from the intransigent magpie. *"He who hesitates*—SCRAWKK!—*flourish only for an omen*—hrreet!—MOMENT!"*

And, just as his rump tips and smacks the ground, they are on him: wolves, boars, apes, moles, toads, dancing camels, plucked daws, serpents, spiders, snails, incestuous cocks and shamming cats, hares, asses, bats, bears, swarms of tongueless gnats, fleas, flies and murderous wasps, bears, beavers, doves, martins, lice and dungbeetles, mice and weasels, owls, crabs, and goats, hedgehogs and ticks, kites, frogs, peacocks and locusts, all the fabled denizens of the forest, all intent on electing him into the great democracy of the dead. A boar wounds him with a blow from its flashing tusks as he sprawls there, paws high, a bull gores him in the belly, a mosquito stings his nose, a cowardly ass kicks him in the forehead.

But even as they convene upon his body, something stirs in the enfeebled lion, something like joy or pride or even love. The rage of. His battered head rears and roars, his pierced muscles flex, his blunted teeth and claws find flesh to rend, bones to crush. The air is thick suddenly with blood and feathers and smashed carapaces, shrieks and howls, mighty thrashings about. He even, for a splendid moment, feels young again, that renowned warrior of old, king of the beasts. He no longer knows which animals he's embracing in this final exaltation—one eye is gone, the other clouded, an ear is clogged with bees, his hide's in tatters—but it doesn't matter. It is life itself he is clutching bloodily to his breast in this, his last delicious moment on earth, and it's the most fun he's had since he sneezed a cat.

But then, through the flurry of beaks and antlers and the blood in his eye, he sees the fox skulking toward him, head ducked, an insolent smirk on his skinny face. "No, wait!" he roars. "*Not yet!*" But he should have known better, take pity on such a creature, you get what you deserve. And what he gets is, too soon, oh much too soon, the treacherous villain at his throat. "You fool!" he gasps, while he's still voice left. "I can't help it," snickers the miserable wretch, nuzzling in. "It's just my—hee hee!—nature..." With a final swipe of his paw (he is being invaded from below, he knows, a seeding of teeth in his plowed-up nether parts as though to found a city there, but it has ceased to matter), he slashes the fox open from heart to groin, then hugs him close, locking his jaws around his nape, their organs mingling like scrambled morals. "It's all shit anyway," he seems to hear the devil grunt as his spine snaps—one final treachery! He feels then as though he's falling, and he only wishes, hanging on as the light dies and the earth spins, that his friend the fabler were here to whisper in his ear, the one without the bees in it, one last word, not so much of wisdom, as of communion. Just so… What? What? "*SKWWAARRRK!*" replies the magpie, as the forest extinguishes itself around him.